6/22

TRUST ME,
I'M A BANKER

TRUST ME, I'M A BANKER

A NOVEL

DAVID CHARTERS

Thomas Dunne Books
St. Martin's Press
New York

This is a work of fiction. All of the characters, organizations, and events portrayed in this novel are either products of the author's imagination or are used fictitiously.

THOMAS DUNNE BOOKS.
An imprint of St. Martin's Press.

www.thomasdunnebooks.com
www.stmartins.com

ISBN 978-0-312-60437-0 (hardcover)
ISBN 978-1-250-01519-8 (e-book)

This book was originally published in two volumes in Great Britain under the titles *At Bonus Time, No One Can Hear You Scream* and *Trust Me, I'm a Banker* by Elliot and Thompson Limited

First U.S. Edition: July 2012

10   9   8   7   6   5   4   3   2   1

For Ella, my bambolina

Author's Note & Acknowledgements

THEY SAY that villains always have the best parts. The investment banking industry certainly has its fair share of villains. As an industry it contains all of the extremes – brilliantly talented, driven, ambitious people, operating in a culture of fear and greed, where the pressure is on to have it all and have it now. The rewards can be immense, at least in a material sense, but this is an industry that has long since lost its moral compass. Sharp elbows are the norm, and he who dies with the most toys wins.

I lived the life for thirteen years. It made me rich but came at a cost, not least in a marriage that was driven onto the rocks. The books I have written are inspired by the best and worst – mostly the worst – of all the people I knew and worked with in the investment banking industry. My antihero, Dave Hart, is similarly a combination of all that finally drove me to leave the industry. He is greedy, shallow, vain, fickle, totally untrustworthy and yet at times bizarrely compelling and brilliant in his insanity and his genius – beware in case you end up liking him or even rooting for him.

AUTHOR'S NOTE & ACKNOWLEDGEMENTS

Many people helped me and my gratitude to them should be recorded. Lorne Forsyth, Andreas Haindl, Joerg Illhardt, Roger Lewis, Jane Miller, Joanna Rice, Adam Shutkever, my sister Margaret and my oldest son, Mark, all deserve special mention. But my biggest debt is to the truly awful people who actually moved me to start writing about them.

David Charters
London 2012

TRUST ME,
I'M A BANKER

LAST NIGHT I killed my boss. It was the second time this week, only this time it was much worse. He was sitting at his desk in his big, glass-sided, corner office, looking out at the trading floor with its hundreds of identical workstations, the computer screens, the phones, and us, the worker bees who feed the machine. Looking at us, as we stayed late in the run-up to the annual bonus round, putting in face time to look good, keeping busy, trying to persuade him how essential we all were. Well, I'd had enough. I wasn't essential anymore – at least I didn't feel as if I was – and I was going to act before someone took the decision for me.

I COUGH nervously, glance around at my colleagues who all have their eyes glued to the screens in front of them, and pick up my briefcase from under my desk, leaving my jacket over the back of my chair. Now, this may sound straightforward, but you don't normally carry your briefcase around the trading floor unless you're going home, and when you go home, you put your jacket

1

on. But if I put my jacket on first – at this time of year – the rest of the team will look at me and I don't want to attract attention, not at this stage.

So I leave my jacket but pick up my briefcase and walk in a lopsided way, half hiding it in front of me as I make my way to his office with my back to the team.

I step inside the open door and close it behind me. I reach across and pull the blinds, so we can't be seen from the floor. He looks up, puzzled.

'What are you doing?'

I smile, reassuring, ingratiating.

'Rory, there's… something I wanted to discuss with you.'

He sighs and looks at his watch. 'Okay, I'll give you five minutes, but do me a favour – no more special pleading about the bonus, okay?'

'No, no more special pleading, Rory.' I smile again, a little nervously – still in character – and open my briefcase on his desk, but with the lid facing him so he can't see what I'm taking out. 'In fact no pleading at all.'

I close the lid with a firm click and swing a sixteen-inch machete up in the air.

Now, before you say anything, a sixteen-inch machete may not seem much, but it had to fit into my briefcase, which is not large. Even in London you can't just go and buy a full-sized machete without attracting some degree of attention. As I like to think I'm a little smarter than some mere criminal on the street, I'd bought the machete at auction, at Christie's, along with a collection of other memorabilia of famous nineteenth century explorers in Africa. So when I swing it through a broad arc and bring it down with a thunk into the middle of Rory's perfectly coiffed, fair-haired, blue-eyed skull, I'm actually using a piece of history.

The problem is, it gets stuck. The weapon goes thunk, right into his head, splintering the bone. My arm is driven by the strength that can only come from years of resentment, humiliation, nervous anxiety, pitiful gratitude and festering anger. He keels over, gently and silently, his eyes roll upwards and he bumps his head on his desk with a sigh. Seeing him lying there, helpless, I put one hand on his head and struggle to wrench the machete free for a second go (and to be honest, for a third and a fourth – I'd worked for Rory a long time).

And then he gets up! No kidding, he actually shakes his head, causing me to leap backwards, my eyes wide with fear and disbelief. He pulls himself together, lifts himself up from the desk, blood streaming down his face, eyes wide open, with the machete still sticking out of his skull. He comes round the desk towards me.

'You always were a loser.' His words have an icy venom to them – which I suppose is understandable. 'A loser, a no hoper, a truly second rate, sub-standard investment banker. The clients don't even like you, let alone respect you, half of them only deal with you out of sympathy, and you have no future here or at any other firm.' He jabs his finger in my chest to emphasise the points, and as he finishes, he reaches up, taking hold of the machete, grasping the handle, and pulls it out of his head, allowing a stream of blood to come gushing out of the crack in his skull splashing down over his face onto the carpet. 'You can't do a damned thing right.' There's blood all over the machete as he hands it back to me, and more blood runs down his forehead and face, but it doesn't seem to bother him. 'Now get out of my office. I have work to do – including some key bonus re-calculations.' As he says this, he gives me a long, meaningful stare – one of the ones I always hate, because when someone looks at you like that, you just know they've found you out – and then he flicks a drop of blood off the end of his nose and goes back to his desk.

When I get back to my workstation, my shirt is sticking to my sides with sweat. I pull my handkerchief out and mop my brow. As I glance around, I catch the eye of some of the other team members.

'Brown-nosing again?'

'Looks like it didn't pay off.'

'Rory's got the measure of you.'

And I start screaming. I scream so loud that I wake my wife.

'Darling – darling, are you all right?'

I shake my head to clear it, and reach for a glass of water from the bedside table. Wendy turns the light on.

'It was one of those awful dreams again, wasn't it?'

I nod, too shaken to speak.

'Oh, my darling,' she smiles, trying to be reassuring, and hugs me, though she clearly doesn't appreciate the sweat covering me from head to toe. 'Come on, darling – look on the bright side. It's not long now, is it? Then all this uncertainty will be over. It's... how many days?'

I glance at the clock on the bedside cabinet. Twelve thirty – half-an-hour after midnight, another day has started. 'Fifty-two days,' I gasp. 'Fifty-two days until we know.'

Monday, 25th October

B minus 52

IT WAS 6:30 in the morning. I was sitting on the tube, on the Circle Line to Monument, staring into space, working out what I'd do with a million pounds. Now, before you say anything, let me explain – even senior investment bankers take the tube sometimes. I know that Rory with his chauffeur-driven car would never be seen dead on the People's Underground, and why should he? He's the boss, after all. But for the rest of us, at least those who live in Chelsea, the journey into the City is quickest by Underground, especially first thing in the morning, even if it is a little democratic when it comes to things like getting a seat and who you rub shoulders with. And I know, I know – you don't need to say it. It's true that the man sitting next to me doesn't smell of Armani Mania.

He smells of... well, let's just say he smells. And a lot of these people haven't even made their first million, and many of them never will. That's capitalism. It's enough for me that I know. I don't need to say anything.

But back to that million. We all know a million isn't what it used to be. To begin with, the Chancellor takes forty per cent. So a million is already six hundred thousand. Then the bank won't pay it all in cash. Probably half the balance will be in some form of share-based incentive – options, deferred shares, some weird derivative, or whatever. But it won't be cash and you can't spend it now – it only turns into folding money slowly, over a period of years, perhaps three or even five years, providing you stay at the bank and don't move to a competitor. If you do that, you lose it all. That's why they call these things golden handcuffs. So your actual cash in hand is perhaps three hundred thousand, and these days three hundred really doesn't go far.

Take an example. Have you any idea how much a Porsche costs? I thought not. Well the basic Boxster comes in at a mere £30k, but no one, I mean no one, serious can drive one of those in the Square Mile. The minimum is the 911 Turbo Cabriolet and for that you're talking the thick end of £100k. So already a big chunk of my bonus is gone.

I know what you're thinking – why buy a 911 at all? We already have a Range Rover – Vogue of course, with the usual extras – so why buy a second car? Well the thing is, we have to have the Range Rover. Wendy needs it to do the school run from our flat in Sloane Square to Cameron House, the private nursery school which Samantha attends, at the other end of the King's Road. It's almost half a mile, and kids these days need protection, and so does Wendy – not the world's greatest driver – so a big 4 X 4 is essential driving in Chelsea. It's also good for giving the impression that we have a place in the country, which we definitely don't yet, but would do if Rory ever got off his arse and gave me a decent bonus. And of course whenever Wendy ventures outside Chelsea, she needs protection even more – like when she takes Samantha to her Little Sweethearts ballet class in Fulham, or to her Young Prodigies violin lesson in Pimlico, her Gymnastics for Toddlers sessions in Battersea, or her Little Tadpoles swimming class in Putney. Don't laugh – if you don't do this stuff for your kids, they might not become a rock star, or Prime Minister, or win the Nobel Prize. Even White Van Man pulls over when he sees Wendy weaving down the middle of the road, talking on her mobile, staring into shop windows, at the wheel of a Range Rover.

But back to my car. We ought to be a two car family, because if I ever need to drive to the office, for example on a Sunday, I can't arrive in a Range Rover – at least not a clean one, the way they tend to be in Chelsea. At weekends Rory drives a DB7, but then he would, wouldn't he?

So once I've finally got myself a decent car of my own

– a 911 Turbo Cabriolet – what else do I need? We still owe a hundred thousand on the mortgage on the flat, which we've paid down steadily over the past few years, and it would be satisfying to own it outright, but we already tell people we own it ourselves, so there ought to be something more... demonstrable that flows from this year's bonus. We could think about a place in the country, but then people would expect to come and stay, and we simply don't have the kind of money you need to buy a place like Rory's: two hundred and fifty acres in Sussex, his own shoot, nine bedrooms, two guest cottages, five staff – you know the sort of thing. Or maybe you don't. Anyway, a cottage is definitely out of the question, even though in terms of strict space requirements, Wendy and I, and Samantha (who's three) could technically survive in a cottage – after all, we only have three bedrooms in Sloane Square. But it doesn't matter, because a million doesn't do it, so there's no point discussing it further.

Watches – and jewellery – always used to be a sure-fire sign of a successful bonus round, though these days people are getting more cynical. If Wendy and I treat ourselves to a new Rolex each, or better yet the latest Patek Philippe, people might think I really haven't done well and it's all a bluff.

We could re-decorate the flat. I haven't costed that, but one of those chi-chi interior designers could transform the place for us. The problem is, I sort of like it the way it is, and I'd hate the disruption of having to move out while a bunch of Polish builders and Croatian decorators moved in. And it always costs more and takes longer than they say – we pay Chelsea prices and get Warsaw delivery times.

If I only get a million, a few key purchases around the home are probably the best compromise – an antique dining table with chairs (less than £30k?), a new centrepiece picture for the drawing room (£20 to 25k?), a new set of crockery (£3 to 4K?) and perhaps new curtains (£10k?). We'd still have change for Barbados at Christmas, not forgetting the Porsche, and the balance I'd use to pay off the overdraft.

Overdraft? I can see the question in the thought bubble over your head. Well, yes, I do have an overdraft. I know what you're thinking. Why does a successful investment banker have an overdraft? Well, actually we all do.

NO ONE LIVES on their salary any more. Besides, Rory only pays me £100k a year, and Wendy couldn't begin to live on that. So what do you expect?

At 11:30 I had a meeting with the Finance Director of Pattison Construction. PC – as we call them on the team – is one of the biggest and fastest growing construction companies in the UK, having come from nowhere over the past five years. We took them public on the stockmarket two years ago, and now they've come to us for advice on what to do next. Yes, really – they've come to us for advice.

It amazes me, but people still do that. Naturally, my advice is that they should do whatever will pay the bank the largest fees. In this case, I recommend we list their shares on the New York Stock Exchange, so that they can access US investors, increase liquidity in their shares and send their stock price higher. None of this is true, of course. The most serious US investors already can buy their shares, without the expense and trouble of a US listing. Creating a separate pool of shares in the US reduces liquidity, and in times of uncertainty, US investors would dump their shares pretty quickly and send the stock lower. But that's all detail. I like to think I'm a big picture man. The big picture I'm thinking of today is my bonus, because as you know, it's that time of year.

On reflection, any time of year is that time of year, but the last few weeks running up to bonus particularly so.

Anyway, PC nods, makes all the right noises and I orchestrate the presentation like a circus ringmaster. We explain why US investors have a different valuation approach to the construction sector and will push his stock higher, a representative of our US operation explains why our tiny New York office is best equipped to do the job (after all, why would anyone want to hire a US firm to do a job in the US?), and finally I wind up with my assurance of the firm's total commitment, how much we want the business, how great it will be for them, the strategic vision, the next step forward – sometimes I think I could do this stuff in my sleep. It's not that investment banking is undemanding work, it's just that at times it's repetitive. Like repeating the same script a hundred times. Or a thousand. I've been doing this a while now. In theory you get slicker, more persuasive, more reassuring, but it can come to sound... jaded. Not that I'd ever get bored with my job, of course. I'm committed, not quite in the way that lunatics get committed to an asylum, but committed nonetheless.

Afterwards, he tells me how impressed he is with our presentation, how highly he values our input, and how useful it is to be able to get genuinely sincere, impartial advice. For a moment I look at him and wonder if he's taking the piss, but then I realise he means it.

Christ, I'm good.

WENDY AND I went to a dinner party at the Finkelsteins'. He runs the swaps desk at Hardman Stoney, one of the most successful US investment banks. He never has anything to say, always arrives at least half-an-hour late to his own dinner parties, and always looks distracted – almost vacant, though obviously that can't be right, because he runs the swaps desk at Hardman Stoney.

The Finkelsteins have an amazing apartment in Holland Park – the sort that Wendy dreams of. You come in through a grand reception area with marble floors and twenty-four hour porterage, step into a big mirror and marble elevator, and get out onto a large landing that serves just two apartments. You buzz at double doors, both of which open when your host's butler (hired for the night – don't worry, this isn't Rory's place) receives you and takes your coats.

The drawing room is huge, with a great view and interesting art: a contemporary bronze here, a classical marble bust there – you know the sort of thing. Or maybe not. Anyway, there are a few coffee tables and some couches, but mostly the impression is space and order. And a 'to die for' black babe dressed as a waitress offers you a drink with a 'come to bed and fuck me' smile on her face and a knowing look in her eyes. Where do they find these girls? Why can Wendy only find short, fat Filipinas and Essex girls who claim to know what they're doing, but only spill things on guests, or worse yet, on the furniture?

GLORIA FINKELSTEIN is dressed from head to toe in Chanel – and it's wasted. Twenty thousand dollars, and you still can't defeat nature. That's without the hair stylist, the manicure, the pedicure, the botox, the lyposuction, the personal trainer, the masseur and the expensive suntan. I guess she must do something for Matt Finkelstein (or at least she did once upon a time). A few good memories and a killer of a pre-nuptial can do a hell of a lot for these American investment bankers' marriages.

Wendy on the other hand is wearing Donna Karan – a simple pale blue number to match her eyes that cost us a mere three thousand dollars on our last trip to New York. In Wendy's case it's the jewellery that does it – twenty thousand pounds' worth of 'heirlooms' for Samantha around her neck and wrists (that was how she justified them), mostly from Theo Fennel, with earrings from Elizabeth Gage: stunning, so much so that Gloria Finkelstein pays her the ultimate tribute of ignoring them, and compliments her instead on her new handbag (a mere three hundred pounds from Coach).

I take a glass of champagne from the black sex machine, ignoring Wendy's 'evil eye' and wonder what she would say if I offered her a thousand pounds to go to bed with me. I take a sip and discover – to my utter horror – that it's Krug. Not only that, but just in case I didn't notice, the bottle is sitting in an ice bucket on the sideboard, propped up so the label is on show. If that isn't typically crude one up-manship, I don't know what is. I make a mental note – next time Matt Finkelstein drops by, I must open a bottle of vintage Cristal. (Second mental note: order some).

We exchange the usual pleasantries: air kisses, compliments, how wonderful, it's been so long, you look amazing, how are the children, before we get down to the real business of the evening (and this even before Matt Finkelstein has appeared!) – how are you doing? Sounds like a simple question, doesn't it? Except it doesn't really mean what it says. What it really means is (and at this point Wendy looks nervously in my direction, relenting on her previous irritation at my preoccupation with the black sex bomb): are you going to be paid more than my husband this year, and if so, what does it do to our relative positioning in the social pecking order?

Great, isn't it? As if it wasn't enough that the husbands compete, the wives have to do it too. My husband earns more than yours, he can buy me a bigger house/ car/boat/holiday home and afford a better personal trainer/masseur/ beautician/guru/tennis coach and we can spend even more money than you on exotic holidays/dinners at fancy restaurants/tickets to the boring fucking opera/weekend breaks in stately fucking homes and WE MUST BE FUCKING HAPPIER THAN YOU FUCKING LOSERS. Or something like that. And anyway, since we all do this stuff, it must be right.

Wendy does her best 'confident corporate wife', glancing at me, looking quietly confident, silently gratified at some hidden knowledge that she and I alone can share – I've been told something. Rory must have given me a hint. Obviously I can't say anything: everyone understands that. Especially Gloria. Wendy puts on such a good performance that we don't actually need to say anything. Gloria looks taken aback, perturbed, ever so slightly unsettled in a quite delicious way, and leaves us with unseemly haste when the bell rings to announce the next guests.

To my relief, it's the light entertainment. Gloria Finkelstein, ever the thoughtful hostess, has organised a

Real Loser. He's here so we can all unite against him and reinforce our sense of security and permanence.

Joe Smith ran forward Foreign Exchange trading at SFP – Société Financière de Paris – until June last year. Then they closed down and pulled out of the London market. Not his fault, of course, his team was profitable, but that makes no difference: when he looks at me, and I look at him, we both know. Not that I'd ever say anything, of course. That's part of the fun.

Our wives know too. His wife, strangely known as Charly, is Hong Kong Chinese, and I've always had a soft spot for her – I bet she's a real goer. She's wearing a brightly coloured, vaguely oriental style, silk mini dress of indeterminate origin – oh dear, my dear, no label – with pearls – okay, I guess – and intricately patterned gold earrings that probably come from the Middle East –I bet they don't have hallmarks. She's in great shape, but that really isn't the point. I wonder what she would say if I offered her, oh, let's say ten grand – or maybe fifty, he's been unemployed for nearly a year now...

'Joe, how are you? And Charly, how wonderful to see you!'

Wendy and Gloria rush to embrace the arriving guests, revelling in their superiority. Sweetness and success: moments like this are what it's all about. But it's all relative – imagine what it feels like for a woman to be married to Rory.

Joe is embarrassed, trying not to be defensive, he has

lots of possibilities, he's still exploring his options, obviously the market doesn't help – and yes, we all nod and no one engages with him: because we don't have to, do we? He's a loser.

Before you say anything, I know it's not his fault – he ran a profitable, successful team, he made a lot of money for his firm, had a fearsome reputation in the market, and paid his people well, at least as long as they performed. It's not that he was kind, you understand. After all, kind is for girls. He was ambitious, aggressive, and like most of us, he knew how to smile upwards on the greasy career ladder and shit downwards. But he didn't have friends. Not that any of us do, really. But he made it particularly clear that he didn't care what his peers at other firms thought, and that was a mistake.

Most of us at least go through the motions, staying part of the 'club', because you never know when you might need a helping hand. Of course, for all I know, Joe's a loving, loyal husband and a wonderful father to his kids and helps small, furry woodland creatures in his spare time. But he's still a loser, and we know it and he knows it and Charly knows it too. He committed the Cardinal Sin: when he found himself in the wrong place at the wrong time, he had no friends and no Plan B. He was naked and alone with no one to cry to, and when that happens, the City is a barren place – the sort of place that makes people become unravelled.

Just as the conversation is stretching out deliciously, reinforcing my sense of confidence and good fortune, Matt Finkelstein arrives and pops the bubble.

'Hi, I'm sorry, so sorry – we've just priced the biggest reverse forward equity swap with collars, caps and inverse reference prices that's ever been undertaken outside of the US.'

We all stare at him. Matt Finkelstein has zits. I know I shouldn't raise this now, just ahead of dinner, but if you were here you'd see them anyway. He's tall, skinny and is losing his hair. He would say he's lean, and it's true he does work out, in the special gym set aside for the use of Managing Directors only at Hardman Stoney. He would probably also say he's clever, and in a manner of speaking, that's true – though only in a narrow, specific way that wouldn't really help him; for instance if civilisation came to an end as the result of a nuclear holocaust and he had to fend for himself in the wild. Sure, he goes to the opera, but if you were to ask him who wrote Tosca, he'd gaze vacantly at you, say 'Huh?' and look around for some Eurotrash they'd hired on their graduate trainee programme to answer the question.

'Wow, Matt – fantastic! Congratulations. You must be over the moon.' I don't ask how profitable the trade was, because they don't necessarily know – these swaps guys are so smart, they bullshit their bosses every time they do a deal, book some huge notional profit for bonus purposes, and let their successors unwind the mess in a few years' time when it matures.

But the really clever thing about Matt's trade is that he's done it now. A dollar earned in the run-up to bonus is worth ten dollars earned at the beginning of the year. My last major success was back in March, which gives me a slightly sick feeling. I take a sip of Krug, but that only makes me feel worse.

'Why don't we go straight through and sit down?' Matt steers us through to the dining room, and can't help grinning as he sees the looks on our faces.

Their dining room has been transformed. They have a new centrepiece picture hanging over the fireplace – some contemporary splurge of colour that I'm sure we're all meant to recognise and must have cost a fortune, as well as a new dining suite, at least new to them. It looks Georgian to me – with crockery that I'm sure is also new from the last time we were here. But the real killer is hanging on the wall to my right: it's roughly six-feet by five, very glossy and dark. It's a photograph, by Hiroshi Sugimoto, of a seascape by night. To you and me, it's a six-foot by five-foot dark patch on the wall, but to those who know, it says that this man, Matt Finkelstein, has two hundred thousand dollars to spend on a museum piece of modern photographic art. Since it is completely black, I wonder for a moment if Matt could have sat in a dark cupboard with a camera with the flash disconnected and taken it himself, then got it blown up, but I don't think he has the nerve. If you study these things close up, you can see the wave patterns and starlight in the darkness. Obviously I can't acknowledge its existence by studying it, but he can't take the chance that someone won't. So it must be the real thing.

Damn him! He's got his retaliation in first: he's done all this stuff before the bonus. How could he? I'm sure he doesn't make that much more than I do, and Gloria is High Maintenance in a way that makes Wendy look modest. The only thing I can think of is debt – he must have mortgaged himself up to the eyeballs, and he's counting on the bonus as his lifeline. I smile and find myself reluctantly compelled to pay him the same compliment that Gloria paid to Wendy when she saw her jewellery: I ignore everything and sit down, pretending not to notice.

Wednesday, 27th October
B minus 50

TODAY I SAW a dead rat on the pavement. Now, if you're tempted to say, 'So what?', let me make clear that this is quite unusual for Sloane Square. I'm sure there are rats all over London, in fact there are probably as many rats as people, living off the rubbish that piles up on the pavements, surviving in the sewers and the gutters and rarely seeing the light of day. But this one had chosen to come out of the sewers and die, here on the pavement outside my flat, for me to find just as I'm leaving to go to work.

In case you're wondering, I'm not superstitious, but it did put me in a really negative frame of mind. I wondered if it could somehow be a metaphor for my life, and that made me think about God. Not the Money God, you understand, but the other one – the one I don't really believe in except for social occasions like weddings and christenings. If there were a Real One – just speaking hypothetically, of course – and He were looking down on this ant-heap of a City, scrutinising us, what would He make of us? Would He think we were actually doing any good with our one unrepeatable lives, making a difference to our fellow man, or would He view us simply as parasites, an irrelevance that could be wiped out with a giant aerosol spray, leaving the planet a cleaner and happier place?

You can guess where I came out, as I sat on the Underground and tried to focus on my newspaper. I found myself wondering if there was anything I'd ever done that was worthwhile, not in the sense of generating fees for the firm, but in the sense of making the world a better place. Like Bob Geldof. He was a rock star, and by and large I think rock stars are pretty worthless people – though it has to be said that the big names do make real money. But Geldof was different. He tried to make a difference, not just to his own immediate circle, but to the whole world. Would I ever do that, spinning madly like a hamster in a wheel on this crazy money-go-round?

And if not, should I be worried about it? Would I one day look back and say it was all worthless?

Well, not if I made two million this year. Two million would still not be real money, but it could make a difference. With two million – which after tax and assuming half the balance is held back in deferred shares or options is really only six hundred thousand – I could buy a proper place in the country – obviously with a second mortgage, because six hundred by itself doesn't get you there, but who cares about debt? Sensible leverage is, well… sensible. With two million, I could buy the kind of place where Wendy and I could invite houseguests for the weekend, possibly with our own shoot, and still get the 911 and the extras I was thinking about for the flat. Though on reflection the extras for the flat have less appeal now that Matt Finkelstein's beaten me to it.

By the time I reached Monument station I was feeling a lot better – forget rats, think bonus.

Thursday, 28th October

B minus 49

TODAY RORY was happy. The sun shone and we were all smiling as we sat at our workstations and contemplated our good fortune. Truly, we work for the best of all possible bosses at the best of all possible firms.

Just kidding.

Rory called a departmental meeting. We were all a little nervous as we filed in to the large conference room at the end of the trading floor. We didn't show it, of course – except by the fact of all the joking and light-hearted banter going back and forth. Anyone observing us would have thought we were on something.

When Rory cleared his throat, you could have heard a pin drop. I was staring at the conference table, wondering what the hell was going on. You see, this was not our regular weekly bullshit session, where we take it in turns to try to claim credit for anything that's gone well, distance ourselves from anything loss-making and position ourselves as busy, productive, irreplaceable members of the team. This was a special meeting, called in the middle of the trading day, at theoretically one of our busiest, most productive times, and at this time of year you only do that for one reason: the bonus. I could feel sweat underneath my shirt and wondered if I should have put my jacket on, but that would have been too conspicuous. Anyway, I could see others were sweating too.

'Thank you all for coming.' I could have punched his ugly mug. As if we had a choice. At this time of year, if your boss asks you to stand on your head and sing Yankee Doodle, you ask in what key. 'I have some important news concerning compensation.'

That got our attention. I felt as if I could hear the entire room breathing – all thirty of us. The beating of my heart, my own pulse sounding in my ears, someone's stomach rumbling a few places down the table – everything became surreal for an awful, agonising moment. Let it be good news, dear God, please. Of course it wasn't good news – it couldn't be. It was all part of the softening up process.

Rory waved some papers, which none of the rest of us could see. For all I knew they were blank, just a theatrical prop to help get the message across. 'The department...' He paused, looking around the room. 'The department is thirty per cent behind budget.' A further dramatic pause. 'That can mean only one thing.'

One thing? It could mean several. It could mean Rory had failed to deliver what he promised management, and had decided to do the honourable thing – fall on his sword and resign. His share of the bonus pool would then be divided among his subordinates, whom he so outrageously misled with his misguided strategy, and for which he insisted on taking sole responsibility. No – this is investment banking, after all. It could mean he wanted a presentation prepared, to which we could all contribute, on a fully democratic basis, to explain to management that the budget was never realistic, but merely a ploy to get him paid more last year, and that it should therefore be revised down to a more achievable level. No – he'd never admit to mere human fallibility. Most likely, it meant we were going to tighten our belts, fire some juniors, and have our expectations managed downwards.

'This means we are going to have to tighten our belts.'
Bingo! 'We need to get control of our costs. With
immediate effect, First Class travel will be restricted to
members of the Executive Management Committee only.'
Around this particular table, that means him. 'Travel to
the airport will no longer be by taxi or limousine, but by
public transport, excepting those employees whose terms
of employment specify their means of transport.' Him
again – a chauffeur's included in his contract. 'Overnight
subsistence rates will be cut, and the list of approved
hotels reviewed for those employees who do not have line
responsibility for costs. In other words, if you're not liable
to carry the can directly with management for costs
incurred, you will be obliged to make economies.' He's
the only one with that responsibility in this room, so I
suppose he can work out for himself which hotels he'll
stay in and whether he really needs the Presidential Suite.
'This is going to be tough on us all.' No, it's not. You're
exempt. It'll be tough on the rest of us. 'But we have to
keep our costs under rigorous control. I will also be
reviewing the staffing requirements of our various
business activities in terms of junior support.' True
leadership – be decisive, fire some juniors, just before the
bonus. 'And it goes without saying that compensation
prospects for all of us are less rosy than they would have
been had we actually delivered on what we all signed up
to.' Now steady on – none of us came up with that
budget. That was yours. We just get to pick up the tab.

We all nodded our heads in agreement. Then came a flash of inspiration.

'Rory, we're with you on this all the way.' I could see heads turning in my direction, envious scowls distorting their features. 'Not only will we focus on costs – we'll focus on revenues too! We need to really go for it this side of Christmas, show management that we can deliver and that we really are the best team in the City of London!'

I can see I've pissed off everyone in the room, except Rory, who's nodding sceptically in my direction, but then beams at us all and agrees vigorously, causing others to do the same. Soon the whole room is full of nodding, smiling, happy faces, as we all agree with the wisdom and intelligence of our Beloved Leader.

DID I TELL you Rory has five homes? Yes, just the five. He has a five-storey house in Belgravia, with four staff, not counting his chauffeur, who's paid for by the bank. Then he has his 'place in the country', in Sussex, which I've already told you about. He has a chalet in Verbier, which as far as I can tell he never visits, and only has two staff; a villa near Antibes (four staff – he tries to spend most summers there, leaving early on a Friday afternoon and coming back on Monday mornings when he can't actually take a whole week off), and finally an apartment in New York (two staff), overlooking Central Park, in preference to the suite at the Four Seasons that he always used to take when he went on business. Someone said the firm might even be paying for his place in New York as part of his contract. Anyway, that makes five homes and seventeen staff, not counting the driver. He's a one-man employment machine, providing jobs and opportunities for so many people, his contribution to third-world development alone must make him a dead cert for a place in heaven.

By my calculations – based only on rumour and speculation – Rory must have been paid over twenty million pounds since he joined the firm four years ago. But do you think it makes him happy, all that material wealth? You bet it does. It makes him as happy as a pig in shit.

Wouldn't it make you happy?

Monday, 1st November
B minus 45

THINGS ARE HOTTING UP. I was sitting in my usual cubicle in the gents, reading a copy of *The Sun* left there by one of the traders, when I overheard a whispered conversation between two colleagues.

First voice (sounds American, I'm not sure who it is): 'Jackie's suing!'

This must be Jackie Thornton, a Vice President who was once considered a rising star, but seems to have had a bad year.

Second voice (Bill Mackay, who sits at the next but one

workstation to me): 'Is that right? But do you think it's true?'

'Nah – but right now she's desperate. All she has to do is threaten to sue and she becomes ironclad. Not only can she not be fired – assuming anyone other than juniors will get fired – but she has to be well paid.'

'But the guy she's accusing is gay – she must know, surely? Everyone else does. He's the last person who would ever touch her.'

I almost start laughing at this point. They must be talking about Nick Hargreaves, who as far as I know is the only gay member of the team, and incidentally one of the top producers. The idea of Jackie, who thinks she's so smart, suing the only gay member of the team for what must be sexual harassment just makes me want to laugh out loud. But naturally I don't, because getting caught eavesdropping in the gents' is definitely not good form.

TALKING OF sexual harassment, the head of the Paris office was in town today, lobbying Rory ahead of the bonus. I've always liked Jean-Luc. He has the widest smile you ever saw, struts like a cockerel in a three-piece suit with a gold pocket watch, exuding a total confidence that he is the handsomest, coolest, smartest man ever to walk the planet (even though he's overweight and has a shiny bald head and glasses with inch-thick lenses). Only a Frenchman could do this.

Naturally, as he was on expenses, a few of us went out

with him after work to catch up on developments in the French market, exchange views on business strategy, compare notes about marketing and origination, and get laid.

Did I say 'get laid'? I thought I did.

I suppose I owe you an explanation. One of the things about the pressure cooker environment of investment banking is that you need to let off steam. People do that in various ways – drink, drugs, gambling, you name it. In Jean-Luc's case – being a Frenchman – it's women. He's a member of a very exclusive club, called Andrea's, just off Dean Street in Soho. We piled into a cab and headed off there.

At Andrea's – where I am not a member – you ring the bell (naturally, there's no sign outside), wait while they scrutinise you on camera, then get buzzed in and go downstairs to be checked in by giant doormen, who are very respectful, and call you 'sir' and 'gentlemen', but everyone knows who's really in charge. Then you go through to a pretty mediocre, dimly lit bar, and pay nearly a grand a bottle for fairly average champagne, which you drink in discreet booths, designed to prevent you catching the eye of the other patrons. Just in case you know them.

Sounds awful, doesn't it? Well, it is awful, until you 'go outside'. 'Going outside' is shorthand for leaving the bar to visit the other part of the club, where the girls are (and if you're so inclined, guys too). Of course, being married, I've only ever heard stories of what happens when you 'go outside'. It usually takes Jean-Luc about half an hour, which is not long, and afterwards he just wants to smoke cigarettes and stare wistfully into the fireplace. If he's in a particularly expansive mood – or wants to get you on side for something, like putting in a good word for him ahead of the bonus – he might invite you to 'go outside' too – on his expense account, of course.

Naturally, as a happily married man, I've never been outside.

There is a story that when Jean-Luc first joined the firm, he was taken to Andrea's by one of the old directors, long since departed in some bear market cull, who went outside to find a girl for his guest. When he brought her into the bar to point her in the direction of Jean-Luc, suggesting to her what she might want to do to him, she giggled, 'Oh, you mean Jean-Luc? I already know what he likes. We all do.'

I did say he was a Frenchman.

Which brings me on neatly to the Kai Tak Convention. If you've never heard of it, I'm not surprised, because it doesn't exist, at least outside of investment banking circles. The Kai Tak Convention is the unspoken code whereby investment bankers on business trips never, ever reveal on their return anything that might – hypothetically speaking, of course – have occurred in the course of their trip. Because that wouldn't be in anyone's interest, would it?

It's rather like the old joke about the patient in the dentist's chair. Just as the dentist is about to start wielding a particularly nasty looking drill, the patient's hand shoots out and takes hold of the dentist's testicles, gently but firmly, whereupon he looks the dentist carefully in the eye, and says, 'We're not going to hurt each other, are we?' Well, investment bankers don't hurt each other either. At least not when it comes to little things like minor peccadilloes on business trips to Hong Kong, Manila, Bangkok, Moscow, St Petersburg, New York, Milan, Paris, Amsterdam, Stockholm, Helsinki, Berlin, Prague, Madrid...

Anyway, without being crude about it, we get to earn a lot of Air Miles. It's one of the compensations of the job.

So there we were, sitting in Andrea's, drinking champagne, with sensual delights by the roomful just the other side of the wall, and what did we do? We talked about the bonus. You know a man is serious about something when he isn't distracted even by the pleasures that one of London's top clubs allegedly has to offer. Dedication is the name of the game – at this time of year, we all stay faithful to our purpose.

Anyway, that's all you need to know.

Tuesday, 2nd November
B minus 44

AFTER LAST NIGHT, I feel rough. I look at myself in the mirror. It's one of those awful self-awareness moments. I can deal with the lines and the bags under my bloodshot eyes, the shadows and the first grey hairs. I can deal with my paunch, and the way I seem to be perpetually stooping after years spent hunched over a workstation. Those are almost a badge of office. What I can't deal with is the fact that I'm a loser. I hate my job. I hate my boss. But my biggest fear is that I'll get fired. Am I fucked up or what?

Don't answer that – I had a late night and now I'm feeling terrible, so give me a break.

And besides, there's something else. Last night the dream thing happened again. Rory was running through a forest in the moonlight, the ground covered in snow, working hard so that his frozen breath puffed out in front of him and desperate to escape, but I was faster. I was wearing an ice-hockey mask, overalls and carrying a chainsaw, which roared every time I squeezed the trigger, making him panic, blubber and run all the harder, though he knew and I knew that in the end he couldn't escape. What happened next is... well, you can probably guess what happened next. Wendy shook me, I was soaked in sweat, the sheets were drenched, and I actually looked at my hands to see if they were covered in blood and bits of gore from where I'd first sliced his arms and legs off and cut open his torso. My hands were actually shaking. I looked at Wendy and wondered if I was really losing my marbles.

I sat for a while on the edge of the bed, and Wendy fetched me a glass of water, though she had to hold it to my lips to drink, because I was shaking so much. She looked at me. I could see the question in her eyes.

'Just a dream. A bad dream. I'll be all right in a minute.'

Wendy never questions me. We're a team. We're on life's great journey together, and where I go, she goes.

I couldn't sleep for the rest of the night, and I looked like shit when I arrived at work. Mercifully, when I looked around the team, I could see I wasn't alone. There were a lot of other pale faces and dark-shadowed eyes. It's the time of year. Nick Hargreaves was the worst. If what I'd overheard in the gents was correct, I could understand why. And then I spotted something. On his desk he had a copy of a Christie's catalogue for an upcoming auction – 'The Christie's Africa Sale'. I got up and asked if I could take a quick look at it, and there, on page seventeen, I saw the machete from my dream.

Now this really freaked me out. This was weird. I mean, in the movies, yes, stuff like this can happen – but not in real life. Or maybe I'd seen a poster somewhere advertising the sale. Maybe somewhere in my subconscious I'd registered something without realising it. I looked at the date of the auction: three days before the bonus announcement. Weird.

THERE ARE times when I wish I was Rory. That may sound strange, but it's true. I happened to be passing his office late this afternoon, when I heard his secretary confirming a business trip for him. Naturally, his chauffeur would pick him up from home to take him to – Biggin Hill! I suppose the name doesn't mean very much to you. It's a former Second World War airfield, you might vaguely recall it from watching old movies.

In investment banking circles, it means a whole lot more. In investment banking circles, Biggin Hill has real resonance. It means freedom – freedom from the burden of travelling with the general public on ordinary flights from airports crowded with ordinary people. To us, it means seniority, privilege and success. Biggin Hill means smokers.

Smokers? Let me tell you. A smoker is a private jet, and Rory gets to fly in a GV. You don't know what a 'gee five' is? I'll explain. The Gulfstream Five is not just any old executive jet. On the team we call it Air Force One. Rory once flew between four continents in twenty-four hours, changing flight crews as he went, juggling the kind of schedule that only global investment bankers can manage. The GV can technically take up to fifteen people, but Rory's jet is equipped just to take him and up to five colleagues. It goes at Mach .885, and flies at up to 51,000 feet, higher and faster than commercial airliners – public transport – literally leaving them in its wake. The firm doesn't own it. That might look bad to shareholders. We lease it. So not only does it make Rory's life more efficient, but it's tax-efficient too. And it's very efficient indeed when he wants to get away for a long weekend to relax and reflect on the future direction of the business, in Rhodes or Capri or Monte Carlo, maybe with his wife, maybe without. I'm sure if it was properly costed, we'd realise how much we save by providing Rory with the GV – it's a bargain and if anyone were ever to ask me – not that anyone would – I'd tell them I'm all in favour of Rory having whatever jet he wants. Or anything else, for that matter, at least this side of the bonus.

Though, in strictest confidence, there is one thing that really pisses me off. I've never been aboard the GV. No, not even once. Jackie has. In fact when she first joined, she and Rory used it for a whole load of strategy weekends and off-sites. But these days it looks as if she's grounded, the same as the rest of us.

Sometimes I feel as if I'm destined to live my life with my nose pressed against the window, a permanent outsider desperately peering in at where the real action is.

'He'll be flying alone, and he'd like the same stewardess as last time.' His secretary's words say it all – this man has arrived. 'No, he prefers the '85 Dom Perignon.'

What can I say?

WHICH BRINGS me to the subject of expenses. In the good old days, it was understood that senior investment bankers didn't really need to worry about expenses – the market was roaring away, share prices were rising, we were all making money, and expenses were a detail. We actually used to authorise each other's expenses. An extremely workable arrangement. Today things are different – we live in a tougher climate. Accountants and financial controllers actually have influence, and management listens to them. They have the authority to question things like the two thousand pound bottle of Yquem I ordered at dinner with the Chief Executive and Chairman of Pattison Construction a few weeks ago. The total bill for dinner for four was a little over five thousand, which would not be unreasonable as part of the softening up process of an important client about to award us a major mandate. The irritating thing is that neither of them was actually present at the dinner – yes, I admit, it was one of those dinners, but God knows, we are all guilty of a little exaggeration now and then. Anyway, had they been at the dinner, it would have been a great opportunity to broaden and deepen our relationship. Instead, I took Wendy and her parents to dinner, and must have accidentally used the corporate credit card instead of my own. We've all done it from time to time.

The problem now is how to explain. And the worst part of it is that the person I have to explain to is an underpaid, uncouth, unpleasant individual named Samuelson, who thinks people like me are overpaid, arrogant, unreliable and probably dishonest. He's sent me a note, asking me to justify the expenditure, and copied it to Rory. If I ever find myself in a position of authority, little shits like Samuelson will be toast. Then a light goes on in my head. I have the solution.

I prepare two replies. The first is to Samuelson, apparently copied to Rory.

I GROVEL and schmooze and weasel my way around the issue, saying that the chairman of Pattison Construction chose the dessert wine, and that there were four of them on their side, not three, as originally suggested (I just had a salad, instead of a main course), and pointing out that in fact three thousand pounds (thereby excluding the cost of the Yquem, which I had been obliged to buy out of courtesy for the client) for dinner for five people, of whom four were clients, was expensive, but not totally unreasonable, and had to be seen in the context of the development of the overall relationship, and imminent business prospects which I was not at liberty to reveal to him for reasons of confidentiality relating to price sensitive information. Just the right mix of taking him seriously, flattering him, sharing hints of 'inner circle' information with him, apparently treating him as an equal, but then reminding him who generates the revenue around here. And I apparently copied it to Rory, who would also see that I was taking him seriously, which could do his bonus prospects no harm at all. But then my masterstroke – I prepared a second version of the note to Samuelson, which I would actually copy to Rory alone. It was much brusquer, sharper, reminding him of the importance of carefully targeted, well thought through 'rifle shot' entertainment of the right people in the right way, emphasising the false economy of entertaining key clients on the cheap, and citing a ten million dollar revenue-generating transaction which we are very close to, but which is still highly competitive. To Rory, this is a reminder that I'm out there playing in the big league, swinging through the corporate jungle with the big hitters, there's a large deal just around the corner, and I'm not taking any shit from bean counters. When Samuelson fails to challenge me – which he would in a second if he saw this version – Rory will realise who gets respect around here. A masterstroke.

Afterwards, I worry that I've never actually met the Chief Executive and Chairman of Pattison Construction – I only know the Finance Director. But I guess that's a detail.

Wednesday, 3rd November

B minus 43

TODAY my worst nightmare happened. Well, not quite my worst nightmare, but something pretty bad. I got stuck on the Underground. To anyone accustomed to travelling by Tube, this may not sound too frightening – irritating, yes, even inconvenient, but not life-threatening. And for anyone used to living in the Third World country that modern Britain has very nearly become – at least outside the Square Mile – it was almost normal. Except that today we were launching a deal.

Today the European subsidiary of All Nippon Rubber were bidding for the Great Western Chassis Company. The bid would be announced at the market opening and I had to be there, so I left half an hour early to get into work. I didn't actually have anything to do with the bid, and had never met the client, but it was essential to be around when the deal happened.

It was actually Nick who was working on the deal, having been briefed by the Corporate Finance team, and I had only learned about it last thing yesterday. But that really didn't matter. If it was well received, I'd make a point of going around to anyone senior and influential to tell them about the deal, so that they first heard about our role in it from me. I could bask in reflected glory, while Nick was still too busy actually doing the deal to take any laps of honour himself. On the other hand, if it went badly, I'd keep my head down and carefully pick my moment to wander over to anyone who was around from the Management Committee. Shaking my head sorrowfully, I'd let them know that it really was Nick's baby, and maybe he'd been just that little bit too ambitious, just a tad too aggressive, perhaps a little impatient – all great qualities in an investment banker, providing they weren't taken too far. He always had the best of motives, of course, and naturally he'd learn from this one and I for one was still optimistic about his long-term potential...

So that was the plan, but half way into work, midway between stations, the train stopped. To begin with, I wasn't concerned. I glanced at my watch, then carried on reading my paper. The carriage was crowded, but I had a seat and I wasn't sitting next to anyone too objectionable. After a few minutes, people started to complain. An old lady standing in the middle of the carriage, barely able to reach the straps hanging from the ceiling, started giving me 'meaningful' looks, as if she thought I was going to offer her my seat. Instead I just gave her one of my wide, beaming smiles, nodded encouragingly and went back to the FT market report. Still nothing happened, and then a very large, very pregnant, very ugly woman pushed her way through to me and asked in a thick Midlands accent if I'd mind giving her my seat. She was probably in her early thirties, but looked older. Her bushy, unplucked eyebrows very nearly met in the middle, she had a teenage boy's moustache, a mole on her cheek with long bristly hairs coming out of it, a sweaty sheen across her face and was wearing crimplene and polyester with clumpy, square, practical shoes. Why on earth would anyone ever breed from her? I looked around indignantly, but all the other seated passengers seemed to be very old, very infirm, and mostly women. Damn – this is what happens when you have a means of transport without First Class.

'Qué?' I look at her, putting on a puzzled look, doing my best dumb Spaniard impression.

'You're reading an English newspaper.' She says it as if she's talking to a moron. Her accent doesn't help. Shit. I'm never at my best in the morning.

'Be a gentleman – can't you see the poor soul's expecting?' It's the old bag who was staring at me earlier, the one who tried to exert moral pressure on me. Some judge of character she turned out to be. The problem now is that having started out by pretending to be Spanish, but reading an English newspaper, I have to decide whether to keep up the pretence that I'm Spanish – which I can't, because I don't actually speak it – or admit that I'm English and offer her my seat. Just as I've decided to do neither, and ignore the lot of them and carry on reading my paper, there's a big jolt, and the train moves forward. The problem is, the pregnant woman, who would not be the lightest or slimmest I've ever come across, even without being pregnant, stumbles and falls onto the floor of the carriage, crying out in pain. As the train lurches forward in jumps and starts, everyone stares at me accusingly, as if I'm somehow responsible.

'Oh, for fuck's sake,' I sigh, and fold my newspaper and prepare reluctantly to get up and offer her my seat, when an older man steps forward through the crowd and kneels beside her, comforting her, trying to stop her idiot sobbing – I can see she's cut her knee on something, and it's bleeding quite badly – and then shouts across to the people nearest to the door, 'Pull the communication cord. She needs to get it seen to.'

I glance down quickly to check she hasn't bled on my shoes or suit. I'm wearing shoes by Lobb of St James's and my suit is hand-tailored at Gieves and Hawkes. A close shave. As he turns back to her, he also gives me a hostile stare. What is it with these people? Am I expected to take responsibility for everything?

The cord is pulled just as we pull into the next station – Westminster – and the train stops, but the doors don't open, while station staff go up and down the platform looking for the source of the trouble. I check my watch. 'Jesus Christ – I'm going to be late.'

Now they're all staring at me.

'We're launching a deal.' I emphasise the word 'deal', in case they really can't get it into their dumb, bovine skulls that there are some things in life that rank ahead of a blubbering woman with a cut knee. Eventually some station staff open the carriage door and come to help her out. I breathe a sigh of relief, check my watch again, and calculate that I might still just make it, but then one of them asks if anyone saw what happened, and the old bag points to me and says, 'He pushed her.'

Can you believe that? This wicked, evil, malicious old bag accuses me – quite wrongly – of an act no gentleman would ever dream of. And they all stare at me again, and no one intervenes to put her right.

'That's nonsense. I never touched her.' I almost add, 'I wouldn't touch her', but luckily I stop myself.

'Yes, he did.' She sticks her jaw out stubbornly, with one of those 'I will not be budged' looks that old people who are really long past their sell-by date sometimes put on. You just know there's no reasoning with her, and I have an almost irresistible urge to punch her.

The other passengers get out of the way as two of the station staff – young men in uniforms, who don't earn a bean compared to me, but infuriatingly take authority in absurd situations – ask me to get off while they call a police officer to establish exactly what happened. I look around helplessly, but no one is willing to meet my glance and I have no choice but to get off the train, inwardly raging, and wait while a policeman is called to question first me, then the old bag. The policeman – when he eventually arrives – looks like a child. I wouldn't even hire him as a graduate trainee, but I have to listen respectfully and go through the motions of taking the whole situation seriously, all the time glancing at my watch and realising that the deal will be launching any minute. The 'victim' – who could potentially sue me if they believe the old bag! – has been taken to hospital for stitches, so she can't corroborate anything, but then the old bag relents and says she may be mistaken, and after leaving my contact details I'm finally allowed to go. Can you believe all this? I could kill her. It takes forty minutes – forty minutes of precious, irreplaceable deal time.

Inevitably, there is now a delay. The next train will be along in fifteen minutes. As I climb the steps from the station to try to hail a cab outside, I look back and glare at her. She deserves to die. I actually thought we lived in a free country run according to principles of decency and fair play. How naïve am I?

By the time I get to the bank, Nick's deal has been

announced, everyone's smiling, high fives all round, and he's a hero. The shares did rise unexpectedly just ahead of the announcement, which is odd, but otherwise it was flawless. Nick grins at me.

'Where were you?'

'Oh – I... er... I was detained... I mean – held up. Well done, Nick. Congratulations.'

Damn. The only thing worse than a colleague having a deal go wrong is a colleague having one go well – and getting to claim the credit for it.

Thursday, 4th November
B minus 42

I'M ON MY way to New York for a day and a half of business meetings, sitting in the Heathrow Express, which I've discovered is actually convenient, quite comfortable and really fast, though of course that's not the point. I should have been collected from the flat by a limo service. Even if it takes longer, and costs more, it's a question of doing – and being seen to do – the right thing.

As I catch sight of my reflection in the window, I ask myself again if I'm looking at a loser. On the surface, everything looks fine: the steely grey eyes, the wavy brown hair, the dashing good looks that captured Wendy's heart almost ten years ago. But I can't escape reality. I'm thirty-seven years old, a Managing Director who has no one reporting to him. I share a secretary, I have to request the support of members of the graduate trainee pool if I need help on something, and I'm not even properly paid. Last year I got a useless, insulting, mediocre six-fifty, before tax, and half the balance was paid in options that are so far away from being meaningful that I feel like papering the bathroom with them. Surely life has to be about more than this? Three years ago, on the back of a monster year in a raging bull market, I got nine hundred. A lousy, hopeless, useless nine hundred in what was otherwise a fabulous year. How am I meant to live? How am I meant to support my wife and child? Wendy has aspirations – it's only natural. And so do I. I don't think it's anything to be ashamed of – I want the best for myself and my family. We all do. That's why we're prepared to make the sacrifices we do.

And talking of sacrifices, here I am, travelling on the Heathrow Express, to board a BA flight where I'll sit in Business Class, not even at the front of the plane in First. There was a time when we used to joke about not knowing how to board a plane and turn right, but these days we're made to travel with the masses. Personally I think it's a bad business decision. The fact is that investment bankers ought to feel good about themselves. This is necessary in order to project an image of confidence and success, to reassure clients and win business. It's not as if we don't work hard – tell me how many other people you know who work the hours we do, who travel as much as we do, who ruin weekends as consistently as we do – and for what? It's clear I'm not even going to make a lousy million this year.

I stare out the window, too depressed for words. I need that million. It's not for myself, it's for Wendy and Samantha. In fact I really need two million. Fat chance. And all the time I have this nagging doubt that Rory doesn't like me. Yesterday he walked past the desk, stopped to exchange a few words with Nick Hargreaves, then chatted to a couple of the juniors, but when he passed my workstation and I looked up and smiled in a confident, relaxed way, he walked straight past, into his office, and closed the door! He didn't even glance at me. What is it – have I turned invisible all of a sudden? Am I totally transparent? And it's not the first time. Last week something similar happened by the coffee machine at the end of the trading floor. Rory doesn't use the coffee machine, because his PA brings him proper filter coffee from a machine in the corner of her office, so it was quite unusual to see him chatting to some of the guys, and I hurried over to get a refill. I smiled and nodded and said, 'How's it going?', just as he turned to go. I looked around, but he didn't even acknowledge me. What am I supposed to make of that? It can't have been an oversight – he cut me stone dead. Don't try telling me he had things on his mind, because we all have things on our mind at this time of year. It just doesn't make sense, unless... well anyway, it doesn't make sense.

YOU MAY find this surprising, but bonus time can bring out the worst in people. Sitting on the plane, sipping my first glass of champagne – before you ask, no, it's not vintage, what do you expect in Business Class, sitting with the oiks? – I remember a Swiss German on our team a few years ago, called Richard Fresser. He pronounced Richard as if it was 'Rick–hart', but it made no difference, because we all just called him Dick. And that's what he was, three years ago, when Rory called him into his office to pay him. Dick felt the amount was so small as to be insulting, and he did a very Swiss Germanic sort of thing – he got up and stormed out of Rory's office, back to his workstation, where he swept the entire contents onto the floor, and then walked out, shouting Swiss Germanic insults in the direction of Rory's office. Only a Swiss German would act like this over money – talk about a provincial, small-minded, little prick. The rest of us would have been much smarter. The next day, he realised that even the insultingly small amount he had been paid would never reach his bank account if he was no longer an employee of the bank in a month's time, when the cash actually got distributed. So he tried to come back in. Can you imagine? Naturally, Rory's PA had immediately cancelled his staff entry pass to the building and his corporate credit card and had cut off his company mobile phone. So when the security guards called from reception to ask if he could be allowed up, we all went downstairs for a laugh. The best part of all was that he never really saw the funny side. It must be a Swiss German thing.

WE'RE AN hour away from landing at JFK, and I haven't slept a wink, though the lights have been turned down and the rest of the passengers in Business Class seem to be sound asleep. There's a very attractive stewardess, who keeps fussing around me, asking if there's anything else she can do for me. Her name badge says she's Donatella, which I suppose is Spanish or Italian, and she has a slightly dark complexion, which I don't usually go for – being a gentleman, I prefer blondes. But I've worked my way through most of a bottle of champagne, and I'm finally starting to relax, so that I can appreciate the way the top buttons of her blouse are undone and the tilt of her head and all the eye contact. I look at her and wonder what she would say if I offered her dinner in Manhattan. She looks interested and I'm the only passenger still awake in Business, so we could potentially... And afterwards, naturally I'd stand her up. I stare at her and ponder the possibilities.

Have you ever had sex on an aeroplane? I thought not. It's actually not that great, especially in Business – or so I've heard. In First, where you have seats that fold flat, turning into beds with small wooden partitions around them, the girl can slide in under your blanket and you can quietly, unobtrusively get on with it – at least that's what I've been told. In Business, forget it. You have to use the toilet cubicle, which is not only unbearably cramped, but by this stage of the flight isn't exactly fragrant.

Did I ever tell you about Piers Hawkins? Piers was an Englishman with the 'right' connections who worked on our team for a couple of years and then joined a German firm. The reason he moved – the real reason – was that no one on the team took him seriously after an episode on a flight to Hong Kong. It seems he made out with a stewardess in the toilets, when he thought everyone else was asleep. But the first time they did it, they made too much noise, banging up against the door and the partition wall, and woke a few people up. That would have been okay if they had discreetly exited, one at a time, and called it a day. But after a pause and a change of position, they started again, and a few more people woke up. By this stage, things were pretty tricky, but they might still have got away without too much embarrassment. But then – and at this point I have to give him full credit – he had another go. Yes, that's right – jet-lag be damned, they really went for it. This time they woke up everyone, and when they finally emerged, the cabin lights were on, everyone was staring at them, and they got a round of applause.

Naturally, no one took him seriously after that, particularly his soon to be ex-wife.

Which brings me to the question of infidelity. No, not infidelity to Rory – that would be unthinkable, at least this side of the bonus. I mean good old-fashioned fooling around. Looking at Donatella, who has quite an athletic figure, I could imagine having a really good time with her – briefly. Should I be concerned that Wendy would be upset if I did this? Well, yes, technically she would be upset, if she knew. And if she ever played away, I'd kill her. But is there really anything morally wrong about the brief enjoyment of purely physical pleasure by a man without any emotional commitment or betrayal? Some of the team say that it's no worse than the physical, sensual pleasure you get from an old-fashioned shave in a barber's shop, or a really invigorating massage: the person you're with is faceless, unknown to you before or afterwards, simply providing a service. It just happens that in this case, the part of the body that gets serviced is… well you know the parts that get serviced. It's all a question of relative values. In some cultures it's perfectly normal and widely accepted, and if anyone should be able to stand above the constraints and the relative norms of everyday morality in one particular society, surely it must be global investment bankers who benefit from a truly international perspective. We really are different from the rest of you, so there can't be any moral problem. Can there?

I'm glad we settled that. But the real question is, do I need the complications now, when I'm utterly stressed out about the bonus? I'm not even sure I could perform right now, so – nah, I won't bother. Not this time. I look away from Donatella, close my eyes and pretend to go to sleep. By the way, you remember the terms of the Kai Tak

Convention, don't you? I only shared this with you because we're on an aeroplane. I'm a happily married man, after all.

Friday, 5th November
B minus 41

I'M A BAD traveller. My first morning in New York, I always wake up ridiculously early. It doesn't matter, because I call Wendy, tell her it's 5:00 am and I'm already up rehearsing for my first presentation of the day. It never fails to impress her, though today she's in a hurry to get me off the line because she's running late and she's trying to squeeze in a session with her personal trainer before she goes to have her hair done. Anyway, New York is a great town, and I love to press the switch that pulls back the drapes – electrically operated, of course, to give me a perfect view of Manhattan. Then I order room service, so I can feast on eggs benedict while I enjoy my first blow-job of the day. And then my second and my third – perfect bliss with no interruptions.

Did I say blow-job? Damn. Well, yes, actually I've switched on the pay TV so I can get myself in the mood for what might come later. Shit. I said 'later', didn't I? I told you I'm not that sharp in the morning. I meant to say 'when I get home to Wendy'. I'm a married man, after all, and I'm here on business.

Saturday, 6th November
B minus 40

IT'S THE WEEKEND. Saturday morning, I'm mildly jet-lagged after my exhausting trip to New York, and there are only forty-nine shopping days to Christmas. Samantha's nanny has weekends off, and Wendy claimed to be worn out by all the sleepless nights I've been giving her – did you get that: I've been giving her! – so I had to go and get Samantha when she woke up and give her breakfast. It's not my fault that Wendy's so shattered. Her personal trainer gave her a couple of really hard workouts while I was away. She said he really stretched her. I'm starting to resent him. I think he's the reason I'm up early on a Saturday morning, seeing to Samantha. Can you believe I have to do this? Now's the time I could use some juniors: pour her muesli and her juice, make sure she finishes, wash her face, brush her teeth, get her dressed. I'm a Managing Director of a major investment bank, and still I have to do this stuff!

Of course I love her dearly. I always wanted a perfect, little blonde just like her mother. She looks so cute in the back of the Range Rover, wearing her Ralph Lauren dungarees and Baby Armani roll-neck sweater. But first thing in the morning she's... well, I would have said a drag, but how can anyone you love so much ever be a drag?

Later, when we're all ready, we go shopping for

Christmas presents. Now, this is a challenge. How much should I spend? If it turns out to be a good bonus, I'm happy to be extravagant on the present front. But if not, well it might still make sense to be generous, though generosity born of guilt about failure is not true generosity. It's a way of concealing inadequacy. It's a way of diverting attention from the real issue: Daddy, you're not a real man because you didn't even make a million. Little Mickie's Dad made two million...

We take a cab to Harrods, and I go mad in the toy department, leaving Samantha with Wendy while I organise almost three grand's worth of toys for delivery: every Barbie they have, a full set of Sylvanian families, a hand-made wooden doll's house, you name it, my little girl can have it – because I love her and I want her to have the best. Well the most, anyway.

Sunday, 7th November
B minus 39

TODAY I WENT to church. Well, when I say I went to church, what I really mean is that I walked past the church, went fifty yards down the road, heard the organ playing and a hymn being sung, turned around and went back, to peer inside. You can probably guess my views on religion. I had my fill of compulsory church services at boarding school. It's not that I mind how people choose to spend their Sunday mornings, but it has to be said that traditional religious belief sits uncomfortably alongside the life of the global investment banker. We serve markets, rather than gods. Or perhaps the markets are our gods. Anyway, truly efficient markets are morally neutral, and our role, as the people who service those markets, facilitating global trade and economic development – the very foundations of our civilisation – is to be completely unaffected, some would say indifferent, in the face of the choices we have to make between different courses of action. If we have to recommend a choice between a strategic restructuring of a huge conglomerate, resulting in massive job losses, or an enormous investment programme, leading to huge job creation, the moral and social consequences of any decision have to be put rigorously aside. We have to focus purely on the financial and economic results of any eventual decision. Which one carries the biggest fees?

That brings me back to church. I pulled the heavy oak door open and peered inside. There was a typical Chelsea crowd, singing in a desultory fashion, off-duty management consultants, lawyers, journalists, a television presenter whom I vaguely recognised, plus assorted spouses and children. What were they doing here? It was Sunday morning, the time when some of us have only just surfaced, unshaven, to venture out and buy a paper, and here they were, scrubbed, shaved, dressed, and worst of all, actually smiling. It was as if they'd all been given monster bonuses, and didn't have to worry any more. But

I knew – and in their hearts they had to know too – that they were running away from reality. Whatever they got from church wouldn't buy them a 911 Turbo Cabriolet, or His and Hers Rolexes, or even a week in Barbados at Sandy Lane (the only place to be seen there). I shrugged. Losers. I closed the door, quietly, making sure not to disturb them and wandered on to the newsagents, feeling hard-nosed and aggressive, my mind in overdrive again as I started working through bonus scenarios and how I'd spend the money. As we say in investment banking circles – he who dies with the most toys wins.

Monday, 8th November
B minus 38

THE MONDAY morning meeting. It's amazing how everyone at this time of year suddenly discovers enormous prospects for new deals, new clients, new business, just around the corner, conveniently after the bonus gets paid. There is a view, to which only a cynic would subscribe, that the bonus is not really paid for past performance during the year at all, but for your perceived productivity going forward, particularly in the next financial year. That's why if you can, you put off really big ticket deals until late in the bonus year, so they're fresh in everyone's memory when those key meetings of the Executive Compensation Committee take place. Like I said, a dollar earned early in the year isn't necessarily wasted, but it doesn't carry as much weight as a dollar earned the week before the Compensation Committee meets.

So today we all sit around and see if we can out-bullshit each other as far as exaggerated claims go. Rory sits and looks bored, until Jackie's turn. She smiles at him, flutters her eyelashes, and starts into a classic line that we've all heard a thousand times before.

'I'm working on some major prospects in the Middle East. It seems the Sand People really want to re-structure some of their portfolios in the light of...'

'Who?' Rory's voice cuts right across her. We all look up to see what's going on. Surely Rory isn't going to object to the old chestnut of enormous Arab wealth, huge trades, vast oil riches that need recycling – we've all used it. But he's leaning forward in his chair and staring intently at her, like a predator stalking its prey, about to spring. She looks flustered and blushes as we all gawp at her.

'The... I meant to say, the Arabs.'

'Do not – I repeat – do not use racist terms again.' Aha – now I see what's going on. 'It's unacceptable in this firm, or, I suspect, in any other. I will be taking appropriate disciplinary steps.'

Well, how about that? I look down the table for Nick Hargreaves, who's grinning. An ambush! It was a fucking ambush. She didn't know it, but Rory was waiting for the chance to nail her. Sitting there at the end of the table like a nodding dog, he was waiting for her to take one step out of line – and she did. He's playing a pretty aggressive game here, though he has a roomful of witnesses on his side, and at bonus time we'll make sworn statements to anything he wants. If the rumours are right, she's got a formal complaint in hand against Nick, which most people know can't be true, but she's done it to strengthen her own position ahead of the bonus round. But Rory, bless his little cotton socks, has decided to take her on. Why would he do that? He couldn't care less if Nick gets hung out to dry. But on the other hand, it might reflect badly on him, as the head of department, if sexual harassment can go on right under his nose. So he must be... yes, that's it. He must be planning to turn it around, to put her in the spotlight, maybe even suggesting she's homophobic as well as racist, and turning the tables on her. In theory, according to the firm's Diversity Code, we must never make any kind of comments, jokes or allusions which run up against the '–isms': racism, sexism, ageism, you name it, we can't do it. Except that Jackie just did. And so today, Jackie my girl, today the Big Beast of our particular Jungle has decided you're going to be lunch.

Jackie goes deathly pale, stares at the table and nods in acquiescence.

Thursday, 11th November
B minus 35

JACKIE LEFT today. Or at least, she didn't show up for work, and later I heard that a letter had come from her lawyers. It looks as if Rory's in fighting mood, and we've all been told we may be called upon to give evidence. Hell, right now I'd give evidence that she was guilty of cannibalism if it got me paid. Yes sir, your honour, I saw her with my own eyes. She lured passing children in off the street, offering them sweets as bribes, and after that, well I hesitate to explain in polite company what I witnessed with my own eyes... but all of it's true, I swear... at least until after the bonus.

The sad fact is that it won't make much difference. I've no idea exactly how much she was paid last year, but my guess is not much more than two fifty, which wouldn't make much difference, whether it was split evenly thirty ways across the whole department or just seven ways among the Managing Directors (which it won't be: I'm sure if Rory's going to this much trouble, he'll keep it for himself).

She didn't even have many decent clients for us to fight over. In fact she had one or two very difficult and badly paying clients that most of us would want to avoid. Maybe that was why she left. Anyway, she was here less than three years, and now she's history. Let's think no more about her, and instead think about... the bonus! On the way into work this morning I did some more scenario planning. I started with three million, but stopped when I realised just how ridiculous that was. Or put it another way: if I get three million, I won't have a problem thinking what to do with it.

So instead I thought about some of the worse case scenarios – a bit reluctantly, I admit, in case thinking about them made them more likely to happen. It's not that I'm superstitious, you understand, but you never know. Anyway, I started with six fifty, the same as last year. That was disastrous. As I've already explained, six fifty gross means three ninety net, and that in turn means less than two hundred in folding money – which is a catastrophe. Take off the overdraft, the 911, and Barbados, and that's it... it's all gone... an entire year of my life... and for what?

Then I went further. I started thinking about five hundred. At five hundred (three hundred after tax, one fifty in real money), I couldn't even pay off the overdraft, once I'd bought the 911 and paid for our winter holiday.

I shouldn't have done it to myself – God knows, my life is stressful enough already – but I then ran through four hundred, two fifty and one hundred. Each was more surreal than the last, each more terrifying as I worked through the consequences. At anything below two fifty I might as well not bother to get paid. Could it really happen? Was I really just torturing myself unnecessarily? I thought I knew the answer, but then I passed Rory in the corridor, and he didn't even glance in my direction – again. I felt like grabbing him by the shoulders and shaking him. Does he know the effect he has on people?

TONIGHT I got home and Wendy wanted to make love. We don't usually make love at all during the bonus season, not because it might be bad luck, but because it's impossible to concentrate when this huge uncertainty is hanging over you. Can you imagine having sex with your beautiful, expensive, wonderful, expensive, loving, expensive, adoring, expensive wife while all the time you're wondering whether you'll make a million, half a million, two-fifty, or just a useless, hopeless, utterly disastrous hundred thousand?

Anyway, I walked in the door and looked into the dining room. I could hear music. The table was set and candles were lit. For a moment I almost freaked – were we expecting guests? No – the table was set for two. And when I wandered through to the kitchen, there was no Samantha – she'd been put to bed early. And Wendy – well, Wendy looked terrific. She was wearing a low-cut, simple black gown by Armani, high-heeled stilettos from Fratelli Rossetti, a white gold necklace from Tiffany and amazing diamond and pearl earrings by Kiki McDonough. She looked complete, the way my wife should. And when she came and kissed me, with one of those lingering lips-half-open kisses, I thought... well, I thought what if I make two million? Think what I could buy her then. Now that is true love.

Anyway, she took my hand and guided it to her thigh, so I could feel what she was wearing underneath her gown. I probably haven't mentioned this before, but I'm a sucker for lingerie. Okay, all right – I admit it – not lingerie, just stockings, preferably black, with suspenders. And no panties. Now I'm blushing, because I've told you too much, but what the hell – when I say stockings and suspenders, I naturally mean La Perla, and no, when you buy one of these outfits, you don't get change from a hundred pounds. So if you don't know what I'm talking about when I say how much I appreciate this stuff – I understand.

Wendy had prepared a simple supper that started with beluga caviar, beautifully presented on crystal dishes filled with ice. It was followed by smoked salmon and a superb Grand Cru Chablis that I'd never heard of, but was delicious and which she must have picked up during the day to surprise me.

And afterwards, well you can probably guess what happened afterwards. She whispered in my ear, told me how she knew it was always tough on me at this time of year, and led me into the bedroom...

As if...!

What actually happened when I got home was Wendy in tears, because the useless, hopeless, ugly, hairy-armpited Bulgarian shot-putter we employ as a nanny had stomped out after a row when Wendy caught her stealing again. It's not that we're materialistic, it's just a simple matter of principle. Another pair of ear-rings had gone missing, and some cash that was left lying around, and a few odd CD's, and then Wendy saw her late in the afternoon going through her handbag, and that was it.

You can guess the rest – Wendy had the full hell of the late afternoon and early evening and no one to help her. First the trauma of bathing Samantha at the most difficult time of day, when she's at her most awkward, putting her pyjamas on, reading her bedtime story, getting her to sleep, obviously having to cancel the session she had booked with her personal trainer, so that just when she most needs help to de-stress, she maxes out on STRESS. Anyway, I walked in and she was on her third gin and tonic. To be honest I can't blame her. Not that that stopped me. I work damned hard and I don't expect to come home to a wife who's half-cut, hasn't even thought about my supper and just unloads a whole bunch of trivia when the whole time I'm in a huge panic about the only matter of substance in our lives right now – the bonus.

I slept in the guest bedroom.

Monday, 15th November
B minus 31

DINNER AT COLON, the new 'in-place' on the King's Road. This was something of a coup, because it's only just opened, and it's really hot. Apparently Hugh Grant's a regular, and someone told me Madonna and Guy have been there. The reviews say the food's mediocre, the service slow, the surroundings 'airport-lounge' bland, and the prices outrageous, but that's not the point, is it? When I called to make the booking, they said there were no free tables, even on a Monday night. This really pissed me off. The maitre d's at these places think they're so fucking important because they have power. They have the power to allow the rest of us to feel good about ourselves, which is absurd, because they don't get paid a bean and mostly they're seriously inadequate people who have to get off on jerking real people around – people like me. Anyway, I had a moment of inspiration, and called back a few minutes later, putting on a different accent, and tried to book a table in Rory's name – and it worked. The idiot who took the booking even said how much he was looking forward to seeing me again. Rory has a permanent inside track to all the hottest places. Don't ask me how he does it, but he does – only tonight, he was renting it out to me!

Sometimes, I try to dissect Rory's life, to work out how he does what he does and still succeeds as a global investment banker. Not that I'm envious, you understand, or somehow left in the shade, but sometimes I do wonder. Did I tell you he went to breakfast with the Prince of Wales? It was a breakfast for business leaders. Obviously nothing concrete or specific came of it, and no one was expecting anything to come of it, but it was a great event to be invited to – it sent a signal, it said that some people had arrived, and others hadn't. Clearly, I hadn't. And then he was invited to a garden party at the Palace. How did that happen? Who puts the invitation lists together? Do they go around the various firms, filling slots with senior people? No – because generally speaking, investment bankers hardly ever get invited – I can't imagine why. So what is Rory's inside track? And how does he juggle all this social stuff and still play the role of investment banker? And it's not as if he's just any investment banker – he's the Leader of the Pack.

It really fucks me off.

But tonight at least, I was briefly a hero... well, at least in Wendy's eyes. I called her from the office to tell her where we were having dinner, and she was over the moon – it went some way towards healing the rift after last night. But then she had to hang up, which irritated me, because her personal trainer was coming to the flat to give her a massage.

Anyway, we were having dinner with the Harrises. He works for Schleppen- heim, the US investment bank that made its name in the arbitrage business. They're aggressive as hell, towards each other as well as the competition, and this time of year is sheer murder for him. By halfway through the evening, I was actually starting to feel sorry for him. It's good to get a sense of perspective now and then, which you can only do if you meet someone really unfortunate. Last year he made a million and a half, but that's not the point. He's seriously overweight, drinks like a fish – though only after hours – looks pale and pasty-faced, and I'd rate him a serious health risk. When I look across the table at him, I see myself in a worst case scenario in, say, ten years or so –

except Bob Harris is two years younger than I am. He's thirty-five years old and looks like an unhealthy fifty-year-old. He has bad skin, eczema, and dandruff. He's rich as Croesus, but I know he'll never enjoy it. I really like being with him.

His wife is called Trish, they were childhood sweethearts, and I suppose she doesn't notice how overweight he is, or his bad skin or dandruff. She's plain, dumpy, has no idea how to dress, and has come out tonight wearing a two-piece suit that could have come from M & S. How can she do this to him? I can tell Wendy really likes coming out with her too.

Conversation centres on – guess what? – the bonus. Schleppenheim have had a terrible year. They placed a couple of big bets early on, using the firm's own capital, and both went terribly wrong. They went through a huge upheaval, even fired some of their management, which shows just how bad it was, and haven't recovered since. Naturally, no one feels sorry for them – those who live by the sword...

He shovels his food into his mouth as if he's worried someone will take it away from him. Maybe they do that at Schleppenheim. These US firms can be really aggressive. And he drinks like a fish, slurping great gulps of Chassagne Montrachet as if it was beer. Between courses he smokes – filthy French cigarettes that I know will make our clothes smell horrible, and which cause other diners to complain. But somehow I enjoy seeing him do this to himself. Thank God Colon hasn't succumbed to the tyranny of the health Nazis and still allows smoking.

The thing about dinner with Bob and Sally Harris is that I always come away feeling good about myself, and terrific about Wendy. Compared to Bob Harris, I'm Brad Pitt. And Wendy – well, Wendy's Jennifer Anniston. For once, even the money doesn't matter, because these guys are just rich losers. They've stayed so true to their working class roots that they wouldn't know Giorgio Armani if he bit them on the arse – which he might, if he saw how they dress. I don't know what they do with their money, but they certainly don't spend it – at least not as far as I can tell. They don't even own a car. Can you believe that? Bob doesn't drive – he just never learned. They live in a big house in Balham – yes, Balham. They have four kids, and no nanny. That's right – no nanny. Someone even told me they have no cleaners or other help either. She does it all herself. Yes, really. Everything – the cooking, the cleaning, the school run, even the ironing. I heard they give away a huge amount of their money each year to charity, though you'd never know it – they don't say a word. Wendy and I do our bit too, of course – but we do it publicly, at charity auctions where we can show what we believe in by bidding for items donated by generous sponsors. Last year we spent five grand on a two week yacht charter in the Caribbean (actually worth ten if you paid the full retail price, but we did it for Pro-Motor, the motorists' lobbying group against bus lanes); we paid three grand for a week in a really plush ski chalet in Zermatt (actually worth four and a half, but I did it at a riot of a livery dinner for the Honourable Company of Stock Jobbers), and we picked up five cases of vintage port for four grand (worth at least half as much again, but we did it for the Poodle Sanctuary). We all do our bit for charity, but why not give it a competitive edge?

Anyway, back to the Harrises. I've noticed how he not only bolts down his food, but he always goes for the least healthy items on the menu too. I wonder if he has some kind of unconscious death wish, a desire to escape from his awful life, the sole Brit in a firm that epitomises American corporate aggression on steroids, a house in Balham with no help, and a fat wife who can't dress to save her life. No matter how much he gets paid, I always know that when we meet for dinner, Wendy and I will look like the stars, and the other diners will assume we're taking our poor cousins from the country to see the sights.

But tonight was different.

It pisses me off now just to think about it. It started to go wrong in the most horrific way imaginable. We'd just finished our main course, and Wendy and I were feeling good about refusing dessert, while Bob and Sally ordered crème brûlée, when I heard a familiar voice calling out from across the restaurant.

'What a surprise – fancy seeing you here.' It was Rory – Rory!!! He was sitting at a table on the far side of the restaurant, with a fantastically beautiful woman whom I thought I recognised, though I couldn't be sure. How could he actually be here, on the very night I'd booked a table in his name? What had the maitre d' said when he arrived? Coincidence can stretch so far, but this was insane!

I beamed and got up as he came over, his hand outstretched and a warm smile on his face.

'Rory – it's great to see you.' I wiped my sweating palm down the side of my trousers and held out my hand in greeting as I prepared to introduce him to Wendy, Bob and Sally, all the time searching desperately for an excuse about why I'd used his name to book a table.

But he walked right past me. He walked right past me and shook Bob by the hand. Bob! Of all the people he could shake by the hand, it was this loser from Schleppenheim, this shabbily dressed, overweight, unhealthy guy with dandruff.

Bob didn't get up but kind of grunted and shook Rory's hand in the gruffest, most perfunctory manner possible.

At this point I had some catching up to do. 'I... I... er... didn't know you two knew each other.'

They ignored me. Rory started talking with huge enthusiasm about some charity that Bob was funding for asylum seekers. Asylum seekers! I mean – what on earth is going on – and Rory approves! Has he lost his marbles? Has Bob? Or have I?

They talk nineteen to the dozen for almost five minutes, with Sally joining in, while Wendy and I just look on, nonplussed, irrelevant and by-passed, until finally Rory says to Bob – yes, to Bob – 'I didn't know you knew these people.'

These people – he hadn't even said hello, let alone gone through the motions, which one would normally do, of being polite to an employee's spouse. He feels he can call Wendy and me 'these people'. We're fucking REAL PEOPLE, in case you didn't know it, and yes, I might have stepped mildly out of line by booking a table in your name, but it's not the worst crime in the world and right now our life is hell because of you and your fucking bonus.

Obviously I don't say this. I smile, Wendy smiles, Sally smiles, and Bob, whom I could kiss, says, 'We're really old friends – we go back a long way.'

'Really?' Rory seems genuinely impressed, and for the first time looks at me, a little perplexed. 'Let me introduce my wife.' He walks halfway back to his table, calls over, 'Darling, come over here for a moment, would you? There are some people I'd like you to meet.'

She smiles, a beautiful, dazzling, radiant smile and gets up to come over. She's wearing a dress by Dolce and Gabbana, shoes by Manolo Blahnik, she's carrying a Gucci handbag and wearing jewellery by Graff. Everything is top of the range – things you have to wait in line for, personally designed, with no compromise – if you need to ask the price, you needn't bother, and no queue jumping, no matter who you are or how big your wallet. At least a hundred grand is walking across the restaurant towards us, and the body is perfect. Toned, tanned, and above all, elegant. She moves across the room in an almost stately fashion, impervious to the looks and stares of every woman in the place not to mention every man. It must be my imagination, but it's as if a hush descends on the restaurant as she makes her way serenely towards us, oblivious to the effect she's having. I can feel that my tongue is hanging out – metaphorically, of course – and I want to take her clothes off there and then and... but then I turn and stare at Rory as he says, 'Bob and Sally, may I introduce my wife? Claire, darling, let me introduce you to two of the greatest philanthropists in the City of London.'

What? Did he really say that? Philanthropists? I want to shout 'Give me a break – you've just said he gives money to asylum seekers'. But of course I don't. After Bob and Sally have shaken hands with Claire, and Rory still hasn't introduced Wendy and me, I hold out my hand and say, 'Hi, I'm Dave Hart – I work with Rory.' I turn to Wendy and smile. 'And this is my wife, Wendy.'

Her eyes don't exactly glaze over, but it's as if somehow she doesn't quite see us.

'For me.' It's Rory. He's looking at his wife, and then at Bob and Sally. 'Dave works for me. Not with me.' He's speaking very quietly. I can feel myself blushing, stupidly, and I nod and grin. Can you believe that? I actually nod and grin. Am I a monkey or a nodding dog or what? And all for that fucking bonus, which isn't going to be any good anyway.

Wendy and I look on as awkward, sidelined teenagers while the grown-ups have a conversation, and when it's over, Rory and Claire return to their table and don't even say goodbye to us. Bob and Sally's crème brulées have arrived and they start spooning it in, looking fat and content as if nothing had happened. I sit and wonder guiltily if Rory knows I booked the table in his name or not. He might not – I could easily imagine him asking for a table for two and no mention at all even being made of my booking. On the other hand, if he does know, and worse yet if he was actually embarrassed, he'll wait for his moment. With the bonus just weeks away, it won't be long coming.

I want to scream.

Tuesday, 16th November
B minus 30

LAST NIGHT was bad. I was entering a large stately home, the sort you see in films about the great families of the eighteenth century nobility. There was ivy growing over the outside of the house and I used it to climb up to a balcony where the windows were open and I could enter a bedroom. There was a huge four-poster bed with drapes drawn closed around it. I was wearing black clothes, a mask like Zorro, and carrying a sword. I pulled the drapes back at the side of the bed, to reveal, lying naked before me – Claire! And then... then I woke up, and Wendy went through the usual ritual: glass of water, arm around my shoulder, ignoring my sweat and my shaking hands and chattering teeth.

I was going to rape Claire.

There, I've said it. I was actually going to rape her, to repay Rory for the way he insulted not just me, but my wife as well. Our honour was to be restored by taking hers – and implicitly his as well. God – I shake my head and wonder how far all this will go, whether I'll ever get used to bonus time, whether I'll ever put all this behind me.

It's 2:00 am I can't get back to sleep, so I go into the kitchen, make a pot of tea and sit staring out of the window.

What's it all about? Is it just money? It's an awful question. I think I know the answer to that, so I make my thoughts go elsewhere. How much longer? I'm thirty-seven. How many more Christmases will be dominated by The Bonus? How much longer will it rule my life, validating my existence, determining my self-esteem? Should I be working on an escape tunnel, building a glider on the roof of the bank, to carry escapees away to freedom? But what is freedom and where would I go? I know almost nothing about anything worthwhile or – God forbid – useful. If Wendy tells me a cupboard door needs fixing, I tell her, 'So get a man in to do it.' But what is a man?

I reach, sadly and with an air of resignation, for the whisky. Not ordinary whisky, you understand: this is a special Macallan, a rare bottling from the Second World War, and not available for sale to the general public. I've always thought Macallan make the best, but this is the best – and the rarest – of the best. Every drop is irreplaceable, and as I sip it – with just a dash of water – I feel better about myself. How many people in London tonight are drinking whisky like this? Or in the country? Or the world? Not only can very few people afford it, but even fewer know of its existence. This is a truly rare malt. I doubt if even Rory has ever tasted it. It was bought as a gift to present to an important client after a major deal, but somehow the celebration dinner kept getting postponed and finally never happened. I can't even recall how it found its way to my flat. Oh well. Needs must and all that. I take another sip and feel better. This is what it's all about.

Wednesday, 17th November
B minus 29

RORY IS LOOKING at me, he's stopped ignoring me, but it's odd. I don't feel comfortable, almost as if he knows that last night I was going to rape his wife. He can't, obviously. Still, it's a little unsettling. I even find myself wondering if he can smell the whisky on my breath, and might ask whatever happened to the presentation bottle of Macallan ordered for the Chairman of WunderKorp.

I really can't decide whether it's better to be noticed, or not to be noticed. I know that sounds facile, but frankly speaking (NB: whenever an investment banker says 'frankly speaking', remember he's not speaking frankly – maybe I should have told you that sooner, though you've probably worked it out by now) – I think there's a higher risk profile involved in being noticed than not. Some would argue that at bonus time the best rewarded people are those regarded as uncontroversially good, high achieving, apolitical individuals whom everyone respects and nobody has strongly negative views on. Yes – really.

And then there's reality. You knew I was bullshitting just now. This happens when I haven't slept, I've been out to dinner the night before, and when I can't sleep during the night I hit the whisky. It's a stupid, ridiculous formula, and at thirty-seven I really ought to know better, but – well, you can guess the rest.

Let's talk about Rory. No, not about me – you know enough about me. Rory is forty-three years old. I know, he's just six years older than me, and I know what you're thinking. He read history and got a First. But then, he would, wouldn't he? I read history too, at Balliol College, Oxford, and got a Second. Rory was at Exeter. No, before you ask, Rory didn't go to Exeter College, Oxford.

He went to Exeter, Exeter. Yes, that's right – the place in Devon where the yokels come from. And before that he went to a comprehensive school. Seems unthinkable? He was one of the beneficiaries of the broadening of the City's catchment area after Big Bang. It should never have happened. They wanted to go fishing in a bigger talent pool, where they wouldn't be limited to people like me, but could instead hire people like... him. Don't ask me why. The result is that he's part of the City's *nouveaux riches*, the new generation of high achievers who've made it without showing any respect at all for the finer traditions of the Square Mile. I'm a third generation stockbroker, a man with his roots in the City. My father was a liveryman like his father before him, a member of the Honourable Company of Stockjobbers and Brokers, and ended his career as the partner in charge of settlements at Carruthers and Stroud, before it was acquired after Big Bang, and my grandfather was a private client stockbroker at the same firm. As an only child it should have meant that I was set up for life, but somehow it never happened that way. Grandfather was a drinker and a womaniser, and he spent his money. At least my father didn't drink, but he did get through his too. I last saw him three years ago, when he brought his latest wife to see Samantha, his first and only grandchild. I forget her name – Susie or Floosie or something. She was younger than me, so I made a point of asking if she minded me calling her Mum.

I haven't seen them since.

Anyway, this isn't about me. Rory's always been a Golden Boy. Youngest ever member of the Executive Committee. Hoping to be the youngest ever Main Board Director. Some say he's Sir Oliver's heir apparent. He's certainly heading for the top. A fast track with a rocket up his arse. Me, on the other hand... but this isn't about me.

He has two children – apparently. I say that not because I doubt they exist, but because I don't see how someone as perfect as Claire could ever have had children. Unless she's immune to all the things that affect other women – or buys her way out of them. The really irritating thing is that she seemed not only beautiful, elegant, lively, adoring and bright, but a nice person as well – at least if you were part of her universe, which Wendy and I evidently were not.

In this business, it's easy to forget what a nice person is. Elsewhere, I'm sure you see them all the time: nurses, for instance, or teachers, firemen, ambulance crews, even social workers. I bet they're all nice people. Or most of them, anyway. But investment bankers? You must be kidding. We eat nice for breakfast.

So what does Rory think of me? You might wonder whether he doesn't see me as just another faceless, brown-nosing, unprincipled whore, who'll do anything for money. Would you like to sleep with my wife, Rory? Sure – go ahead, why not? You pay our bonus, after all. Humiliate me, stop me sleeping, give me ulcers, high blood pressure, a heart condition. Why the hell not? I'm yours, Rory, yours for the duration. So go ahead – abuse me, the way you kick a puppy and it comes back, nervous, frightened and ingratiating, always wanting more.

Except you wouldn't treat a puppy like this.

Monday, 22nd November
B minus 24

AN AMAZING thing happened tonight. I'd waited until Rory finally left the office, around eight, before packing up my things to go. The rest of the team were doing the same, once someone had checked that the coast was clear, and I went down to the main entrance to walk towards Bank underground station. It was dark and pouring with rain, and for some stupid reason I'd left my umbrella in the office, so I was splashing through the puddles when a car horn sounded behind me. I turned around and saw a dark grey Bentley flashing its headlights. Rory's car! It pulled up beside me, the rear window slid down and Rory peered out at me and said, 'Get in.'

For a split second, an impulse of pure madness almost overcame me and I found myself thinking how fast I could run to get away, whether I'd make it to Bank underground station before the car could catch me.

But of course I smiled meekly and got in.

'How are you?'

My jaw dropped. As if he could care. Actually Rory, I'm going out of my mind worrying about what I'm going to be paid in three weeks' time – as you know only too well, you bastard. In fact you probably have the numbers right there in your briefcase.

'Great,' I smile back confidently.

Rory nods to the driver, who slides the big car smoothly back into the traffic, muscling his way elegantly into the correct lane and heading for the Embankment, which is vaguely in the right direction for me, although Rory hasn't actually bothered to ask where I'm going.

'Good.' He stares out of the window.

'It's a filthy night. Thanks for picking me up.'

He ignores me and the silence stretches out. I look at the Bloomberg screen in the back of the car, the walnut desk top that folds down from the back of the front seat for him to place his laptop, so he can work on the way home, and the walnut cabinet where he keeps his whisky. I could use a glass right now, though of course I don't say anything. The Bentley's a slightly stretched version, so there's plenty of leg room, and the seats feel like armchairs. This is definitely the way to travel.

'Where did you first meet Bob?'

'Bob?' I'm genuinely puzzled.

'Bob Harris.' He glances at me, irritated, as if he thinks I'm playing a game.

'Oh, sorry – well, Bob and I go back a long way.'

'How far?'

'We were at university together.'

'Really?' He turns and looks at me again. 'Weren't you at…?'

'Balliol.' I say it almost guiltily, weighed down with the shame of the privileged under-achiever.

'That's right. Did Bob go there?' He seems slightly incredulous, his eyebrows raised as if it's somehow inconceivable that someone as clever and successful and different from the rest of us as Bob Harris could have gone to Oxford.

'Yes.' I can't help a note of petulance creeping in.

'What did he get?'

I pause and look away. 'I'm not certain – he was a couple of years younger than me. But I... I think it was a First.' Actually, I know it was a First, but who cares what class of degree people get anyway? It really doesn't say much about the sort of person you are.

Rory just nods. 'Do you think he'd come and work for us?'

Now I'm startled. 'Bob? Work for us?'

'That's what I said.'

'But... what would he do? Do you mean actually work on our team?'

'That's right.'

'But, it's not his field. He does arbitrage.'

'He could learn.' Rory turns and looks at me again, with what I think – hope – is a twinkle in his eye. 'We could break him in doing your job.'

I try to laugh, but it comes out as a sort of half-strangled gurgle, and I'm almost sure I catch the eye of the chauffeur in the rear-view mirror, sneering at me.

'Don't worry.' Rory slaps me on the thigh – yes, he actually slaps my thigh! We've just driven down the sliproad onto the Embankment and Rory leans forward to tap the driver on the shoulder. He pulls over to the side and stops, while Rory turns back to his laptop and starts tapping into it. I realise it's my cue to get out, and open the door.

'Goodnight.'

Rory ignores me, and I could swear the driver's grinning. I close the door and pull my collar up to protect myself from the rain. It's a damp, dark night, the nearest tube station is ten minutes' walk, and there isn't a cab in sight. Did he do this deliberately? Is he really thinking of hiring Bob? And if he is, surely he doesn't think he'd take my job? Bob's a heavy-hitter. No heavy-hitter would ever want my job.

Would he?

Wednesday, 24th November
B minus 22

THERE ARE rumours abroad.

I know that rumours are worthless, empty, unreal garbage that aren't worth the paper they aren't printed on. But it's twenty-two days till the bonus – twenty-two fucking days – each of them twenty-four hours long, with sixty minutes in every hour and sixty seconds in every minute, and those of us who have to live through each one of those seconds, wondering, speculating,

79

enduring the uncertainty, need something to keep us going.

There are three principal rumours. The first, which no one believes, is being spread from Paris by Jean-Luc, who claims to have heard that Rory is planning a team move to an American firm. Team moves were flavour of the month a few years ago when the market was booming and the Germans and the Swiss were hoovering up talent like it was going out of fashion – until of course it did go out of fashion, they dropped a bundle, and now we have to sit tight and wait while the market naturally corrects itself, the indigestion works through the system, and the next wave of dumb money comes along. But the Americans aren't dumb. Greedy, sharp-elbowed, vicious, single-minded and utterly ruthless, yes – but they're not dumb. And anyway Rory and most of the team would hate working for an American firm – if you think we have a tough time, you have no idea what an American firm does to its people. So this first rumour, that Something Is Happening on the team, is bullshit. Because if something were happening, I'd know about it. Wouldn't I?

The second rumour, which is only slightly less implausible, is that the entire bonus is going to be waived, because the firm as a whole is barely profitable (thanks partly to fixed income trading, and partly to private equity, neither of which has anything to do with our area, though that wouldn't necessarily matter). The idea of the entire bonus being waived for the entire firm is ludicrous –

even in the worst bear market, which this is not, you still get paid something. This rumour probably comes from management, and is more softening up to make us feel pathetically grateful for whatever scraps eventually come our way. Do they think we're stupid, or what?

It's the third rumour that intrigues me. Someone on the team has been insider dealing – using confidential client information to make a killing in the stockmarket. My first instinct is to dismiss it. Who on our team would ever break the law? Well, on reflection I suppose it would depend what was at stake. Would I break the law for a million? No, probably not – at least, not unless it was a dead cert that I'd get away with it. You wouldn't either, would you? Would you? To take a real risk, I'd need to make real money – five million upwards, and I'm your man. Oh, come on – don't be so shocked, not after what you thought just now. I look around the desk and wonder who it could be – and how it is that the rumour has started. You actually have to be quite brave to break the law, and I don't see any heroes on our team. Has someone confided in someone else, perhaps after they had a drink too many? I can only gaze around and wonder.

The good thing is that this takes my mind off my latest dream. Did I tell you about the latest one? It happened last night, and it was Claire – again. I'd tied Rory to a chair, bound and gagged, but not blindfolded, so he could see what was happening. I'd tied her to the bed, the big four-poster, naked and frightened, her wrists and ankles bound with silk, while he watched, powerless to intervene. I straddled her, naked myself save for a black leather mask, her master, her dominator, all-powerful – until my fucking dick went limp. Can you believe it? I think it was Rory, sitting there bound and gagged, but still in control. His eyes said all he needed to say: have her if you will, but I'm still the one who'll pay you.

Or not. And actually thinking about it, I went limp. Just like that – in a matter of seconds I went from a strutting master to a servile wimp. But then, with Rory's evil eye on me, it's hardly surprising, is it?

Friday, 26th November
B minus 20

TODAY AT WORK I did the headhunter trick. It backfired terribly.

You've never heard of the headhunter trick? Well, it goes like this. I pretend to have a call on my line. I get up and turn away from the rest of the team, as if seeking privacy, and as I do so I hit the 'Privacy' button on the dealerboard that stops other people picking up my line or listening in to the call. This usually acts like a beacon to attract everyone's attention. It generally means either a row with the wife, a call from a lover, trouble with the bank manager, or a headhunter. Now, you can go into a private conference room at the edge of the trading floor, where everyone can see you talking through the glass walls, but most people prefer to try to be inconspicuous by hiding themselves in the general buzz of the desk.

So I stand there, talking quietly to myself, saying, 'Sure... How much?... Guaranteed for how long?... Sure... you've got my home number?...Okay. I can't talk right now... Okay, bye.'

And do you know what happened next? Nick Hargreaves – yes, Nick, the gay guy I felt so sorry for – gets up, grinning at me, and walks over to Rory's office. He closes the door and sits with Rory, and points out at me. Yes, he fucking points at me! And Rory looks up and nods – and laughs. I can't believe it. I can feel I'm going stupidly red, and I pick the phone up to call home – not that I need to phone home, but I need to be busy, and right now anyone will do.

And then it all gets worse, because a man answers, and I don't know who it is, and I realise I've dialled the wrong number. In my stupid anxiety I've dialled Rory, and now he puts me on the speakerphone, so he and Nick can hear me.

'Yes?' It's Rory's most superior, supercilious voice.

'Oh... er...' God help me, right now, please dear Lord, if I can only play one of my jokers now, let me do so. And then it comes to me. 'Rory, are you planning to visit Paris for the football? I only ask because Dominique Dupont was angling for an invitation, and he's given us a lot of business over the past twelve months. I'm going to be in Frankfurt, but if you were free, I'm sure he'd be flattered.

Obviously I wouldn't ask you to go especially, but if it could be combined with one or two other visits, it might...'

'Definitely.' He interrupts me, and I can see Nick is nodding seriously now, the laughter wiped from his face. 'Put me down for it, and I'll arrange to see some other people as well.'

He clicks off the line and I close my eyes – Rory loves football. Thank you, God, I owe you one.

Monday, 29th November
B minus 17

SOME BASTARD broke into my car. I couldn't believe it. Why do people do these things? The driver's window was smashed, so the alarm must have been going on and off all night. Lucky for us it was parked around the corner. They couldn't take the radio, which is built into the dashboard, but they ripped the front off the glove compartment, which was empty, and then they took the fire extinguisher, which I found lying, empty, in the gutter. And they scratched the side of the car, all the way along the side, and for what? What do they think they're doing? What are they actually achieving? They stole nothing, but caused hundreds, maybe thousands of pounds of damage. Who are these people? Who are these faceless, feral creatures who prey on the rest of us? I bet they don't have to scare themselves shitless worrying about the bonus. They just fuck things up for honest, law-abiding people who work hard and try to do their best. Wendy had to take a taxi for the school run – it was that or walk – and she was seething with anger. I called the garage to collect the car and get it taken in for repairs and respray, and the insurance company to see about getting the repairs authorised. By the time I'd dealt with that, I was twenty minutes late for work, and this is not the time of year to be late for work.

Bastards. I'd hang the lot of them, except that would be too quick.

Which brings me to justice. Not justice in the legal sense, but what might be termed appropriate compensation – people getting what's coming to them. I'm a great believer in the principle that what goes around comes around. I knew Rory by reputation some years ago when he was at Swiss Credit, who were our great competitors for a piece of business that my then boss, Harry Braithwaite, was after. I was very close to Harry, I'd been to his house for dinner many times, and he'd even agreed to come to our flat once for supper – at the time we lived in Kennington, so it was quite a commitment on his part. So we turned up for the beauty parade at the client's offices, and there was Rory, leading their team, sitting in the foyer when we arrived and trooped in with our presentations and handouts.

Rory set the tone at once. 'Oh, here come the coach party.'

Harry said nothing, but was obviously seething, and headed off to make some calls before we were summoned to present to the client's top management. The rest of our team were stony-faced, ignored Rory's remark, and sat down to wait.

I know you're going to ask, so let me tell you – I smiled at Rory's remark, made eye contact and nodded to him: as one professional to another. I'm not quite sure why I did this – he was a competitor, after all, and we needed to win the business. But anyway, we didn't, Rory did, and Harry was fired.

This was a source of great regret on the team, because Harry was the closest thing I've known in the City to a popular team leader. But popular, as they say, is for girls, and within days of Swiss Credit winning the business, Harry was gone.

And then his successor was appointed – an outside hire, there was a lot of buzz going around about the amazing package the firm had come up with, and suddenly the announcement: Rory was joining to head our team.

Naturally, on his first day in the office, we all went to see him, offering our observations on the rest of the team, trying to get the measure of him, putting ourselves forward as his obvious deputy and right hand.

And he didn't like me.

I can't say for sure that he disliked me, but when he looked at me, there was no respect, no warmth, none of the familiarity that had briefly existed between us for one tiny instant when he had insulted my boss – and, I suppose, my team and my firm, in fact technically myself too – and I had smiled and nodded to him. It was almost as if he didn't recognise that this wasn't reflex ingratiation with a powerful, senior figure from another firm, or subconscious arse-covering in case I ever wanted to apply to him for a job, or he became – as he now had – my boss, but instead the natural acknowledgement of one bright, quick-witted, high calibre individual by another.

So there's no justice now, but one day there will be. One day I'll have my moment in the sun. Because Rory should have acknowledged that we had history together, that we had connected before he even met the rest of the team, and that we were two of a kind. But he didn't then, and he hasn't since.

It's okay. I can wait. My time will come. You don't believe me? Just wait and see.

Tuesday, 30th November
B minus 16

A LUCKY BREAK. Rory noticed I was late yesterday, and called me in for a chat. Apparently the verdict on the team is that my acting was so good about the car being broken into that it couldn't possibly be true, and someone – probably that slimy sycophant Nick – had spoken to him.

He actually appeared solicitous, as if he cared. He asked me about Wendy – he called her Mandy – and what our plans were for Christmas, and how things were going, and I could tell he was looking me over, trying to work out if a loser like me really could take another firm in sufficiently for them actually to make me an offer.

Would it bother him to lose me? It's not as if I actually do much, but then none of us really does much, though the hours are long and the travel is punishing. But enough business always seems to come our way that when the markets are strong we can talk the board into paying us and covering our overhead and expenses and the whole great bandwagon keeps trundling on.

After that, I decided to take a lunch break. No, I didn't have a client lunch – not even one of those 'client lunches' that the firm pays for but the client never actually makes it to (usually because he hasn't been invited – hey, no one's perfect!). No, this was an actual lunch break. The sort everyone is theoretically entitled to, but which our macho culture means that no one actually takes. A sandwich and a bottle of juice at the workstation, because markets are moving and we're too essential, too committed, too serious about our work, to do anything as frivolous as taking a lunch break. It's just about acceptable to slip out for forty minutes to play squash or work out at the gym if the markets are quiet, but taking lunch is for cissies.

So I took lunch – God knows why, it was just a moment of madness brought on by stress and anxiety – and now Rory really was worried.

When I got back, he called me in again.

'I thought things were clear between us. What's going on?' This time he looked positively hostile. At least I thought it was positive, because it showed he was concerned. One way or another, I was on his radar screen, and payday was just around the corner.

I played it cool. Yes, idiot that I am, I actually played it cool. 'I just went out for lunch.'

This clearly perplexed him. 'And?'

'And that's it. I was grateful for our chat this morning, I know you've got my best interests at heart – that's it. It's an important time of year, and I trust you.'

'Ah.' He leant back in his chair and made a bridge out of his hands, resting his elbows on the arms of the chair and staring at me. 'I see.'

At this point I felt somewhat less cool and confident than I had a few moments earlier. I realised I might have overplayed my hand.

'So you've dealt.' He was really fixing me, looking for the slightest clue.

'D – dealt?' I had to cough to clear my throat. 'What do you mean?'

He gestured out to the trading floor. 'This doesn't matter any more. You'll wait to be paid, and then you'll be off. You've done a deal with another firm. You're leaving.'

I experienced an almost irresistible urge to be violently sick. I could feel myself blushing. This was a disaster – if Rory thought I was definitely going to leave, there would be no point paying me. That would be a catastrophe, compounded by the thought that 'my' money would go to some undeserving bastard like Nick Hargreaves. Imagine him spending my money, while I sat at my desk, watching as the days went by and I felt more and more naked and Rory and the whole team waited for me to resign – except I had no job to go to. I'd never be taken seriously again.

'Rory – I'm not leaving.' I tried to put on my firmest, most resolute voice. 'I'm not saying I haven't been tempted, or that there aren't other opportunities out there, but this works for me, and this is where I'm staying.'

Even as I said the words, I could see his expression change as he realised that now I might be telling the truth and he struggled not to laugh. And then it dawned on me. This time I'd really fucked myself. If he believed me, which he apparently did, he'd have no reason to pay me well at all – he'd concentrate his firepower on the people who might really leave.

'Thank you.' He said it with an almost syrupy sincerity. And yes, I believe that at that moment he was sincere, because I'd just saved him several hundred thousand pounds that he could use on someone else.

Oh, God – why me?

Friday, 3rd December
B minus 13

A FUNNY THING happened today. I got in just about on time, feeling grim after yesterday, but determined not to be ground down by the everyday horror of my life. I'm a survivor, after all. In fact, that's a common trait among all investment bankers – we're all survivors. If there had been investment bankers on board the Titanic, everyone else might have drowned, but the investment bankers would have made it to the lifeboats. The women and children might somehow have been left behind – but not the investment bankers. The rescue ships would have arrived and found a few lifeboats and rafts containing... investment bankers. Because whatever happens, we never give up. It defines us. It determines who we are. And if anyone, ever, is inclined to dismiss us, to despise us for our unprincipled greed, or our egotistical superficiality, or the urgency and desperation of our lust for money and material possessions, all I say is this: could you do what we do?

Anyway, Nick left the Christie's catalogue on my desk. On my desk. I don't know why. He and I never discuss things like this – collecting antiques, buying at auction, personal things like that.

But there it was, and I flicked it open – and saw again the machete from my dream. It was only a few weeks ago, but it feels like a lifetime. I stared at it for an age, and when I looked up, I saw Rory looking at me from his office. I slammed it shut, got up and went straight to the gents. When I got there I splashed water on my face and stared at myself in the mirror. This was freaky. Did he know? Could he have any idea about the dream? Did he have a sense that somehow our destinies might be linked?

No, he was probably just bored and wondered what I was reading when I should have been working. It took me a few minutes to compose myself before returning to the floor. When I did, I saw that Rory had a visitor. Sir Oliver was with him. I looked around at the team.

'What's Sir Oliver doing with Rory?'

Nick looked up from his workstation. 'Chairman's annual visit to the trading floor, I suppose. Came down to chat with the team, put names to faces, he said – given the time of year.'

'But – but, I wasn't...'

Nick smiled. Yes, he actually smiled. 'That's right – you weren't here. But I don't think he wanted to see you. He didn't say anything, anyway.'

Of course he wouldn't say anything – but I would have. I'd have told him how much business I'd done during the year, thrown in a few names of key clients, talked about the prospects for next year, how excited I was, the huge potential that's out there, just waiting to be had – and I missed my chance because I was in the gents'. In my mind's eye, I'm planting the machete from my dream in the middle of Nick's forehead, splitting his skull wide open and letting his brains spill out onto the floor.

But of course I smile. 'No problem. Maybe I'll catch him on the way out.'

'Maybe you will.'

After that I don't move from my seat, alert for any sign of Sir Oliver getting up to leave. And then, when he does leave, Rory gets up and walks out with him, the two of them with their heads down, engrossed in conversation, and Rory seems to steer him away from the desk, so that he leaves the trading floor by the far exit. In my mind's eye I play out the scene from that Arnold Schwarzenegger movie when he pilots the Harrier jump-jet, coming up in the hover alongside a skyscraper full of terrorists and sweeping the whole floor with his cannons. Only this time I'm the pilot and I'm sweeping the trading floor, smashing workstations and glass-panelled meeting rooms and doing my best to lower the headcount this side of the bonus.

I look up and see Nick grinning at me.

I'M TAKING Wendy to the Barbican for a concert, and I have to go and collect her. It makes no sense, but she's tired and fraught and when she's in this mood it's no use arguing with her. Apparently she was due to see her personal trainer this afternoon, but at the last minute he cancelled her appointment because he had to see another client, and now she's pissed off. So I leave the City by underground, go home to change into my dinner suit and then drive her back towards the City in the Range Rover, intending to park at the Barbican. I wouldn't bother, but we're entertaining one of my more important clients and his wife.

Needless to say, the traffic is appalling. As I sit on the Embankment and fume, I curse Ken Livingstone and his useless congestion charge. What's a fiver, for God's sake? If you really want to keep poor people off the roads, make it a tenner or more. Or introduce special lanes for rich people who can either pay an extra charge or get their firms to pay it for them. That's the way they used to do it for the old Communist Party officials in Moscow. Why can't we do it properly and learn from people who really knew how to run a country – they never took any shit from their poor people.

When we get there, stressed out by the drive, we spot our guests, but we're running dangerously late if we're going to have a pre-concert drink. Our guests are the director of the London office of Nippon Heavy Rollers and his wife, Mister and Mrs Kanehara. They're an ill-matching pair. He's wearing what looks like a Moss Bros DJ that's two sizes too big for him, with an elasticated bow tie, which is positioned off-centre, but I daren't put it straight, because that would make him lose face, whereas she has an evening dress that looks like Catherine Walker and copious strings of pearls, possibly Mikimoto. She's small and cute and probably in her mid-thirties, whereas her husband is much older, maybe early fifties and a lifelong corporate man. I wonder what she's like in bed, and how much her husband makes – what would she say to a quick £10k?

Time is short, so after we apologise for being late, I shoulder my way through the crowd to the bar. I need to get a bottle of champagne, quickly, and get a few glasses down them as fast as possible. The Japanese are hopeless at holding their drink, so the sooner he's half cut the better.

As I push my way to the bar and shout my order, an old woman standing beside me hisses, 'Do you mind? I've been waiting here nearly ten minutes.' A funny thing happens at this point. It's as if my life is so full of shit that I have to take from all sorts of people, that to begin with, I just assume I have to take it from her as well. But then I do a sort of double-take as I realise that I've no reason whatsoever to be afraid of her: even at bonus time, she has nothing on me. I make a point of ostentatiously handing over a fifty pound note and telling the barman to keep the change as I pick up the ice bucket in one hand and four glasses, stems carefully intertwined between my fingers, in the other. Then I lean close to her and whisper in her ear, all the while smiling my usual friendly, engaging smile, 'Could I make a suggestion?'

'What?' She looks puzzled, as if I might have something genuinely useful to say.

'Why don't you go fuck yourself?' She tries to take a step backwards, but the crush around the bar is too great, and so she has to stay where she is, her face inches from mine as I continue my beaming smile. 'Just a suggestion – feel free to ignore it.'

I shrug and smile again as I shoulder my way back through the crowd. YES! Sometimes it's nice to bite back.

We down a few glasses, but then the bell sounds and we all rush in to take our seats. Within minutes I'm asleep and only wake up when Wendy nudges me because I've started snoring.

It's when the lights come up at the interval that I focus on the programme on my lap – it's open at the list of individual sponsors of the evening's performance, and there at the top of the list of Platinum Supporters is... Rory.

I close my eyes and take a deep breath, trying not to lose it altogether, as I imagine this all-knowing, ever-present being pursuing me during my every waking – and sleeping – hour. Wendy casts anxious glances in my direction, recognising the symptoms, and ushers our guests out to the bar.

When I emerge a few minutes later, my normal self-control restored, Wendy and the Kanehara's are talking to an old woman who seems vaguely familiar – it's the old bag from the bar. I'm about to duck behind a pillar when Wendy sees me and calls me over.

'Darling – come over and meet Lady Gore-Williams. Her husband is Sir Brian Gore-Williams, the governor of the Bank of England.'

Wendy is delighted. She obviously thinks she's Made a Useful Contact, someone with whom I can Network. Don't you just hate those pushy corporate wives at drinks parties who positively insist you meet their husband, because he's the director in charge of internet strategy at Amalgamated Lawnmowers, and who get pissed off when your eyes glaze over and you look over their shoulder for someone more interesting? Anyway, right now I look at the old woman, look at Wendy, look at the Kanehara's, and imagine spraying an Uzi sub machine-gun round the room, wasting everyone in sight, blazing away until the magazine is empty, peace descends and my last cartridge rolls across the floor amongst the bodies.

Lady Gore-Williams surprises everyone when she nods at me and smiles. 'Oh, we've already met. Your husband passed on some very useful advice to me, which I'm sure my husband will appreciate. Did you say your name was Hart? I must mention your advice to my husband – I do believe he's been invited to lunch with your chairman, Sir Oliver Barton, next week. He was saying to me only yesterday that he didn't think they have much to discuss, but I'm sure I can give him a tip or two.'

The great thing is, she says it all with the sweetest look of utter sincerity on her face – a harmless, lovable little old lady, as she slides a knife between my ribs and twists it sharply round and round. As my heart sinks further, and a horrible feeling of nausea threatens to loosen my bowels, I can't help thinking to myself, Christ, and I thought I was good – she's the one who should be an investment banker.

Saturday, 4th December
B minus 12

TODAY I REACHED the Point of Maximum Desperation. Unlike PMT, PMD comes just once a year – but it's got to be much worse than a whole year's worth of

PMT. It's the moment when I realise just how bad things could be if I don't get paid. Little things can spark it, passing a Porsche showroom or walking down Bond Street, but this year it was the credit card statement. We – by which I mainly mean Wendy – had spent eleven thousand pounds on the credit card in November.

Now, eleven thousand may not sound like much to you, but in certain poor countries whole families can live on that much for a year! I know this may seem ridiculous, but think about it from my perspective – on a basic salary of a hundred thousand, I simply cannot afford to run up credit card bills like that. So when I got home from the concert late last night and found the credit card statement with the mail on the drawing room table, I sat in an armchair and got utterly and completely depressed. I don't mean that I was feeling 'a little low', or 'less than a hundred per cent' – I was FUCKING DEPRESSED! A major league Blackie had descended on me, a whole pack of Churchill's black dogs, and they weren't letting go. As if symbolically, my special bottle of Macallan was empty, reflecting the state of my bank account and my bonus prospects going forward. Looking at it, I could swear it was the bloody Bulgarian shot-putter who finished it, probably as revenge after Wendy stupidly re-employed her, mainly out of desperation that the absence of childcare meant she had to stop her sessions with the personal trainer – apparently she needs his help to de-stress, because of all the pressure she goes through at this time of year.

Anyway, here I was, sitting in a million pound apartment in Sloane Square, a Managing Director of a major investment bank, days away from the annual bonus round, and I was broke. Wendy didn't make it any better by saying how much she'd saved – yes, saved! – by taking advantage of the fact that the sales start before Christmas these days and actually she had found some amazing bargains: a Donna Karan scarf at a thirty per cent discount, another handbag from Coach at a twenty-five per cent discount, and so many new shoes at amazing savings that I finally lost count. How many shoes can a woman wear? But they were all bargains. In fact she had saved us so much money that now we didn't have any left.

The more I thought about it, the more solutions I found. I could always raise the overdraft, get some more credit cards and extend our credit with the various store cards that Wendy uses. The main thing was to act with confidence. We live in a fickle, superficial world, which responds to us so often directly in proportion to our expectation of its response. Of course, I'm rich – very rich, actually. I have investments, naturally, and offshore accounts. So I must be well off. And it must make sense to extend my credit. Otherwise I might take my custom elsewhere, and that would never do, would it? I thrust my jaw out and put on my grim-faced but determined look. I do grim-faced but determined very well. Eleven grand on the credit card was not going to be the straw that broke the camel's back. I was solvent and I had a good job. In fact compared to the vast majority of the population I was among the favoured few. It was important to remember that, to keep a sense of perspective that would allow me to bounce back. Have you noticed how I do that? No matter how bad things are, I always bounce back. I have something called resilience. Nothing ever defeats me. Push me over ten, twenty, fifty times and I always bounce back – another smiling investment banker propelled ever onwards in life by invincible self-belief. Phew.

Tuesday, 7th December
B minus 9

THE CHRISTMAS PARTY. It's strange having it just before the bonus. Normally it's timed to be a few days later, when most people can pretend to each other that they've been fantastically well paid and are happy, successful people, and anyone who can't hide his depression can get hopelessly plastered at the firm's expense.

Only this year was different. Rory sent around an e-mail announcing the date, the venue and most importantly the fact that because of cost-cutting measures, the MD's were picking up the tab instead of the firm. Yes, I said the fucking MD's were picking up the tab, and he hadn't even consulted us. Can you believe that? By now I suppose you can. But the other surprise was the venue. It was going to take place in the staff canteen!

I'd always known there was a staff canteen somewhere in the basement, but I'd never actually been there. It was a place where support staff and juniors went to get subsidised lunches. Front-line revenue generators like me would never be seen dead there – we were either chained to our workstations or lunching clients at proper restaurants.

I tried to work out Rory's game plan. It would look good to management – imposing strict economies on the team – and it would look as if there was a strong team spirit – the MD's, as the most senior and well paid team members, picking up the tab for everyone else. What he hadn't said was how much he would be paying personally towards the cost. All MD's were not exactly equal, so would there be an even seven-way split between us or would he shoulder more of the burden? Someone checked with his PA and you can guess the answer.

So anyway, there we were, thirty of us, drinking sparkling wine and serving ourselves with cheap canapés, while making small talk with people we'd sat next to all year, without our spouses (probably doing them a favour), in a room that could seat a hundred and fifty, and was decorated only with some cheap tinsel and baubles. There was no live music – in the past we'd often had live jazz, which definitely hits my spot – and instead the secretaries had brought in CD's of boy-bands I'd never heard of. Luckily the music was so weird that no one was dancing, so the MD's were excused the need to show what good sports they were by strutting their stuff on the dance floor. The other piece of good news was that the bill at the end of the evening would definitely not be much. No one could dare to get drunk, in case they said something they shouldn't. Everyone was hanging around Rory, who seemed utterly bored and kept looking at his watch.

At nine o'clock, the evening reached its low point: the juniors had made a spoof video. This was a tradition on the team, and a kind of competition among the younger team members, to see who could be the most creative and yet risqué at the same time, pushing the envelope in terms of aggression verging on insubordination towards the MD's – except Rory, of course.

Well this year it was different. The lights went down and we all sat around a giant screen TV in the corner of the canteen, drinking more sparkling wine and munching cheese crackers – which by now we were all sick of – and a series of sketches started as the juniors mimicked the idiosyncrasies of the senior team members.

Except that half of the juniors weren't on the team anymore.

It slowly dawned on me – on everyone – that Rory had quietly fired half of them over the previous few weeks. As I looked around, I caught the nervous glances of the few remaining ones, as they saw their old comrades in arms on the screen. It was a cross between a wake and a memorial service. How was it possible that so many young people could quietly disappear in such a short space of time and no one seemed to notice, let alone comment on it? Were we really so self-absorbed that it simply passed us by? They were real people, after all, they had wanted to be investment bankers, they had worked hard, and now they were... well, they were gone. Afterwards I heard that they had not all been terminated – one had been moved to the library, which is worse than being fired. When it came to an end the lights came up and we all applauded politely and Rory said, 'Well done, everyone,' and left without saying another word. The other MD's took their cue from him and left as soon as he was out of the way.

Thursday, 9th December
B minus 8

BILL MYERS was fired today. You don't know Bill? I'm not surprised. Bill was the quietest Managing Director on the team, a kind-hearted man approaching fifty years of age, married with four children and always looking as if life had dealt him a bad hand. In the high-flying world of investment banking, Bill was undoubtedly a low-flyer, a turboprop, World War One vintage biplane that had somehow survived because he was vaguely useful and despite his apparent seniority not very expensive. He had been at the firm far too long – nearly eighteen years – and constituted the tribal memory of the team, as well as taking charge of the juniors, training and mentoring them, and looking after some of the duller, less important aspects of the team's work, like monitoring costs. Useful but dull, that was Bill. He commuted every day from somewhere near Brighton and always seemed slightly frayed around the edges. Someone told me he had a handicapped daughter, but I knew that would cut no ice with management. The fact was, Rory could present a senior firing as a decisive act of strong leadership without actually losing much by way of revenue. It would be a pain in the neck for everyone else, because other people would have to pick up some of the administrative and personnel duties that he had handled, but for Rory it was a clear win.

I suppose it was the eighteen years' service that really did for him. If he had been a sharp job-hopper, never more than two or three years in any one firm, moving from one guaranteed package to the next, he'd have been both richer and better regarded. But he hadn't, so he was poorer and largely disregarded. When he arrived in the morning there was a black bin liner sitting on his desk, a note from Personnel and a security guard hanging around 'unobtrusively', making sure he did not do anything stupid like smashing his computer screen.

Not that Bill would ever have done anything like that. Bill could define the term middle-aged: balding, greying, stooping, physically pear-shaped, he did not even look like an investment banker. He saw the bin-liner, went deathly pale, picked up the envelope from Personnel, opened it and read the contents. Then he closed his eyes, breathed a big sigh and looked around at the team, a lost, blank expression on his face.

'So that's it?' He looked sad and lonely as we all stared at our screens and pretended to be making phone calls.

As the guard took Bill's pass and company credit card and mobile phone, I glanced across at Rory's office, to see if he was watching. After eighteen years' service, couldn't Bill expect that his boss would at least do the deed face to face? No – the lights were out and the office was empty.

It was only later, in the gents', that I spoke to Nick Hargreaves.

'He can't have been making more than three hundred. He's a lifer, or very nearly, and they never get paid.'

That was Nick's assessment. I nodded. 'Still, three hundred spread around the MD's would help a little.'

'Nah.' Nick gave a smug grin, as if he was somehow privy to Rory's thinking in a way that I was not. He tapped the side of his nose. 'It's all about positioning. Rory can milk this for a lot more than that. You mark my words.'

I left the gents' with a spring in my step. This was the first good news in weeks.

AFTER BILL'S desk had been cleared, I decided to think about Christmas presents. Not for myself, of course – I already felt Bill had given me an unexpected surprise – but for the important people in my life: the clients whose fees pay my bonus. As investment banks' services to their clients get more and more commoditised, and clients find it hard to tell the different banks apart, Bartons has sought to distinguish itself from the rest of the pack. We're the generous bank. We give great gifts to the individuals who run major corporates, and in return, they give us great gifts – of fees for deals they never knew they wanted to do. I think of it as a financial eco-system – we send gifts to the clients, and the clients send us gifts from their shareholders, which in turn pay for more gifts, and so on.

The thing about presents is that you have to pitch them just right. Give too little, and you can actually cause offence, or seem like a cheapskate. On the other hand, if you overdo it, your gift might seem excessive, almost like a bribe, and obviously we'd never bribe anyone. It's in the firm's Code of Practice – we're simply not like that. And what could be even worse, would be if the clients felt obliged to reciprocate, not with business and deals and fees, but with gifts. Who needs gifts? Gifts are for girls. Real men want bonuses.

So I drew up a list of clients and split them into three. The first part of the list was those who really could give me some business, and whose home addresses I knew. The next part was those who really could give me some business, but whose home addresses I hadn't been able to find out. And the third part of the list was those whose home addresses I did know, but who were not in a position to give me any business, although they did know my home address and understood the game.

The best list to be on is the first. A client who really can give you some business is worth cultivating. Not bribing, mind you – cultivating. And if you know his home address, then cultivating him is a lot easier. Gifts that arrive at home obviously ought to be declared by the client to his employer, just in case they were ever to influence him in deciding who to give a piece of business to, but somehow in the hurly-burly of the run-up to Christmas, when there are a thousand and one things to do, some things may be overlooked. Like enormous hampers from Fortnum's, or cases of vintage port, or boxes of Cuban cigars. It's easily done.

The worst part of the list to be on is the second. Gifts delivered to a client's office are subject to whatever regime his firm imposes. Some firms make the recipient donate them to their annual charity auction. Others say the recipient can keep gifts below a certain (ludicrously low) value, but anything beyond that must go into a pool of gifts distributed via a draw at the annual staff party. There's really no point in sending these people anything worthwhile, and so they're the ones who get the desk diaries and the restaurant guides. Later on, when it comes to Ascot and Cowes Week and Wimbledon and Henley, you do your best to make it up to them, but in the meantime Santa's reindeer don't park on their roofs.

The really interesting group are the last one. They're the people who don't have any business to give you, and realise that, but understand how to play the game.

They're the ones you can 'entertain' to dinner at a top restaurant without actually troubling them with an invitation or the requirement to attend: they understand. They're the ones you get the bank to buy Wimbledon tickets for without imposing on them the tedious obligation of sitting in those tight little seats in the Centre Court on a hot summer's day. In short, they're the ones who help you out when the in-laws are in town and you need to make a good impression and it's half way through the year and the bonus is still months away, but you're already overdrawn. They're friends.

Friends are people you look after – because they look after you. So the third list get really special, personalised presents – silver coasters from Tiffany, special gift sets of aromatherapy oils from Jo Malone, a humidor from Davidoff. These gifts are the ones I really think about, because in a manner of speaking, I expect to be on the receiving end of 'presents' from these people all year round. And just occasionally, because they know me too, they send me something in return – at home, of course. It's never anything of value, obviously, or I'd disclose it to the Compliance Department, who exist to keep us on the straight and narrow. No commercial value is the phrase – and after all, once a bottle of Macallan forty-year old's been opened, it really doesn't have any commercial re-sale value, does it?

So we all sit at our workstations, making calls, placing orders, working through our Christmas lists. This is the one area where the firm does not cut corners. We might all have to slum it in Business Class on long-haul flights, we might be forced to take public transport out to Heathrow, but we can still stretch the corporate plastic at Fortnums. There's a hum on the desk, a buzz, like I haven't felt in weeks. We're working, and the team spirit really kicks in. Just one big happy family, looking forward to Christmas and all it brings.

AFTER WORK, a normally pleasant event – someone's leaving drinks. I always feel instinctively good about someone leaving: one less mouth to feed come bonus time. The person leaving – strictly speaking retiring, though he's still a few years away from the official retirement age – is Jeff Ward, one of the longest serving sales-traders on the floor. Jeff is a classic old Stock Exchange figure, a source of advice in difficult situations, a fund of experience such as you rarely find in any firm, and while he does like a drink or two at lunchtime – almost uniquely in the firm, though once it was the norm – his instinct is always to do the right thing. It's as if he's the corporate conscience of the trading floor.

He hasn't had any line management responsibility for some time now, since an unfortunate incident that embarrassed the firm and left everyone feeling slightly uncomfortable. We'd done what's called a block trade – bought a huge holding of shares from a corporate seller with a view to selling them on at a higher price. Jeff didn't want to do the business – he said the price was wrong and the market felt dodgy. Naturally the investment bankers whose client wanted us to do the business tried to downplay his views – they didn't understand what he meant when he said the market 'felt dodgy' and instead produced charts and graphs and trend lines and everyone smiled indulgently at the Old Man of the Markets who was trying to stand in the way of a lucrative piece of business.

Except he was right.

We bought the shares and tried to sell them on, but over the course of the morning, the market started to fall and soon we realised we were going to be stuck with a large unsold position – so large, in fact, that we would have to disclose it to the Stock Exchange, which would be a disaster, since all of our competitors would know we had it and the price would fall through the floor. Not only would we look like idiots, but we stood to lose millions.

Naturally we had to do something about this, and the first instinct of the investment bankers was to conceal the information internally and work out a game-plan. So far, so good, but one of the people they had to deal with was Jeff, and in the simple world he inhabited, if you took a risk and it went wrong, you paid the price. If the position had to be disclosed, then disclosed it should be. He didn't say 'I told you so', but instead set to work trying to think how to hedge the firm's risk.

In the meantime, the investment bankers decided to lie. Not a Big Lie, of course, just an itsy-witsy, teeny-weeny little lie. They decided to say nothing to the market, on the grounds that the amount of unsold shares was actually small enough not to need disclosure – the balance was sitting on the firm's 'normal trading book' and as a 'normal trading position', wouldn't need to be revealed to anyone. As sleight of hand goes, it was not a bad strategy – though of course I would never be tempted to do anything similar myself – but when Jeff heard, he said no. He said that it was almost certainly wrong from a legal perspective, and if they were caught they could go to prison, but it was definitely wrong morally. Morally? Yes, really – he said that no amount of money made on any one trade could ever justify jeopardising the good name and reputation of the firm, and he went over the investment bankers' heads, directly to Sir Oliver, and laid it on the line.

Of course, Sir Oliver was hugely embarrassed. He was caught between a rock and a hard place, and had no choice but to Do The Right Thing. So the firm disclosed the position, the share price fell, and Jeff worked like a dog to hedge it and work it and eventually, three months later, thanks in part to a buoyant market, the last of the shares were sold, at a modest overall profit.

And do you know what they did? They transferred the investment bankers overseas, and then waited another six months to 're-organise' Jeff's division, removing him from any management or decision-making responsibility. And this year, they were going to fire him – but he was a canny old fox, and somehow a little bird had tipped him off, which is why we had the very unusual spectacle of a retirement drinks party several years before he reached retirement age, and just a few days before the bonus. Jeff was leaving in his own time and on his own terms – with dignity and honour intact.

Naturally, the rest of us felt very uncomfortable. It was not that we wouldn't put pride and reputation first, of course, and after a lifetime in the City, Jeff could probably afford to quit anyway. But fundamentally, we all agreed, he was a dinosaur. He'd been in the City thirty years, man and boy, and was simply out of kilter with the times.

Only this dinosaur had teeth. This dinosaur was an Allosaurus – an Allosaurus with a sore head who was looking for a fight.

We all went into the downstairs bar of the Happy Jobber, one of those traditional bangers and mash, sawdust on the floor, pubs that men of Jeff's generation had always enjoyed, and which had somehow survived the corporatisation of the City and the slow but steady disappearance of men who drank at lunchtime. The place was packed. I suppose there were two hundred of us, from all parts of the firm, including most of the heads of department, and Jeff had his credit card behind the bar so we could take full advantage of his hospitality. At around eight o'clock, Sir Oliver put in an appearance, with Rory in tow, and someone banged a glass for him to say a few well-chosen words.

'Your retirement, Jeff, seems like the passing of an era. When I look around the trading floor today, I see no one from the same mould as you. Truly, you have been unique and your contribution to the firm has been extraordinary. We shall mark your passing as a defining moment for the firm as we move forward into a different age, a different climate for the City of London...' and so on. I'm not sure he ever actually said he liked Jeff or would miss him, but I'd had a few glasses of champagne and might not have been concentrating. At the end we all clapped politely and then, instead of letting us all carry on drinking, while Sir Oliver and Rory sloped off, Jeff announced that he wanted to say a few words too.

I had no idea what was coming.

'Thank you, Sir Oliver, and thank you all, for coming along tonight. It's good to see so many familiar faces, because it will help me remember what it is I'll be missing from now on, the people I won't be seeing each day. When I first started at Bartons, Sir Oliver was a mere whipper-snapper, the old Chairman's son, brought in to learn the trade.'

At this point, Sir Oliver smiles politely, but I can tell he doesn't mean it. Rory and the other heads of department take their cue from him and put on corporate smiles – polite ones that they don't mean, and which show that they're really just indulging the old codger because it's his last day and he's probably ga-ga and half-cut anyway.

'Ollie the Wally, we called you – wouldn't dare to now, of course.' A few people, who have obviously had one too many already, snigger at this, but then stop as they realise their mistake. Too late, because Rory's clocked them – ouch, it's a bad time of year to be caught laughing at the Chairman. Sir Oliver's smile has become fixed, frozen in place, while Rory and the others have stopped smiling and are glancing around, looking at their watches, doing their best 'I'm bored and I'm not paying attention' impressions. Jeff seems to savour the moment and pauses to take a deep breath, as if by inhaling the moment, he can capture it for the future. There's a twinkle in his eye as he continues. 'But in those days, everyone called you that – even your special friend from Eton, that nice young man with the wavy fair hair who joined with you. Funny – I can picture him now as if it was only yesterday. Very tall, very elegant, with girlish features and delicate hands with long fingers and the family crest on a ring on his pinkie.' Jeff looks at Sir Oliver in a very unusual way, almost as if he's the predator, and Sir Oliver the prey. This makes me very uncomfortable – the investment banking food chain simply doesn't work like this, at least not normally. 'But then Sir Edward sacked him.' Jeff pauses, as if trying to recollect something from far back in his memory, while Sir Oliver stops smiling and stares ahead, tight-lipped. 'Something to do with the Christmas party, and some misunderstanding, as I recall. Something to do with the two of you. And a broom cupboard. Or was it the stationery cupboard? Anyway, that's not important now, is it?' Christ almighty – I stare at the floor, then glance up again at Jeff, trying not to catch anyone else's eye. He's grinning now, staring at Sir Oliver as if to bait him. 'What was his name? I saw him in the paper just the other day. Oh, yes, I remember – he's the Chief Executive of –'

Before Jeff can finish, Sir Oliver steps in front of him and booms out in his loudest, most authoritarian voice, 'Thank you, Jeff, for that little reminder of the past.' He smiles magnanimously, but it's clear that his eyes are as dark as thunder. 'It's funny how these tales can grow in the telling. Ladies and gentlemen, let's have a big round of applause for Jeff.' Even as he's speaking, he starts clapping as loudly as he can, and Rory and the heads of department join in and look around commandingly, so that we all follow suit, and the applause rocks the rafters and drowns out anything else Jeff might have wanted to say. After a vicious glance in Jeff's direction – the sort of glance that would kill me on the spot, but Jeff just grins – Sir Oliver exits while the rest of us try to push our way to the bar for another drink.

Jeff stays rooted to the spot, staring at Sir Oliver's retreating back, then drains his glass. We're all avoiding him, not wanting to risk being implicated in whatever it was that he just implied about Sir Oliver, aware of the intense scrutiny of Rory and the other hard men from the Executive Compensation Committee, as they search for dissenters, for anyone bold enough even to talk to Jeff, even though it's his retirement party and his credit card that's buying the drinks.

Naturally, we all do the correct thing and ignore him.

Friday, 10th December
B minus 7

A MAJOR SHOCK – Rick Jenkins was fired today. Rick was an Executive Director, a good, solid producer, and everyone thought he was a cast iron certainty to be made up to MD this year, especially after Bill Myers had 'made room' for him. Rick was an operator. Not only had he invited Rory to his wedding last year, but he had even made him godfather to his first child just two months ago. He had the longest Christmas present list on the team, even though he wasn't an MD yet. He really knew how to play the game and work the system, and I'd have sworn he had a great future ahead of him. But Rory had decided his great future was somewhere else.

He was in a state of shock when they walked him out of the building after 'black-bagging' him. He had always talked a good story about how tough he was and the sport he'd done at university, and how he'd personally hang rapists, and any mugger who tried it on with him had better watch out. So I wondered briefly if he would do something outrageous and smash up his desk or trash Rory's office. But he didn't. I suppose executive aggression and the real thing aren't quite the same.

Later, Rory showed up at the desk – he'd been 'held up' in a management committee when Rick was fired – and wandered round, seeing how we all were, taking the temperature of the team and doing a morale-check.

He needn't have bothered. We all smiled great cheesy grins and no one mentioned Rick. His body could have been lying underneath the desk and we would have pretended it wasn't there. After a few weeks, when the smell got really bad, we'd have sprayed aerosols of air freshener around, but no one would have said a word. Not before payday.

AFTER LUNCH, a note went round that there would be an important presentation at 5:00 pm, with attendance required by all executives. Suddenly those stories about the bonus being waived seemed a lot more plausible, although the rumour machine went into overdrive and invented a whole load of new ones too. The favourite was that there was going to be a takeover. Jean-Luc called from Paris to say that one of the big German commercial banks was going to bid for Bartons, and Sir Oliver, as the controlling family shareholder, was selling us out. Don't ask me how he was meant to have heard this in Paris of all places. And then again, if it was true, would it be good news? Would the incoming owners be anxious to ensure continuing staff goodwill and increase the bonus pool – yes, some people really wondered about this – adding some long-term incentive payments to keep us all locked in, or would they announce wholesale redundancies, closing entire business areas, on the grounds that it's a buyer's market for jobs out there and most of us would rather have any job – even without a bonus – than find ourselves on the street?

We filed into the large presentation room on the ground floor and took our places. There was a podium at the front of the room where Sir Oliver was sitting with several heads of department, including Rory. They were all smiling, as if they had some really good news to tell us. This made us all extremely worried. When it seemed as if everyone who could be crammed into the room was there – it seated nearly five hundred, and there was standing room only at the back – Sir Oliver stood up and went to the microphone.

'Ladies and gentlemen – welcome.' He smiled magnanimously around the room. 'It's good to see so many familiar faces here today.' Don't bullshit us – there are several hundred fewer faces because of your pre-bonus cost-cutting. 'Today I have great pleasure in making a significant announcement that will affect all of our futures.' Oh Christ, he's sold the bloody bank. 'Today the board of the bank, under my chairmanship, has taken a major decision.' The board – shit – this is it: the real thing. 'The Management Committee has been fully involved in this decision and briefed upon it at every stage of the way, and is unanimously behind the move.' Bullshit

– all that means is that they've been bought off. 'Ladies and gentlemen, after a hundred and fifty years, the board of Bartons has decided –' Oh God, let it be good news, please. '– to re-brand the bank.' There's an audible sigh of relief around the room. Imagine five hundred people taking a deep breath, holding it until they're going purple, and then releasing it in a single rush, almost like a collective orgasm. 'After a hundred and fifty years of honest, reliable service to our clients, of being known for the quality of our work and the integrity of our people, we have decided it is appropriate to move with the times. We live in an age of image projection, sound bites, spin doctors, advertising and marketing. We must adapt. So ladies and gentlemen, following an eight month intensive programme of brainstorming, research, focus groups, visual identity development and brand testing, I am proud to present: the new Bartons, Bartons for the twenty-first century!'

Incredibly, the SurroundSound speakers in the conference room blare out a trumpet fanfare, and on the screen behind him the word 'Bartons' appears, but in a new typeface and coloured gold, rather than our traditional dark green. An American voice-over introduces 'Bartons, an investment bank for the twenty-first century – Bartons, the bank that's trying harder – trying to succeed.' Yes, really. The whole time we were sweating our guts out, desperately killing ourselves over the bonus, watching as old colleagues were black-bagged, looking on as poor Bill Myers was taken out and shot, the management were working with a branding agency, spending God knows what to change the colour of our stationery. The scene becomes even more surreal as girls from a PR agency walk down the aisles, handing out T-shirts and baseball caps with the new corporate logo – 'Bartons – we're really trying' – and all the time trumpets are sounding and the American voice-over talks about our corporate values, our noble history and our fine traditions, all of which sit so happily with a spirit of entrepreneurialism and innovation for the twenty-first century. And do you know what we do?

We cheer.

Yes, really – none of the polite, measured applause you'd expect from socially inhibited English people – we get up out of our seats and we cheer, with great grins on our faces. Partly it's relief that we haven't been sold, but mostly it's knee-jerk sycophancy, always the safe default position in the presence not only of the board, but so many of one's peers as well. Some people are giving each other high fives, normally sober colleagues hug each other and slap each other on the back, and the room echoes with the noise of our exuberance and enthusiasm.

On the podium, Sir Oliver looks at his colleagues and nods. Rory nods back. They were right. We really are a bunch of sheep.

Monday, 13th December
B minus 3

I TOOK A DAY off sick today.

Before you say anything, I know that investment bankers, in their capacity as masters of the universe, are not allowed ever to get sick. Illness is a sign of weakness, and weakness is a vice allowed only to the competition.

The reason I took this unprecedented step is that after one of the worst weekends in living memory, I did not sleep at all last night. I literally stayed up all night, pacing around, convinced that if I went in to work, I would be the one to be black-bagged.

Wendy was beside herself. She accused me of being crazy – she actually said mentally unbalanced, when in fact I'm the most rational person I know – and if it was going to be me, at least let's find out now, rather than later. She said that running away and hiding achieved nothing, and how on earth had we got ourselves trapped in this worthless life.

You can imagine what I said to that. Worthless? How many other women get to wear twenty thousand pounds worth of jewellery to a dinner party? How many get taken to Glyndebourne, Covent Garden, Garsington, Ascot, Henley and Wimbledon every single year, and always at someone else's expense? How many get to shop at Harrods and Selfridges and Fortnum and Mason and run up credit card bills of thousands of pounds every month?

And do you know what she said? She actually said she didn't care about all that, it was like a bad drug habit (how would she know?) and she'd kick it in a second if we could only walk away from all this.

She said she'd never been happier than when we were first married and living in a rented flat in Battersea, eating takeaway pizza and drinking cheap red wine.

I just about went berserk. Cheap red wine? Who the fuck drinks cheap red wine? No one we know, anyway.

But that wasn't the end of it. There was more. She asked me if I could remember when I last gave her a hug! You can imagine what I said to that. Anyone can give their wife a hug – but how many men give their wives two thousand pound Bulgari bracelets for their birthday? Or three hundred pound bouquets of flowers on their anniversary? Or bring them back a five thousand dollar kimono when they come back from a business trip to Tokyo – and before you say anything, yes I was feeling a little guilty after that trip, and I did charge it to expenses, but that's hardly the point, is it?

When I'd calmed down, and she'd stopped crying and admitted that yes, she understood that I did all this for her, and she'd been confused and foolish and I should ignore her stupid remarks earlier, there was no way I could sleep and so I stayed up and eventually watched the dawn over the rooftops of London, which was very gratifying, reminding me why a top floor flat in Sloane Square commands such a premium.

The problem was, by morning I looked like shit and felt even worse. When I rang my number, Nick Hargreaves picked up the line.

'Nick... it's me,' I croaked.

'Who?'

'Me – Dave. I'm feeling awful. Must be a bug of some kind. I've been throwing up all night.'

There was a silence at the other end. Not a good silence, an embarrassed, awkward silence. A long pause, and then: 'Will you be in later?'

'No. Not the way I'm feeling. Is there any special reason, Nick? Is there anything I should know?'

Another long silence. 'I guess nothing that can't wait. See you tomorrow. Get your strength back.' He hung up before I could say anything. 'Get your strength back'? No one tells you to 'get your strength back' when you're ill. They say things like 'get well soon', or 'I hope you're feeling better tomorrow'. Why should I need my strength? What does he know that I don't? Is there a black bin-liner sitting on my desk with a letter from Personnel?

I put my head in my hands and almost started to cry.

It was only much later, around eleven o'clock, when I woke up on the couch in the study and went in search of Wendy. She looked tired too, and stepped away when I tried to put my arms around her waist and kiss her.

'Please don't.' There was a tightness to her, a fragility that I hadn't noticed before.

'Okay, I'm sorry. Let's just put last night behind us. It's

almost over now. I'm going to take a shower, shave and go out for a breath of air.'

She looked relieved as I headed off to the bathroom.

When I was ready, I stepped out into Sloane Street and headed off, walking aimlessly as I enjoyed an unusually pleasant winter's day, with a clear blue sky and a crisp coldness in the air that sent shivers right through me, chasing away the fatigue of the previous night. I walked and walked, much further than I'd intended, and eventually found myself in Piccadilly. I stopped briefly at the Fountain Restaurant in Fortnum's for a light lunch and a glass of wine, feeling strangely exuberant, like a child playing truant from school. Afterwards I wandered off around the side streets of St James's until I found myself, just after two o'clock, outside Christie's.

The Africa sale had just started.

You know what happened next.

Afterwards, when I emerged once more onto the pavement, it was already getting dark. The air was damp as well as chilly, and I hurried to find a cab to carry my purchases home, thinking how I would explain to Wendy that I'd just blown nearly five grand on a bunch of nineteenth century relics of the Great Age of Exploration.

Tuesday, 14th December
B minus 2

I WENT IN TWO hours early today. I was at my

workstation at five-thirty, while the cleaners were still vacuuming, and searched everywhere for evidence of either a black bin-liner or an envelope from Personnel. When I was sure there was nothing waiting for me – I even checked the contents of my drawers three times – I looked on everyone else's desks, checked their drawers and then tried Rory's office, though that was locked. Nothing. I wondered then if Nick had been playing some cruel trick on me yesterday, trying to spook me. Or maybe someone else had gone. I looked around, but none of the other workstations looked particularly vacant.

There was a time, about two years ago, when someone played a cruel trick at Hardman Stoney, during the annual cull to thin out the headcount immediately prior to bonus, and placed a black bin-liner and an empty sealed envelope on a colleague's desk. It was meant to be a laugh, a hysterical, quite near the knuckle, risqué joke. But it backfired. The individual concerned arrived, saw the bin-liner and the envelope, threw the bin-liner on the floor and took the envelope into the Heads of Department meeting, where his boss was discussing the business of the day ahead with his opposite numbers from around the bank. He grabbed his boss, pinned him to the table, and tried to shove the envelope down his throat. You can imagine what happened next. By the time he was restrained, and what was left of the empty envelope had been opened, his team had removed the bin-liner – doubtless fearing the worst – and swore blind that they knew nothing about whatever it was he was alleging. He was summarily dismissed, of course, saving his boss another tough decision ahead of their annual payday. As they say on Wall Street, all's fair in love and the bonus round.

I hung around, drinking coffee from the machine, waiting for the others to arrive, and all the time wondering if Nick had been playing something similar on me. Interestingly, he was the first to arrive, and smirked when he saw me, though he wasn't obviously carrying a spare bin-liner to place on my desk.

'You're in early – must have made a full recovery?'

I could have killed him. It actually occurred to me to leap across the desk at him, put my hands around his throat and keep squeezing until his eyes popped out of their sockets and he stopped breathing forever.

Instead I just smiled. 'Much better, thanks. Thought I'd make an early start and catch up. How was yesterday?'

YOU MAY FIND this hard to believe, but I am capable of being both devious and ruthless. Which brings me to my revenge on Nick. I sat seething all morning, thinking of different ways to torture and humiliate him. Just as I was finishing a particularly exquisite fantasy, in which I was appointed Rory's deputy with specific responsibility for compensation and expense monitoring, his boyfriend called. His boyfriend is an interior designer called Charles. I've only met him once, and he struck me as a really nice guy. Naturally that wouldn't stop me getting my revenge.

I only caught one side of the conversation, but it was enough to realise that they were meeting after work for a drink with some friends, and his other half would be downstairs at 7:30 pm.

So I ordered flowers. Flowers? Sure – a huge arrangement, a hundred pounds worth, lilies and white roses, to be delivered to Nick, here on the trading floor, unsigned, but with the message, 'The earth moved for me' and lots of kisses. He was amazed when they arrived, just before six, and one of the security guards brought them over to his workstation amidst much cat-calling and whistling from the traders. When he looked at the message, he went bright red, and looked very unsure of himself. I thought to myself, do you have some guilty secrets, or what? So at seven-fifteen I went down to reception, hung around until I spotted Charles, went over and re-introduced myself, and asked if he was there to meet Nick. When he said he was, I invited him up to the trading floor, and swiped him through the security turnstiles on my card, so that I could take him up to our floor and over to the team area. When he got there, Nick was on the phone to a client in the States, and since I made sure we approached from behind, he never spotted us, until his boyfriend tapped him on the shoulder and grinned.

Nick's face was a picture.

And then I said to Charles, 'What fantastic flowers'. He looked puzzled, and with Nick looking on nervously, still stuck on the phone and unable to stop him, he picked up the card that was lying next to the bouquet.

The thing about revenge is that it can be the sweetest feeling. And when it comes after what has really been a gruesome time, it tastes sweeter still. So when Charles turned bright red with anger, picked up the flowers, hit Nick over the head with them not once, but seven – yes, seven – times, and stormed off, snarling over his shoulder that Nick needn't bother to come home, it was a huge effort on my part to retain my dignity and not to double up laughing. When Nick finally finished his call, he picked up his jacket from the back of his chair, threw a horribly accusing glance in my direction, and rushed after his partner.

Now is that devious, or what? Not as devious as what came a few minutes later, when I wandered over to Rory's office to ask his PA (in a suitably loud voice – Rory was sitting at his desk) if she knew where Nick was, because his jacket was gone from his chair and a client in Chicago needed him urgently.

Now that is devious.

Wednesday, 15th December
B minus 1

IT'S ALMOST OVER, at least for another year. Tomorrow is Bonus Day. The day after tomorrow, the day when We All Know, the start of another year, well... that's B minus 365.

Yesterday I caught Rory staring at me from his office. He looked away, turned to some papers spread out on the desk in front of him, shook his head and scratched something out with his pen.

This was very unsettling, but not nearly as unsettling as what happened next. Nick was fired!

It was the last thing any of us expected, obviously including him, because even by investment banking standards, firing someone on the day before bonus is pretty brutal.

But Nick had been a naughty boy, and someone had tipped off the Compliance Department, the internal 'police' who keep us on the straight and narrow. Nick had been dealing in shares.

Now, before you say anything – yes, it was Nick's job, in a manner of speaking, to deal in shares. But these were illicit dealings, unauthorised by the Compliance Department, for his own account. The earlier rumours had actually been true, though I would never have imagined that Nick would be the guilty party. He had opened a personal dealing account with another broker, based in Geneva, and had been using inside information to profit at the expense of our own clients. When he heard a big purchase order was coming in to buy a particular company's shares, he quickly bought some of the shares in question himself, for his own account, and then waited for the big purchase to push the price up higher, making him a tidy profit. Quite illegal, of course, it's called dealing ahead of a client. It was common practice in the old days, but today we're all too ethical to do this stuff – unless, like Nick, we're in such a hurry that we're willing to break the rules.

So who'd have thought it? Rory's blue-eyed boy is escorted off the floor to an interview room, where the police are waiting to talk to him. Now, normally I wouldn't spare a second thought for the dear old boys in blue, who after all earn next to nothing compared to investment bankers, and funnily enough don't live in top floor apartments around Sloane Square or eat at Colon, but this time I really admire them and wonder how they actually caught him. Apparently they were put onto him by an anonymous tip-off, but who could have known? Certainly not me, or I wouldn't have bothered to play the flower trick on him – I'd have done for him this way instead. Privately, I'm relieved, because I know he knew it was me, and he would have wanted his revenge too, and these things have a way of getting out of hand – turning into vendettas. Publicly, I'm delighted. We all are – think about it. Any nervousness that I felt about tomorrow evaporates as I think what Nick might have made. He looked as if he was onto a winner, he'd been so far up Rory's arse for the past month that only his ankles were showing, and now that money is up for grabs. This could be a great year.

Then comes the bad news. Jean-Luc calls to say that Rory could be in trouble. Where he gets his information I can only guess, but word spreads across the floor like wildfire. Nick is going to be charged. He'll probably go to prison. There'll be no cover-up on this one, they're looking for someone to make an example of – and Nick has just been volunteered.

Can you imagine, an investment banker going to prison? It's absurd. Even Nick doesn't deserve that – prison is for other people, ordinary people: criminals. But anyway, Rory now has to see Sir Oliver to account for what's happened. He's brought the reputation of the bank into disrepute – in a hundred and fifty years, nothing like this has ever happened before. Or at any rate, no one's been caught, which must say something for the calibre of people we hire. Our moral standards are of the highest and our reputation is our greatest asset – at least that's what it says on the corporate website. Worst of all, Rory's judgement may be called into question. All of the numbers might have to be re-visited. This is terrible.

On the other hand, it could be great. What if Rory gets fired? What if his enormous share of the bonus pool is up for grabs? What if the board needs to find a successor in a hurry? I could do that job – and if I don't, someone else will. I glance around the desk. Has it occurred to anyone else? Let's hope not.

Cometh the moment, cometh the man. With trembling fingers, I dial Sir Oliver's number. Amazingly, his PA says she'll put me straight through. There's a click and a faint background noise that tells me I'm on a speakerphone.

Jesus, I'm playing for high stakes, but fuck it, you only live once. As I'm about to introduce myself and ask for a meeting so that I can formally offer to step into the breach and lead the team forward, a gravelly, older voice growls at me, 'Were you after me or Rory, who's sitting here beside me?'

Then Rory's voice cuts across him, 'What is it, Dave?'

I hold the phone away from me and stare at it. It's another nightmare. It can't be real. Why hasn't Wendy shaken me awake yet? What is it with me and phones?

I hang up.

I cannot believe I did that. What if they call back? What about when Rory returns to the desk and asks what that was all about? What if they're re-doing the bonus numbers right now and I've blown it? I might just have blown a million pounds.

I run for the gents' to be sick.

Later, much later, I emerge cautiously and sneak a look at Rory's office. He's in there, talking to his P.A., dictating something, I think. I walk boldly back to my workstation to resume pretending to work. A flashing light blinks at me and I pick up my phone. I freeze as I recognise Rory's voice and turn to see him staring at me from his office.

'Dave, could you join me for a moment, please?'

I nod, gulp, swallow air, and finally, because I can't actually speak, raise a thumbs up in his direction and hang up. I do my deep breathing exercises, but I'm already sweating as I make my way towards his office, my mind a turmoil as I desperately grope for some kind of rational explanation for my idiocy.

For a ridiculous moment, I wonder whether to tell him the truth. He's a lousy boss and I think I could do better. I really do. You don't doubt that, do you? Success in this business is all about confidence. We're all stark naked all of the time, but some get away with it and some don't. I could get away with it, if only I got the break.

But not today.

Today I open the office door and try to do an engaging grin – which emerges as a toothy sneer – while Rory's PA brushes past me, contempt oozing from her every pore.

'Don't sit down.'

I stop and stare at him. This is not a good start. He's busy studying columns of names and figures – bonus numbers.

'Dave – what was that call you made to Sir Oliver while I was there?'

'C... call?'

'Yes.'

'Oh, you mean that call.'

He puts his pen down, looks up and nods. He's poker-faced, impossible to read. 'Which call did you think I meant?'

At this point I want the ground to swallow me up. 'I... I was after you.'

'Me? What for? Why didn't you wait until I got back?'

'I wanted to catch you before you went in. But Sir Oliver's PA put me straight through. I d... don't know why she did that. I –'

'Why did you want to catch me before I went in?'

All sorts of stupid thoughts fly through my mind – and this time I can't say I wanted to offer him tickets to the soccer or the rugby or the opera or the mud wrestling or any damned corporate entertainment opportunity. 'I... I wanted to say good luck. That was all.'

The effect is amazing. He rocks back in his chair, a look of utter bafflement on his face. I'm helped in part by the fact that the words come out very quietly – because I'm shitting myself – and sound sincere. Now, on the whole, investment bankers don't do sincere – at least not with each other. We do sincere with clients, when we're pleading for business, begging for fees, swearing undying loyalty and total commitment, but we don't actually mean it. This time, I sound as if I mean it, and Rory is completely thrown. He may never have come across a situation like this before and his face betrays a mixture of emotions – gratitude, quickly replaced by suspicion, followed by guilt (about my bonus number? – Aaaaargh!) and finally bewilderment: this does not compute. He coughs.

'Thank you, Dave. I appreciate it. I really do. In fact everything's fine. Sir Oliver's very supportive and we've agreed a press release. As far as the team's concerned, it's business as usual.'

'That's great, Rory. No one's more delighted than I am.'

Great. I'm doing well – in fact better than just well. I'm doing fantastically. And so of course I have to blow it.

'Rory – one thing just occurs to me. What will happen to Nick's – ?'

I don't get the chance to finish the sentence, because Rory goes bright red and explodes with anger.

'IS THAT WHAT THIS WAS ALL ABOUT? DO YOU NEVER THINK OF ANYTHING ELSE?'

I think there may be a few people on the far side of the trading floor, possibly somewhat deaf and in need of new batteries for their hearing aids, who don't actually hear Rory's response. But on reflection I'm probably wrong.

I shrug, desperate once again for the right response.

'Well, it is that time of year…'

'GET OUT!!!'

I run. I don't mean I walk at a brisk pace while trying to preserve my dignity – I mean run. I don't even bother going back to my workstation to collect my jacket or my briefcase. I couldn't have moved faster if there was a T. Rex on my tail, or a Lottery jackpot ticket lying unclaimed at the other end of the trading floor. And where do I run? To the gents', to hide in a cubicle and cry, silently, so that no one else can hear me. Around nine o'clock that evening I sneak back to the trading floor, after checking that everyone's gone, get my things and go home to sob my heart out with Wendy.

Today has not been a good day – and it's not over yet.

WHEN I GET home, the flat's in darkness. I call out to Wendy, check in the kitchen, the dining room and the bedroom. The message light is flashing on the answerphone, so I press the Play button. It's Jean-Luc, his voice sounding remarkably cheerful as he says there's a rumour going round the Paris office that I've been fired. I hit the Delete button and tiptoe into Samantha's room, which is empty. Finally I spot an envelope on my desk in the study. It has one word written on it, in ink, in Wendy's unmistakably childlike writing – _Dave_. She's underlined it as if to emphasise the finality of whatever it contains, and I pour myself a whisky before sitting down to read it.

She's gone.

But you knew that, didn't you? She's left me for someone else, someone who has become very close to her in recent months, and she wants to start again with him. They're going to lead a different life together from the one we had – a simpler, easier, better life. All she wants from me is the flat, the car, half the bonus, half the proceeds when I eventually get my hands on my options and unvested shares, maintenance for herself and Samantha – whom she'll allow me to see on alternate weekends – and whatever else her lawyer recommends. Oh, and I'll have to pay her legal expenses. She hopes I'll understand, she's not trying to be unreasonable, but the pressure was too much, and she wants to turn her back on material things and be with a man who truly loves and understands her. She's already taken her clothes, her jewellery, some pictures and other bits and pieces of artwork, the car, and 'as a precaution' has drawn some money from the bank – increasing the overdraft. She hopes we can do this amicably, if only for Samantha's sake, because it's her we should think of first and foremost.

Shit.

But she's right of course. I'd be lying if I said our marriage had been the greatest ever union of two people, and it's not as if I haven't occasionally – well, you know – but as it sinks in I feel a curious mixture of emotions: relief, that now I can go out and get laid whenever I want; concern that people might think I've somehow failed; anger that she's going to rip me off financially in what seems certain to be a terrible year; optimism that I can effectively trade her for a younger, more beautiful, more amenable model; outrage at what she's already taken – including my daughter, my own flesh and blood – and ultimately despair, because even my resolution and capacity for rationalising any setback are finally exhausted. I've lost my wife and daughter. I've lost my right hand, my trusted aide and confidante, my ally as I fought my way through the corporate jungle. She was the reason I did all this – well, her and the money and the lifestyle. I'll probably lose my home and most of my possessions, and with my bonus prospects down the toilet, I just can't see how I'm going to dig my way out of this one. Forget Barbados, forget the Porsche, forget the makeover for the flat – in fact forget the flat altogether. I'll have to go and live somewhere terrible like Fulham. When I look around me the brutal finality of it all sinks in. I feel physically sick. It's over.

How could she do this to me? I gave her everything – everything – a woman could want. Well, maybe not an actual place in the country, and okay, the flat's not as nice as the Finkelsteins', but we would have got there. At least I didn't make her live in Balham like Bob and Trish Harris. And I know that Wendy would have looked great cruising down the King's Road on a sunny day in the 911, with the top down, wearing her Gucci shades. There's a new range of brushed gold jewellery from Tiffany that she would have looked amazing in – I already had my eye on the necklace and ear-rings as a post-bonus surprise for her. And then there's Barbados. She always loved Barbados.

I'd like to say that I cried myself to sleep, curled up in a ball on her side of the bed, sniffing her perfume on the pillow.

But of course I don't. I decide that activity is key, so I check the tickets for Barbados and leave a message on the answer-phone at the travel agents, asking if hers is transferable, and start thinking who I might take in her place. Then I call round the various credit card firms to cancel her cards, and leave another message for the bank. On a whim, I phone the police and tell them the car's been stolen – that should be worth a laugh in the morning. And finally I go to the storeroom where she kept her mementoes of childhood and schooldays boxed up in an old chest, and take the whole lot down to the basement and tip it into the rubbish skip. It's not exactly progress, I know, but at least it keeps me from hitting the bottle. It's not yet midnight, and I'm all alone, worn out, and desperately in need of a good night's sleep before tomorrow.

So naturally I hit the bottle.

One whisky becomes two, two turn into three, and soon a nearly new bottle is empty. And then, when I should be at my lowest point, when lesser men would be thinking of despair or even suicide, from deep inside me comes a strength I never knew I had. This is not it. I know I have to carry on, I can't give up now, because people like me simply don't do that, and while I still have the presence of mind to do so, I set the alarm for tomorrow morning before passing out sobbing on the sofa.

Even in my sleep, I'm troubled. She's left me for a fucking personal trainer. How shallow is that? Mind you, it could have been worse. In my dreams, my tortured mind plays tricks on me. What if it was Matt Finkelstein? Or Bob 'Fat Man' Harris? Or Jean-Luc? Or Rory... Or all of them...

Thursday, 16th December
Bonus Day

I WAKE AT 4:00 am, well before the alarm, and start pacing round the flat in the darkness. My mind's a blur of racing, crazy thoughts. I check the answer-phone three times for messages from Wendy. Nothing. I call her mobile, but it's turned off, and I don't want to leave a message. I stand in front of the mirror, naked, and stare at myself. Overnight I seem to have aged about five years. My hair is wildly tangled, streaked with grey that I never seemed to notice before. My eyes are bloodshot from a combination of whisky and tears. My hands are shaking. I think that perhaps I'm going mad. I won't ask what you think.

I steel myself. Today is Bonus Day. The most important day of the year. As they say in the movies, this is not a drill. It's the real thing, and I have to get in early. Get in early and be on the phone, talking to a client – a real one, if I can find one that early, maybe someone in Hong Kong or Singapore – and avoid eye contact with any of the surviving members of the team. There's no point in not showing up at all, because if there's a chance, for the sake of one day and a little more humiliation, I might as well collect whatever's coming my way.

I ignore the empty flat, my aching head and back, and force myself to take a shower and get ready for work.

And then there's my briefcase. I want to get in early to get my briefcase under my workstation without anyone asking what's in it or why I don't just leave it open on the desk where it usually sits.

Today's the day, and there's no reason not to.

WHEN RORY comes in, half an hour later than usual, I have final confirmation that I've blown it. Yesterday was the last nail in my coffin. He sweeps past me, makes polite remarks to a couple of the others, then goes to his office and closes the door. After a few minutes, his PA takes his coffee in, and when she re-appears, she has a list of timings for us each individually to see Rory to get paid for the year. He's left me till last, making me wait until he's seen everyone else on the team, even the juniors – hanging me out to dry, no doubt to savour the moment. I look up, catch his eye and he curls his lip disdainfully.

Well, that's it. I've had enough.

I cough nervously, glance around at my colleagues who all have their eyes glued to the screens in front of them, and pick up my briefcase from under my desk, leaving my jacket over the back of my chair. But you know all this, don't you? You know how I walk over to Rory's office, in a sort of lop-sided way, half concealing my briefcase from the watching eyes of the team, go in, close the door behind me and draw the blinds. You know how this makes him look up, puzzled.

'What are you doing?'

I smile, reassuring, ingratiating.

'Rory, there's... something I wanted to discuss with you.'

He sighs and looks at his watch. 'Okay, I'll give you five

minutes, but do me a favour – no more special pleading about the bonus, okay?'

'No, no more special pleading, Rory,' I smile. For an awful, tantalising moment, a voice inside my head seems to be saying that this isn't inevitable, it doesn't really have to happen this way. There is an alternative. But then my eyes fall on the paper in front of him, a list of names ordered to match the sequence of meetings. The name at the bottom is easy to read, because it's mine.

Twenty five thousand pounds.

I glance quickly up the list. Rory doesn't even attempt to cover it up. He wants me to know that mine's the smallest number. A number so small that no Managing Director in the history of the firm has ever been paid so little. In this business, size really does matter. Even the juniors are getting more than me. It would be kinder to fire me.

I smile and shake my head as I rest my briefcase on his desk and flick the catches to open it.

'No, Rory – no more pleading at all.'

PART II

WHAT WOULD it take to make you kill someone?

I'm standing in the glass-box corner office of Rory, my fair-haired, blue-eyed boy wonder of a boss, waiting for him to gratify himself at my expense, waiting for him to enjoy his moment of supreme power and domination of another human being. That human being is me. It's bonus time, and he's about to pay me.

Only this year it's different.

This year I've had enough. This year the pressure is too much. The waiting has nearly killed me. All my hopes, all my aspirations, have gone out of the window. He was going to nail me, and laugh at my expense.

It doesn't help that Wendy, my beautiful, high-spending, attractive, money-loving, high maintenance wife, has left me for her personal trainer, probably figuring that she's spent the bonus year with me, as well as all the other years, and she'll collect handsomely for 'our' achievements. Or maybe she's figured that it isn't worth hanging around. It doesn't help either that she's taken Samantha with her, our darling three year old, the apple of her father's eye, the child for whom I could never buy enough.

So I'm alone. A man who has lost everything. A man who has become dangerous. And in my briefcase, with the lid open so that Rory can't see it, is a machete. A special machete, bought in the Africa Sale at Christie's, used by explorers carving out the Dark Continent. It's going to carve something else now. I'm about to slice Rory's neatly coiffed skull wide open. That's why I closed the blinds when I came in, shutting off the view to the trading floor. It's payback time.

Rory has left the list of departmental bonuses on the desk in front of him, so that I can see it. He wants me to know that at twenty-five thousand pounds, I'm setting a new record for a managing director at the firm. I'm to be paid the lowest bonus of all time.

So I do what investment bankers always do in meetings. Even though I don't mean it, I smile. And as I swivel the briefcase round so that he can see what's inside, I lean forward across the desk, grasping the handle of the machete.

It's a perfect moment. Rory's eyes follow mine to the briefcase, widen as they take in the machete, his mouth drops open, and he turns and stares back at me.

I nod and grin. Over the years I've done a lot of nodding and grinning at Rory, smiling as he told me I had to do another all-nighter, or cancel a holiday, or that the bonus couldn't be quite what I was expecting because Fixed Income had had a tough year, or there were big losses in private equity, or whatever. But this time I'm grinning because I'm in charge. In the world of executive aggression, I'm breaking the rules. I'm introducing the real thing. And the man with the machete is always boss.

The colour has drained beautifully from Rory's normally tanned face, and his Adam's apple is bobbing up and down in his throat. He's facing a madman. Harvard Business School doesn't teach you what to do next, does it, Rory?

'Dave... wait...' He raises a placating hand, and at the same time pushes his chair back from the desk. His eyes flicker across to the door, but the beauty of one of these large corner offices is that the door is a long way from the desk. A long way to savour the discomfort of the wretched people summoned here sweating to be told the result of a whole year of their lives. A long way to cover, with a madman swinging a machete at you.

All I do is grin. I never knew this could be so much fun. He's human, just like the rest of us. And he's shitting himself. Quite why he ever thought he could carry on messing with real people's lives the way he did is beyond me. Out there on the street, people get mugged for a walletful of notes. In here we're talking millions. What would you do for millions?

'Dave – we need to talk about this.' His mouth is dry. He's finding it hard to get the words out, and joy of joys, he's perspiring.

I shake my head. 'Talking's over.'

'Dave – I have a wife, children – please don't do anything rash.'

'This isn't rash. I've had a long time to think about this.'

'Dave – we're investment bankers. Investment bankers don't kill each other.'

'The rules just changed.' My voice is a whisper, but it's

totally calm, not a hint of the excitement, the bloodlust, the adrenaline pumping through me. Rory crumples at his desk and puts his head in his hands. His shoulders start heaving to and fro and a strange noise comes from him. I look at him, vaguely embarrassed. He's sobbing.

And then the door opens.

The bubble bursts as a film crew appears. There are three of them. They are led by a tall, skinny woman with mousy hair wearing a dark grey trouser suit who looks almost but not quite beautiful in an uptight, bossy, reporter-like way. She is flanked by a scruffy, shaggy haired camera man and an even taller, skinny guy in jeans and a T-shirt, carrying what looks like a very large sound recorder and a long-handled microphone. Behind them, Rory's PA is trying to get past, looking apologetic. Before she can get a word in, the woman, whom I've recognised as a pushy dimwit who asks idiotic questions on NTV Cable Business News, marches across the room with her hand thrust out.

'Amie Short – we're here to do the piece on this year's bonus round in the City. Which of you is Rory?'

Possibly for the first time in my life, I experience one of those moments when everything happens very slowly. Rory has leapt to his feet, knocking over his chair, and I watch as he rushes forward to grasp her hand in both of his, swivelling her around so that she's standing between him and me. She doesn't know it, but she's his human shield.

'Me – I'm Rory, that's me. Welcome, come in, all of you, come in.'

His voice is unnaturally squeaky and high-pitched, he's breathing hard, and he has sweat patches under his arms.

For a deliciously crazy moment I wonder whether to bring the machete out of my briefcase and start swinging and slashing at everyone in the room. I imagine blood splashing over the carpet and the blinds and the desk, limbs and lumps of raw meat flying around so the place looks like an abattoir. I imagine standing triumphantly amidst the corpses – 'NTV Cable Business News regrets to announce the death of our reporter Amie Short and her film crew. Amie was covering this year's bonus round at Bartons, the blue chip UK investment bank, when she got caught in the middle of a discussion between star investment banker Dave Hart and his boss…' But instead, I drop the machete back into the briefcase and click it shut, closing the lid that shielded it from the film crew.

Rory is standing, panting, next to Amie, ignoring her, staring at me. She's looking at him curiously, and follows his glance in my direction.

'Are we interrupting something?'

No, of course not, you brain-dead moron. Try rubbing both brain cells together and see if you get a spark. I was just about to kill my boss, you dimwit. It's the sort of thing that happens at this time of year. Or at least this year.

I smile confidently and nod back. 'No, no problem.' I turn to Rory. 'I think we'd covered the ground. Rory, I'll see you another time. We need to pick up where we left off. Maybe I'll pop around to your place tonight? Or if not tonight, then some other time. I'm sure I'll catch you again.'

He just stares at me, open-mouthed, to the obvious puzzlement of the film crew. I walk purposefully out of his office, swing by my desk to grab my jacket from the back of the chair, smiling at the team, who have probably been laying bets on how I would do, and head out of the building fast, before Rory can wake up and call security.

It's only when I emerge from the Underground in Sloane Square and dump the machete in a rubbish bin, having wiped the handle fastidiously with my handkerchief and wrapped it in a newspaper, that I realise I've utterly blown it.

If you're going to kill your boss, you really have to do it. No half measures. I return to my empty, barren flat and start re-running the whole scene in my mind over and over again. I knew what I had to do, but I couldn't even get that right.

Without Wendy and Samantha, the flat seems soulless. Half the cupboards and wardrobes are empty. All the familiar sounds and smells are gone. I spend the rest of the day moping around the place, wallowing in depression, waiting for the doorbell to ring and armed police to arrest the maniac who thought he could kill his boss. I stare at myself in the mirror, noting the first grey hairs at thirty-seven years of age, the lines on my face, the slightly sagging belly. How did it all happen?

But then I start to wonder. I'm an investment banker, after all, and we're nothing if not resilient. The doorbell hasn't rung, neither has the phone, and when I fire up the computer and log in to my e-mails, it's all routine stuff, some banter from the team about the bonus round, but nothing about me. Then I start to think about the situation. What will Rory do? What can he do? Make some crazy allegations? Where's the proof? Who would believe him? Of all the people in the world, Dave Hart must be the least likely ever to bite back. And if they didn't believe him, and I was still out here, on the loose, watching and waiting and knowing where he lives – I have the addresses of all of his homes – he'd be the one who was scared. In the safely cocooned, insulated world of the global investment banker, no one actually gets hurt – at least not physically.

Finally at around five o'clock I make a decision. I experience a burst of what is known in the markets as irrational exuberance. I was going to kill my boss, but I didn't. And so far, I've got away with it. Nothing's happened. I'm a free man, and who knows what possibilities lie ahead? I go out and buy a half case of champagne, plus whisky, vodka and gin, replenishing the stocks that I've exhausted over the previous weeks of uncertainty, call up a couple of drinking buddies and decide to have a party. It may be the last party I'll ever have, so I might as well make it good – the condemned man and all that.

The buddies I call up are Dan Harriman, who runs European equities at Hardman Stoney, and Nigel Farmer, the number two on the oil trading desk at Berkmann Schliebowitz. Both are single men, in the sense that they are divorced – Dan recently for the second time – and both know how to party. You might think three guys sitting around in my flat drinking is a pretty sad sort of party, but I haven't told you about the hookers.

Hookers? Well, no, not exactly. Escorts. High-class escorts. These days you can find them on the internet, whole galleries full of them. Not the firm's internet of course – the firewall stops you browsing from the office.

That's why we all have these rinky-dink, tiny personal laptops with Wi-Fi connections. You didn't think all those young men sitting on public benches in the 'Wi-Fi village' at Canary Wharf were checking stock prices, did you?

And let's be absolutely clear what happens when you book these girls. You're paying for their time and company only. Anything else that happens is a private matter between consenting adults. Yes, really.

So around ten o'clock that night, Dan is sitting on the sofa in my living room, his shirt off, exposing his flabby, hairy belly, his trousers and underpants around his ankles, and blonde-haired, twenty-three year old Ilyana from Kiev is going down on him. Nigel, similarly half-dressed, is standing by the drinks cabinet, pouring himself another large Scotch, while dark-haired Carla, twenty-one, from Brazil kneels at his feet and services him. I'm totally naked, sitting in the large armchair, while red-haired Helena from Warsaw straddles me. On the rug in front of the fireplace Patricia from Spain, a brunette whose hair reaches almost to her waist, and Beatrice, a beautiful black girl from Columbia, are lying head to toe, servicing each other for our entertainment and pleasure. All of the girls are naked, obviously, and their clothes and lingerie are scattered around the apartment, on the furniture, on the floor, a g-string here, a micro-bra there. Half empty champagne bottles and glasses are similarly spread around, there's a suspicious scattering of white powder on the glass coffee table, and on the huge, flat screen wall-mounted TV over the fireplace there's a hard-core movie showing a stunning blonde from California kneeling on all fours and being serviced at both ends by a couple of studs who are hung like gorillas.

You might think this is the kind of thing that goes on every night in those exclusive apartments around Sloane Square, but in fact I haven't partied like this since before I was married. Honestly. At least not at home.

The drugs and the porn were not my idea. Dan brought those. I don't use drugs, and I regard porn as a poor substitute for the real thing. The escorts, okay, I take some of the blame, but how was I to know what these girls would do? And the only reason investment bankers get dragged into these murky areas is because their clients want it. Honestly.

So there we were, the party in full swing, and it wasn't yet late, when I could swear I heard a key in the front door. I look past Helena, who is moaning and groaning at the top of her voice, throwing her head around, rolling her eyes and doing an amazing fake orgasm impression, and there, standing shocked and amazed in the entrance to the living room, is Wendy. She's wearing a sober dark grey skirt and jacket by Armani, with a white silk blouse, and discreet emerald and pearl earrings from Elizabeth Gage. She looks stylish and beautiful in an understated, luxurious way. And terribly small, frightened and vulnerable. My heart goes out to her and for a sickening moment I think I can remember why I fell in love with her.

'What... is going on?' Christ. She's shaking her head as she takes in the scene around her, and giving me one of those 'this is too horrible, I just can't believe it' looks.

Dan looks up from the sofa, and reaches across for his crumpled jacket, momentarily ignoring the bobbing head in his lap. He's got a crazy look on his sweaty, florid face. He pulls out his wallet and looks up at Wendy.

'Here's five hundred quid. Get your kit off. Bend over the coffee table and I'll have you next.' Dan's never met Wendy. He's holding out a pile of notes, and frowns as she screams and fixes me with a half-crazed stare.

'I wanted to come back! I wanted to stand by you! I wanted to give you a second chance!' She turns and runs back towards the front door.

'Wendy! Darling! This isn't what you think...'

The front door slams and Dan looks at me and shrugs. 'Women...'

I NEED TO get away. Anywhere. Fast.

I've hardly slept since Dan and Nigel and the last of the girls left, around three a.m. Yes, that's right – three a.m. Of course we carried on partying after Wendy left. What else could we do? We'd all taken Viagra – my one concession to chemical assistance – there were five girls already in the apartment, with a new shift due to arrive at midnight, and we were flying.

But now it's eight a.m., I've hardly slept and there are ugly monsters crawling out of the darkest corners of my mind, monsters with names like conscience and trust and integrity. I think if I stay here any longer I'll go mad.

And what if the police come? Rory's had a whole night to ponder what to do. I bet he hasn't slept either. Should I call him? By now he'll probably have his phone lines monitored. He's not a man to under-estimate. What if he's hired someone to come after me?

That makes me think. Could he? In the movies he would. But in real life, if you don't mix with the criminal classes – other than smart, white collar criminals, who don't actually hurt people, but do things like running hedge funds and dealing on insider information – how would you know where to go to hire a hit-man? That's one service you can't yet order over the internet.

I'm spooked. I admit it. I rush frenetically around the flat, picking up used condoms, clearing away empty bottles and glasses, hoover up every last trace of powder around the coffee table, search under the cushions for Ilyana's missing g-string and put it down the waste disposal, and finally collapse, exhausted and still feeling guilty, and stare around my prison cell. The terrifying thought strikes me that it could so easily be swapped for a real prison cell, and investment bankers just don't do prison. Prison is for little people, the great unwashed, the huge unwealthy masses who toil in the industries whose fate we decide with our clever deal-making skills. It's not for us, at least as long as we stick to the unspoken code. But I didn't. Machetes aren't covered by the code.

I need to leave town. Somewhere hot, far away, with a beach, a complete change of scene, and of course hot and cold running nymphettes. I know where I need to go. Hardman Stoney had their MDs' off-site there last year, and Dan can give me the low-down on the local scene. I go on-line, make a few calls, and to my surprise and good fortune strike lucky, picking up a last minute cancellation. I pack a bag and call a cab to take me to Heathrow. I figure that I've lost my job – I can't see Rory having me back – and with my debts and overdraft, the balance of the mortgage, and my imminent divorce, I'm as close to being insolvent as anyone who plays in the high stakes casino of the Square Mile and loses. So I do the obvious thing, use my corporate credit card – amazingly still working, what is Rory (not) doing?! – and book a First Class ticket. Jamaica beckons – Caribbean sunshine, reggae music and nubile black bodies. I have to escape.

It's the pre-Christmas rush, and when I get to Heathrow, thousands of wannabe holidaymakers are thronging in the departure hall. My Gold Card doesn't help, because I haven't had time to pick up a ticket, and need to queue to get an e-ticket from a machine. When I finally do get my ticket, I need to queue again to get some currency – Jamaican dollars for out of pockets, and US dollars, as the global currency of available young women everywhere. Then, privilege of privileges, I get to queue again, this time for security. After all this, I get to line up to board. I'm late, and there doesn't seem to be a separate line for First Class passengers to go ahead of the waiting throng.

In front of me in the line is the family from hell. The father, who I gather by eavesdropping is called Mick, is a forty-something, shaven-headed thug in a tracksuit and perfectly unblemished white trainers – presumably freshly shoplifted for the holiday from Lilywhites or bought from 'some bloke down the pub, can't remember his name, officer, honestly' - with an earring and a sour, hostile look on his face. The mother is a flabby beast soaked in an overwhelming aura of cheap scent and wearing tight pink leggings and a bulging white vest that leaves her bare arms and shoulders exposed to show off her tattoos. I can tell she's an ugly slapper with attitude just by looking at her – I don't need her to tattoo herself to spell it out. Jason and Kennie are aged about seven and nine, just old enough to have acquired their father's surly resentment. *You lookin'* *at me? You want some?* Despite their age, every second word starts with an 'f', until their mother catches my eye and tells them to 'stop that bloody swearing'. I'm wearing a blazer from Brooks Brothers, slacks and an open shirt from Gieves and Hawkes, with tan leather lace-up shoes from Fratelli Rossetti. To her I probably look like some kind of authority figure. She looks back to me, as if for approval, but I turn away, scowling.

What pisses me off most, apart from the fact that I have to stand next to them, is that they probably all live on benefits, paid for out of taxes raised from people like me. In fact, when I think about all the money I've paid in taxes in recent years, even without getting anything like my fair due at bonus time, I probably support a whole village full of idiots. And Rory, well he must support a couple of large towns of these people. Maybe they should name one after him, or call all of their first-born sons Rory? Between the MD's at the firm, we must support a whole county. Add in the other top investment banks, and the hedge fund industry, and the pension funds and insurance companies in the City, and pretty soon you're funding a whole underclass of work-shy, uneducated, irretrievably incapable parasites. All they can do is consume and breed and occasionally fight, while someone else picks up the tab. People in the real world may not like the privileged élite who work in the Square Mile, but what would they do without us? Who else would pay for their social failures, allowing them to indulge in the notion of a caring society? Let's hear it for capitalism.

BEHIND ME is another family, and they're almost as bad. Toby, Jasper and Monty must be aged between four and eight, wholesome, well-scrubbed, terribly well-spoken well beyond their years, and immaculately dressed in identical clothing from some middle-class mail order catalogue. Their pretty, tired but enthusiastic, cheerful in adversity, long-haired thirty-something mother is wearing loose, practical trousers and a white blouse and cardigan, probably from Marks and Spencer, and is actually holding hands with her very tall, slightly other worldly, professorial husband, who's staring around the departure hall, as if he hasn't been in one before. They are the hard-working, fair-minded, serious, law-abiding, aspiring lower middle classes at their nauseatingly cheerful worst. Announce that there's a six hour flight delay, and they'll shrug their shoulders and say, 'Oh well, never mind. Let's see where we can sit down – isn't this exciting, children?' and start to play 'I spy' while mum gets out packs of home-made sandwiches and a flask of tea. They are probably schoolteachers, or civil servants at the Department of Social Security. For all I know he might even be a vicar, and no matter how well they do, how hard they work, they'll never know what it feels like to make a million dollars at bonus time. In their world, it simply doesn't happen.

I'm too young to be a grumpy old man, and I know it's wrong to sneer – though I've never quite worked out why – but people like this make me sick. They lead plodding, one-track lives, where the most exceptional thing that happens is falling in love, getting married, having kids, raising them, and launching a whole new, self-perpetuating cycle. Eventually they have grandchildren and then they die, without ever making a bean. What are these people for?

I'm beginning to feel stressed by the delay, so much so that I start taking deep, relaxing breaths. What if I can't actually leave the country? What if the inscrutable official at the desk looks at my passport, glances briefly at me and presses some hidden button to call the police to take me away? 'Fugitive investment banker caught at Heathrow' – I can see the headlines now.

There's a commotion ahead. A lot of people are shouting, and some are moving forward, crowding around what looks like a middle-aged man lying on the ground. Women are saying things like 'Oh, my God', and one of the airline ground staff is making an urgent phone call from the check-in desk.

I can't bear this any longer.

'Excuse me! May I come through?' I surprise myself with the strength of my voice, as I step forward and the crowd parts and people look at me expectantly. 'Excuse me – may I come past? Thank you.' They automatically step aside as they hear a voice of authority. Several people are kneeling helplessly beside a grey-haired man in a crumpled tropical suit. He looks very pale and it's not clear if he's still breathing.

'Are you a doctor?'

'No.' I step forward, lifting my feet carefully over the prone victim of what I suppose must be a heart attack, and present myself at check-in. 'I'm an investment banker.' I turn to the check-in attendant. 'Dave Hart, seat 1A.'

There's a buzz of angry conversation behind me, and the check-in girl seems reluctant at first to take my passport and ticket, but I stare her out and she finally lets me through. I can feel a wave of hatred hitting my back from the crowd as I walk down the jetty towards the waiting airliner. Some people would be bothered by this, but not me. I have investment banker's immunity to the feelings of the Little People. This is a result. Instead of standing in line like some gormless twerp, I can get on board, relax and order my first glass of champagne.

I'M ON MY third glass, munching canapés, sitting in the best seat on the plane – seat 1A, the only one that Rory would consider on the rare occasions when he used public transport, rather than taking the corporate jet. I've booked a suite at the Bay Club, Jamaica's hottest new property, with scuba diving, water skiing, tennis, golf, a Givenchy spa, and the closest thing you'll find to *haute cuisine* dining in the English-speaking Caribbean. I've also got Dan Harriman's list of hot numbers to call. I may be a fugitive from justice, as well as from my soon-to-be-ex-wife, with no job, no prospects, and no future, but life is good, at least for the moment. First Class is almost empty, which is how I like it. Just a few business types quietly sipping champagne and reading.

The plane was thirty minutes late taking off, because they had to remove the bags of a passenger who had been taken seriously ill before take-off. I'm philosophical about these things. It allows me time to chat to a very pretty blonde stewardess called Maxine, who's half-French, has small boobs and a cute backside. It's all going really well, until she explains that the announcement they've just made isn't strictly accurate. The man who was taken ill actually died. And one of the First Class passengers apparently stepped over him in order not to be delayed at check-in, while he was actually dying! We look around at the other passengers and wonder who it might be. After that I lose interest in Maxine.

I glance at the curtain that separates First Class from the rest of the plane. Back there in World Cattlemarket Class I can imagine Mick and Jason and Kennie arguing over who gets the last plastic chicken korma from the trolley, while Toby, Jason and Monty munch contentedly on mum's sandwiches, probably made with gluten-free, organic wholemeal bread, low-fat margarine and cold breast of free-range chicken. Any time now the adults will be served their last alcoholic drinks, the lights will be dimmed, the air conditioning turned off so that the cabin gets hot and stuffy, and the cattle will doze off and start snoring for the duration. Gross.

There is a story that Rory once took his family on a holiday to Australia. Naturally, they all had seats in First Class, along with the nanny and the au pair. But it was a long flight and the kids started misbehaving. Rory, as a man accustomed to being in charge of his destiny, found this all a bit too much and finally lost it, threatening the kids that if they didn't behave, he'd send them 'back there' – he pointed to the curtain – where they'd never been before. His kids were pretty scared and took a peep behind the curtains. All they'd ever done in their lives was board an aircraft and turn left. They didn't know what happened if you turned right, and probably thought that behind the curtains on the right was where the baggage was kept, and the fuel was stored, and where the engines were. When they saw there were actually whole rows of people asleep back there, they really freaked out, got the point and came back to sit down and be quiet for the rest of the flight. It made a real impact on them. They were terrified.

And the best thing of all? They weren't even looking at Economy Class. Behind the curtain was Business Class, where Rory made the rest of us sit on corporate trips.

After dinner and a movie, I doze for a while and finally wake up to the welcome news that we'll be landing in half an hour. As a jaded long-haul traveller, I don't usually get excited any more about flying, but this trip is different. I feel like a kid who's been let out of school early.

In the baggage hall I grab a porter, and I'm delighted to see that First Class baggage really does come off before Mick's. I watch while Jason and Kennie climb all over the carousel, and wonder if it will start up and slice their fingers off. They look sweaty and filthy, their T-shirts covered in the spilt remains of whatever food they were served in-flight. Toby, Jasper and Monty are still looking well scrubbed – probably cleaned off by mum in the toilets half an hour before landing, while dad – the vicar – is staring around the arrivals lounge, obviously never having seen one before.

I'm through Immigration in a flash – no arrest warrants here – and a beaming black man in a white suit is holding a name card with 'Mr D Hart – Bay Club' on it. While Mick is still waiting for his baggage, I'm in the back of an air-conditioned stretch limo, sipping a glass of mineral water so cold that I fear it could crack the enamel on my teeth. This is living.

I HATE the Bay Club.

For starters, they don't allow hookers. Why any businessman would ever stay here is beyond me. On my second night, after conquering my jet-lag, and with no sign that anyone was after me from the UK, I decided to have a party. Not quite on the scale of my last party in London, but a party nevertheless. I made a couple of phone calls, took a shower, put on my hotel dressing gown, and sat on the sofa in my suite nursing a large Scotch and water. Then the phone rang.

'Mister Hart?'

'Who is it?'

'It's reception, sir. There are two...'

There was an awkward pause. 'Yes?'

'There are two... young ladies here. They are asking for you, Mister Hart.'

'Excellent. They must be my nieces.' I chuckle knowingly, as if sharing an in-joke with the man on reception. 'Why don't you show them up?' I've used this line before, and generally it works. The guy on reception knows they aren't my nieces, and he knows that I know that he knows. And what I'm suggesting is that he shows them up, rather than sending them up, because obviously I'm going to slip him a couple of large denomination notes for being accommodating.

'I'm sorry, Mister Hart, but it's against hotel policy.'

'What? Are you saying hotel guests can't entertain visitors in their suites?' I raise my voice to emphasise the point. 'In their thousand-dollar-a-night suites?'

'I'm afraid so, Mister Hart. Would you like to speak to the night manager?'

'Certainly not. I want to speak to you. Right now. In person. Kindly come up straight away, and bring the young ladies with you.' As I say this, I reach over to my wallet and reluctantly start unpeeling hundred dollar bills. Whoever this fellow is, he takes his job seriously. This is going to be expensive.

'That's not possible, Mister Hart. I'm sending the young ladies away. There are many other attractions at the Bay Club, Mister Hart. Have you tried the Givenchy facial, or the pedicure? Or how about a golf lesson? Or tennis?'

I can't believe I'm hearing this. 'Do you know who I am?' I positively roar the words down the phone. There's a pause at the other end, and then a different, older voice comes on the line.

'We know exactly who you are, Mister Hart.' This totally freaks me out. Who is this? What does he know? How can he know anything at all about me? I only got here two days ago. 'And you must know that an upmarket family resort hotel cannot allow ladies of this type on the premises.'

I hang up. Damn, I swallowed a Viagra tablet forty minutes ago. Swallow them quickly, they say, in case you get a stiff neck. I should have waited until the girls showed up. Now I daren't even go down to the bar for a drink in case I embarrass myself. And what about the girls? Who will pay for their taxi out to the resort, or pay them for their time, or their trip home? I imagine some vengeful Yardie pimp with a revolver slipping into my room at night and firing round after round into my sleeping body. I sit in my room, torturing myself and steadily draining the mini-bar.

The next day at breakfast I have the feeling that everyone is looking at me. Not just the staff, but somehow I get the sense that the guests know all about the scene last night at reception, when a couple of hookers were turned away. A couple of hookers? Yes, that's right. He wanted two of them, the twisted, perverted beast. I look across at the elderly couple spooning up mouthfuls of muesli at the table on my right. They nod cheerfully and smile 'Good morning', but I know that they know.

After breakfast I wander over to the pool to lie in the sun and snooze. Amazingly, every sun-lounger is taken. I look around and can see nothing but an oil slick of nearly naked Germans, Scandinavians and Dutch people, roasting slowly in the Caribbean sun. Where do they come from so early in the day, and how do they get all the best places?

I wander down to the beach, which is the private property of the hotel, but runs alongside a public beach that is open to anyone. Sure enough, members of the public are wandering across our beach. And then it gets worse. Mick is here, with Kennie and Jason, and his appallingly bovine wife.

'Hey, Mister – wasn't you on the same plane as us? Wasn't you the one what stepped over that bloke what was dying?' Kennie is looking up at me from the deep, possibly deadly pit the male members of the family are excavating. It's already up to his chest, and must have taken real labour. Perhaps Mick isn't just a benefits parasite, but works as well, as some of the more enterprising ones do, and digs up roads or operates a digger machine in his working life?

I ignore Kennie and stare out to sea, imagining that I must cut a romantic figure, dressed in my Villebrequin shorts, my Ralph Lauren polo shirt and my Rayban shades – echoes of Tom Cruise.

'We're staying at the Coconut Club – the other side of the bay from this place.' It's a gruff male voice, estuary English, and I realise that Mick is talking to me. 'The beach isn't as nice there, so we come here instead. Belongs to this posh place, but they can't stop us, see?'

Feeling trapped, I reluctantly acknowledge him. 'Really?'

'You bet. And there's a barbecue here tomorrow night as well.' He winks conspiratorially. 'Might even see if we can slip in.'

'Good idea.'

'By the way, that fella died.'

'Really?'

'Stone cold dead. "Brown bread," as we say down our way. In case you was interested.'

'Not really.' I find this exchange slightly surreal. Is he trying to prick my conscience in his slovenly, uncouth way? Doubtful. Probably just trying to make conversation. Under other circumstances, the first thing I'd do would be to tip- off hotel security about gatecrashers at the following night's beach barbecue, but I'm so fed up with the hotel, with the nearly naked Germans, Dutch and Scandinavians, and with the prospect of spending a thousand dollars a night in order not to get laid, that I actually chuckle.

'See you at the barbecue.'

Mick grins and gives me the thumbs up.

I wander along the beach, and it gets worse. The Wholesome Family are here too. Toby, Jasper and Monty splashing in the waves while the vicar stares at people making sandcastles as if he hasn't seen them before, and Missus Wholesome spreads out a blanket and starts slicing up a melon and putting pieces onto brightly coloured paper plates that she must have bought in a local supermarket.

'Weren't we on the same plane?' She looks up and smiles as I walk past.

I shake my head. 'No. You must have seen my cousin, Dan Harriman. Flew out a couple of days ago. We look very similar. He's a total shit, steps over dying people if they're in his way, does drugs, hookers, booze, you name it. Even tried to smash his boss's head in with a machete.'

She tilts her head on one side to stare at me, and I realise that under other circumstances she might be quite attractive – well, at least shaggable – and she laughs. 'It was you. You stepped over...'

'Don't tell me. I stepped over a dying man. I know I stepped over a dying man, although I didn't know then that he was dying, and realistically there was nothing I could do even if I did know. I'm not a doctor, and I'm not a first-aider. At least by getting out of his way I could give him some privacy. And dignity. It's better than standing round gawping at him.'

'Don't sound so defensive. You weren't to know.' She has long brown hair tied up in a bun, freckles and a delightful snub nose. She's definitely fuckable.

'I'm not. Just rational. Are you staying at the Coconut Club with...' I nod towards Mick and his family.

'With Mick? Yes. He told us about this beach.

Apparently there's a barbecue tomorrow night, and he wants us all to gatecrash it. But I don't think Trevor wants to.'

Trevor? I might have known her husband would be called Trevor. He looks like a Trevor.

'Well, I'm actually staying here. I have a suite. Tell Trevor you can all be my guests. See you around eight?'

'We'd love to. Are you sure it's all right if we all come?' She stands up and holds out her hand. 'I'm Sally by the way. Sally Mills.'

I shake her hand and find she has a delightfully firm grip. I love it when women have a firm grip. Anyway, she's wearing a conservative one-piece swimsuit that covers up rather too much and has never been seen by any designer known to man, yet still she looks attractive. For a moment I imagine lying on my back on my bed in the hotel, while a naked Sally Mills sits on my face and goes down on me.

'Pleased to meet you. See you tomorrow. Let's hope it's a big night.'

'Let's.' She smiles and catches my eye, and I wonder briefly if she's flirting. Well, what woman wouldn't, if she met me, on a beach in the Caribbean? Tom Cruise's half-brother. Especially if she was married to Trevor the teacher.

I'M FLYING.

We've got a big table near the barbecue, just a few yards from an improvised dance floor that's been put together on the beach, and waiters are running a shuttle service of cocktails from the bar. Mick has helpfully sat himself next to Trevor, and keeps making him drink more, which he's obviously not used to, while Mick's wife, Claire the Human Pudding, is on Trevor's other side, keeping him wedged in. The kids are all over the place, running round causing havoc.

I'm playing the role of perfect host. I greeted everyone when they arrived, and made them all laugh by explaining how there'd been a bit of tension at the hotel. Apparently the Germans and the Dutch and the Scandinavians were in the habit of going out to the pool last thing at night, and spreading out their towels and magazines and personal odds and ends on the loungers to claim the best sunbathing spots. Well, last night someone went out even later and threw all the Dutch and Scandinavians' things in the pool, leaving only the Germans'. Outrageous, what some people will do, and this morning it nearly caused world war three. We all have a laugh, Mick gives me a sideways glance, but I don't react, and instead we settle down to drinking, which I'm quite good at.

A steel band is playing, and the beach is beautifully lit with burning torches, under a clear, starlit sky. I'm feeling so good about life that I even gaze on benevolently when some of the Germans and the Scandinavians start to heal the tension with a little friendly limbo dancing.

The reason I'm so particularly happy is sitting opposite me, her view of Trevor blocked by the bulk of the Human Pudding, and we're talking as if no one else is around.

'Investment banking is a tough business.'

'Really?'

'Sure. The hours are a killer, when we're on a deal we work till we drop. I once did three all-nighters in a row.

You work weekends, you start by seven in the morning, and if you're lucky you finish by midnight. You travel all over the world, everywhere the business is. It's brutally competitive, everyone's bright, everyone's hard-working, everyone wants to win. Imagine a whole trading floor of alpha males – and females, we have women investment bankers too – and every one of them is convinced he can run the firm. Testosterone on steroids.'

'Sounds exciting.'

'You bet.' I pause to drain my marguerita, then raise the glass and signal to a waiter for another. 'You never know what's going to happen from one moment to the next. It's the market, you see. The market's bigger than any of us. War, terrorism, politics, everything's reflected in the market. You need perfect news flow, and seconds, not minutes, make all the difference. Blink and you're left behind.' I smile in acknowledgement as another glass is placed in front of me. 'But it takes its toll.'

'Oh?'

I put on my sad, mournful look. 'Things didn't work out at home. I'm getting divorced. That's why I'm here... alone.'

'Really? Because of your work?'

No, you silly cow, because I'm a shallow, greedy, philandering piss-head without a decent bone in his body. 'I'm afraid so. And the worst of it is, I won't be able to see my beautiful Samantha again.'

'Samantha?'

'My daughter. She's three.' I could add that she's the one I haven't even thought about until now, when I realised what a great sympathy card she is, and sympathy could be a great way into those no doubt brilliant white, practical cotton panties.

'Won't you be able to see her?'

I shrug and stare into the darkness. 'You know what it's like. It's not exactly an even-handed system.' And thank God for that – what would I do with Samantha for a whole weekend without Wendy around?

'I'm sorry.' Her voice is a whisper, and it looks as if she has tears in her eyes. She glances around to check on her own boys, as if to reassure herself that Toby, Jasper and Monty are not in danger of being whisked away.

'Don't be. I've learnt to be tough. You have to be in my business. I'll get through it. It's just that sometimes you have to let your guard down, you have to open up to someone. It's pretty rare that you find someone you can trust, or feel close to.' As I say this, I look into her eyes. Even in the light of the blazing torches I can see her blush as she glances away. Time for a change of mood.

'Anyway, that's enough about me. Let's talk about you.'

I smile reassuringly. 'What do you think about me?'

That's when somebody screams.

For once it isn't something I've said. We turn and see a group of tall, rangy men with dreadlocks standing on the makeshift dance floor built out over the sand. The band have stopped playing and in the silence we can hear someone moaning. There's a body lying on the dance floor, and I think I recognise it as one of the hotel security men. There are six or seven men standing over him, and they are all carrying weapons – knives, baseball bats, and one of them has a machete.

Suddenly Sally screams, as the man with the machete leans forward and sweeps up a small bundle from the floor beside him. Toby, aged four years and three months, screams 'Mummy!' as the man shouts at us in a spaced-out, half-crazed, vaguely sing-song Jamaican accent, 'Ladies and gentlemen – please be so kind as to hand over your wallets and your watches and your jewellery to my associates. Please be so kind and we all be cool...'

A surprisingly strong hand grasps the sleeve of my collarless white Armani evening shirt and yanks me out of my chair.

'He's got Toby – come on!' Sally Mills might only weigh a little over fifty kilos, but she has the strength of a man possessed. She pulls me out of my chair and drags me forward alongside her as she charges towards the dance floor.

Only she trips up on the sand and falls headlong, releasing her grasp of my shirt in time to catapult me into the dreadlocked gangster holding Toby. I'm wearing a brand new pair of navy blue Gucci loafers and shouldn't slip on the dance floor, but someone's spilt a drink there and as I step forward I skid and fall, throwing my hands out desperately for support. My outstretched hands hit the Yardie full in the chest and he goes down with me on top of him. As he falls, he swings the machete around and I feel something slice past my forehead, which is suddenly wet with some slick, warm liquid. He drops Toby, who scampers off the dance floor into the arms of his sobbing mother, who is crawling towards us across the sand. I cling to the bad guy, too scared to move, sick with fear and adrenaline, not knowing what to do next.

Behind me there's a great roar and I manage to turn my head for a second to see Mick running towards us, holding a chair over his head, which he throws towards the gang members standing on the dance floor. Claire is hard on his heels, screaming with thirty years of ugly bovine rage, a broken wine bottle in one hand. She looks like she's done this before. Trevor the teacher is still sitting in his seat, looking on with a curiously detached air, as behind him a dozen or more large, bearded Scandinavians decide this is not the time for neutrality.

Mick slams into one of the Yardies, bringing him crashing down next to where I am lying on top of their leader, who is dazed but awake and starting to struggle to get free from under me, pushing me away and wriggling towards the edge of the floor, where I can see he has dropped the machete. I grab his arms and hang on for dear life, not daring to think who he will carve up first if he gets his hands on it. Claire comes pounding onto the dance floor and lunges towards another of the gang with the broken bottle. He sidesteps her and swings a baseball bat into the back of her head. She staggers forward a few steps, her eyes rolling heavenwards, and crashes down on top of the Yardie leader, who has reached the edge of the dance floor, dragging me whimpering with him. I hear a distinctive crack and he jerks once, then lies completely still. Claire's full weight has landed across his neck on the edge of the raised floor, forcing his head backwards and sideways towards the sand some twelve inches below. She groans and rolls away, and then there is a rush of heavy, pounding feet as Sven and Olaf and Jerker the Berserker lead the Viking charge, a brief clash of improvised weapons and the Yardies break and flee.

Something sticky is covering my face as I lie on top of the Yardie leader, sick with fear, and black out.

I AM a hero.

I am in a private room in a hospital in Kingston, where a police guard and a member of the consular staff from the British High Commission are keeping the press at bay, while I am stitched up and have the chance to recover. Scattered around my room are press reports from the Jamaican and British press:

BANKER KILLS YARDIE THUG
British Tourist Fights off Yardie Gang, Saves Toddler

and in the *Daily Post*,

BULLDOGS: 1, YARDIES: 0

There are flowers in my room from Mick and Claire, who were the first people allowed to visit me, Claire with a heavily bandaged head, along with Jason and Kennie, who declare me both 'cool' and 'wicked'.

There are flowers too from Sally and Trevor, who visited me briefly – he obviously had not been to a hospital before – and who brought with them Toby, Jasper and Monty, who had made me get well cards with felt tip pens and crayons, and asked how many stitches I'd had in my forehead, and would it leave a scar. Sally held my hand, and I squeezed hers, but luckily there was no chance to say any of the things that were swimming around in my head, like the fact that I did it for her, and was there any chance of a blow-job?

I've had a phone message from Wendy, who had no idea I was over here until she heard my name on the radio and read what had happened in the papers. She's offering to fly over and talk. Talk? Who's she kidding?

More promisingly, Dan Harriman sent a couple of hookers round dressed as nurses, but the Jamaican policeman on the door was nobody's fool and ordered them away. Good old Dan – at least he tried.

I've had lots of messages from people in the City, including some of my old team at Bartons, who seem baffled by what's happened. In fact, the common theme among everyone who knows me seems to be sheer bewilderment at what on earth got into me.

I can't think about what actually happened without needing to throw up. I still feel sick with fear, which the doctors, who clearly admire me enormously, are putting down to concussion. They tell me gravely that I will have a prominent scar across my forehead, that it may fade somewhat over time, but only plastic surgery can hope to reduce this savage mark. It is a high price to pay for courage, but it was only a fraction of an inch from slicing through my skull. They assure me that a machete blow that connected firmly to the head would have caused unthinkable consequences. I agree. I can't think about them either.

I'm still not taking phone calls – claiming headaches – and the doctors won't allow the press to talk to me, so Mick and Sally are the people who get to tell the story. When I see them interviewed on the cable television in my room, I wonder if they are talking about the same incident, or if they are, how much they had had to drink.

It seems I not only charged the Yardie leader holding Toby, knocking him to the ground and wrestling with him, but in a desperate life and death struggle fought him to the bitter end, all the while bleeding copiously from the machete wound that had split my head open. When the Yardies fled, they left their leader dead on the edge of the dance floor with a broken neck, with me lying unconscious on top of him, weakened by loss of blood, but still clinging to him desperately. The news coverage includes photographs of me being helped from the scene, my face and my white Armani shirt soaked in blood, still looking shocked.

I can't quite believe it, but the story's all over the media, so it must be true.

My only bad moment comes when a superintendent from the Jamaican police comes to call. He is respectful, almost wary in my presence. First, he assures me that I'm not going to be charged with anything.

Charged? I almost leap out of bed and grab him, so that I can scream at him that I don't need to be charged because I didn't do anything.

But he goes on to say that there will be a coroner's enquiry, much as there would be in the UK, and that he believes the coroner will return a verdict of lawful killing. I can swear a deposition now and with luck, it will not be necessary for me to return for the hearing, although men like me are always welcome in Jamaica.

Men like me? This man knows nothing. I made three New Year resolutions this year: screw more beautiful women, smoke more cigars, and try to be more shallow. Okay, I'm joking about that last one. Oh, and get a bigger bonus, but that goes without saying. And now he thinks I'm a hero. He tells me that it's rare for tourists to make a stand as the guests of the Bay Club did that night. Tourists generally just panic and scream and hand over their valuables. I nod. Makes sense to me. But he tells me that I inspired them. A number of guests have said that when they saw me take the leader down, they thought they'd have a go.

Then he gets to the bad part. He tells me the Yardies are a dangerous group to cross. The man I killed (that's right – I killed) was a well-known gangland
figure over here, and they have connections in London, where they play a major role in the drugs trade. I may feel I can look after myself, but I should still take 'sensible precautions'. Sensible precautions? I'm a man who thought sensible precautions meant wearing a condom. He totally freaks me out, and when he's gone, I cling to the bedcovers, pale and trembling.

ON THE FLIGHT home, I get VIP treatment. I could get used to this. It's actually even better than Rory would get. The Minister of Tourism escorts me out to the plane, bypassing formalities and taking me directly airside. He shakes my hand, and promises me a warm welcome and a more peaceful stay next time I come to Jamaica. I ignore the photographers, because I've got used to them by now, and anyway they're only the locals. Once I'm on board, back in seat 1A, the cabin crew can't do enough for me, and the other passengers look at me with awe. They know. One of them, an American business type, comes over and shakes my hand.

'I was a marine. Two tours in 'Nam. But I never did anything like you just did. Sir, it's a privilege to shake your hand.'

At Heathrow, there are more photographers, wanting to get a close-up of my battle scar, and some reporters wanting a quote about how good it feels to be home again. The airline has laid on a couple of people from Special Services, who escort me through to immigration. It's only when I'm in a taxi heading home that I begin to take stock and think what on earth I'm going to do next.

There's a pile of unopened mail in the flat. Lots of kind notes from well-wishers, messages on the answer-phone... and a letter from Rory:

> Dear Dave,
> First, let me welcome you home and congratulate you on your very courageous act in Jamaica.

Act? How does he know it was an act? How could he?

> I hope you are fully rested and well on the way to recovery, and that you will forgive me for raising a delicate business matter with you so soon after your return. As you know, before your departure, we were discussing the difficulties of accommodating your full potential within the firm, and I think we had both agreed that it was time for you to move on.

The shit. I'm a hero and he's firing me. How's that going to look in the press, Rory? But there's more.

> As part of the general restructuring plan currently being implemented at Barton's, we are in a position to offer you exceptionally generous terms if you are still of the view that it is best to seek fresh opportunities elsewhere. At a minimum we would be looking at granting you three years' total compensation, based on the average of your three highest earning years in the past five – approximately £2.5 million – as well as the immediate vesting of your options and employee shares. We would give you a very favourable reference, and be pleased to continue paying your basic salary and benefits until the earlier of twelve months or until you find suitable employment elsewhere. We would, however, naturally seek your agreement in writing that this concluded matters between us on a positive and final note, and that as a good leaver you bore no ill-will towards the bank or any of its employees.'

I can't believe it. He's paying me off. He's paying me off because he's frightened. He's offering to spend millions of the bank's money so that he doesn't have to worry about waking up one night to find me standing by his bed with a machete in my hand.

On reflection, it makes good sense. It's not his money he's offering me. And he's running scared. More than scared – he's read the papers. He knows I'm a killer.

There's also a letter from Wendy. She and Samantha are staying with her mother in Buckinghamshire, and she's had a lot of time to think. She acknowledges faults on both sides, and wants to 'try again'. We've both made mistakes – like running off with the personal trainer, though she doesn't say this – and after all I've been through I probably need a period of stability in my life. Could she have got wind of Rory's letter? There's nothing like a few million pounds to bring a woman round.

I put both letters down and call Dan Harriman. He's delighted I'm back, insists we have to celebrate and suggests we meet for drinks.

The best dry martinis in London are served at Duke's of St James's, a small boutique hotel beloved of Americans (who know a thing or two about cocktails) and sadly these days, hedge fund managers. The barmen here say that dry martinis are like women's breasts: two are too few and three are too many. As far as breasts go, I've always preferred four myself, in two pairs, both at the same time, but that's another matter.

We are soon on number three, and Dan is starting to slur his words.

'So you're leaving Bartons?'

I nod. 'Need another challenge.'

'Did they fire you?'

'Course not. But I've had it with being Rory's poodle.'

'Never bothered you before.'

I very gingerly finger the stitches on my forehead. I've developed a nervous tic in my cheek, which gets worse when I'm stressed, lying, or otherwise under pressure, which I'm finding is quite a lot of the time, and I can feel it now. Whenever it starts in my cheek, a pulse becomes visible on the side of my forehead where the scar is most prominent. I feel as if people can read me like a book. 'That was then. This is now.'

Dan nods, unconvinced. 'So where will you go?'

'No idea. Not a US firm – they work too hard. Not one of the old British firms either – too sleepy. Maybe I should start my own firm? Could you see me running somewhere? I quite fancy it. Maybe it's time.'

'Yeah, right. If I were you I'd get my arse back to Bartons in double quick time. Failing that, it's a sayonara job.'

'A sayonara job?'

He nods firmly. Sayonara jobs are the last jobs taken by struggling has-been's desperately clinging on to the City lifestyle, normally after a couple of divorces and a few years of the downward spiral at a proper firm. 'If you're not careful, you'll be head of capital markets at the Korean Farmers' Bank, running a department that comprises yourself and your assistant.'

I'm tempted to tell him about Rory's letter, but I don't. I need to get it finalised first, and whatever happens I need to get more. I know he won't see me, that I'll have to go back to him through Human Resources, who must be baffled by his decision. But if I don't squeeze another half a million out of him my name's not Dave Hart. I raise my glass to Dan.

'Who cares? Here's to the Korean Farmers' Bank, London Capital Markets Department. I'm an undemanding sort of guy. As long as I have a six-figure salary and an expense account, I'll be happy.'

I'm actually quite troubled. Dan could be right. However much I squeeze out of Bartons, I'll burn through it in no time, or if I don't, Wendy will – and then what will I do? The thing about friends is that they tell it to you straight. Dan and I will always be friends. We both know too much not to be.

Dan drains his glass. 'No more for me – I've got a seven o'clock flight tomorrow morning. Fancy a Chinese or an Indian on the way home?'

I shake my head. 'Nah. I think I'll go for a Ukrainian, or maybe a couple of Brazilians.'

It is only much later, when the girls have gone, and I'm alone again in the flat, that I get round to playing the answer-phone messages. I delete a couple from Wendy, and then come to one from a head-hunter.

'Mister Hart, my name is Susannah Grainger. I work for McLintey Dobbs, the executive search firm. We haven't met before, but you come highly recommended, and I wonder if you might be able to help us with an assignment we're working on. I'd be very grateful for your advice on a search we're conducting for someone who can run the London-headquartered investment banking operations of a major Continental European banking group. I'll try you again tomorrow, or if you have a moment, perhaps you'd be kind enough to call me on…'

I scribble the number down. Head-hunters always ask for 'advice', when they are really asking if you're interested. Am I interested? Hell, yes.

LARGE, SLOW-MOVING Continental European banks with huge wedges of capital but small or nonexistent investment banking operations, are like dinosaurs: too much weight and not enough brainpower to turn it around. They typically have highly profitable domestic franchises, based around hard-working citizens who save lots of money and demand little interest when they feed it into the branch network. They also tend to have large stakes in industrial companies dating back decades, often valued at nowhere near the current market price. Their board members see themselves as guarding the legacy of the past, unadventurous types who pay themselves little and take pride in offering their employees a job for life. Their businesses are both profitable and secure, if a little conservative.

Clearly, what these people need is me.

I'm sitting in the offices of McLinty Dobbs in St James's Square, sipping a cup of coffee and reading the annual report and accounts of EFG Bank – Erste Frankfurter Grossbank, one of the heavyweights of the German banking sector. Grossbank in German is a generic term meaning major bank, and these guys were the first one set up in Frankfurt – hence 'Erste Frankfurter'. Luckily someone round there spoke enough English to realise that answering the phone as First Frankfurter doesn't make a lot of sense, so instead they wisely chose to be known simply as Grossbank. Damned clever, these Germans. They only have a tiny London-based investment banking operation, but have recently appointed a new, and apparently thrusting, Chairman. Susannah Grainger is sitting opposite me with one of her colleagues, looking at a printout of my CV, which I e-mailed before the meeting. She's mid-forties, very thin, adequately dressed in a business suit that does little for her, and which I don't recognise, and has no interesting jewellery. I guess she can't be doing that well.

'The new chairman, Herman Schwartz, why does he think I'd be suitable? We've never met. He wouldn't know me from Adam.'

Susannah looks up from my CV. 'To be absolutely honest, I think it's what you did in Jamaica that caught his eye. You got a lot of coverage in the German press, you know. There were apparently some vivid eyewitness accounts of what happened from some of the German guests staying at the hotel.' Eyewitnesses? Shit. My cheek starts twitching. But she looks at me respectfully, as you would someone who has charged a gang of armed thugs, saved a little boy and killed their leader in single combat.

These days, people fortunate enough to be born in the Western world rarely encounter deadly violence. We have to suffer petty crime, and a very few of us might choose to serve in the armed forces, and be sent to dangerous places, but for most of us killing is something we hear about on the news or watch at the cinema.

That's why I'm exceptional.

'I see. And did you... check with Rory, as I suggested?'

'Yes. He confirmed the circumstances of your departure, the fact that you need a broader canvas – that was how he put it – and said very complimentary things about you. He was very helpful, and it's wonderful that someone so senior should make himself available at such short notice. I have to say, though, that he came across as rather nervous. I wonder if he thinks he's made a big mistake allowing you to leave Bartons.'

I can't help smiling. 'Oh, I don't know. How many alpha males can you get in the same room? I think if we're honest it's best for both of us to put some space between us.'

She nods. 'When I questioned him, he said something very similar himself.'

I sit back and smile. 'So when do I go to Frankfurt?'

THE NEW GROSSBANK tower is a landmark on the Frankfurt skyline. I'm whisked into town from the airport in a dark grey S-class Mercedes with a uniformed chauffeur, straight into the underground car park, where the head of personnel is waiting to greet me and take me to the fifty-fourth floor. Two very dour, Brünnhilde-like receptionists – definitely unfuckable, built like wardrobes – give me the once-over, and ask in guttural Germanic accents if I want the bathroom ('No, thank you, I had a shower before take-off'). Then I'm shown into a high-tech conference room with the most staggering view, that surely ought to be used as a film set for the next Bond movie.

Eleven elderly retired bank manager types are sitting around the conference table, staring at me with suspicion and perhaps a little nervousness, as if I've come to steal their wallets. I have. I want to say, 'Relax, guys, I'm the one being interviewed', but I know it would be wrong. Instead I stand at the end of the table, incline my head slightly towards them, just stop myself from clicking my heels and say, 'Good morning, gentlemen.' A few of them – presumably the ones who are not yet dead – incline their heads slightly in my direction, and one or two mutter 'Guten Morgen'. My hand-made silk suit probably cost more than all of theirs combined, and I feel for a moment

185

conspicuously overdressed, but then I remember that they are hiring me to be an investment banker, and it's better that I look the part.

I'm about to sit down, when the doors behind me burst open, and a younger, much more vigorous man in a half-way decent suit strides in. I recognise him as Herman Schwartz – 'Herman the German' – and I'm relieved to see that he's actually wearing an Hermès tie. He pumps my hands vigorously, looking sleek and elegant with his dark, carefully trimmed hair, his perma-tan complexion and his neat, slim figure. I know that he's forty-nine years old, and the youngest Chairman in the Bank's history, but he doesn't look a day over forty.

'Dave – may I call you Dave? – welcome to Frankfurt. We're very excited to meet you, aren't we, gentlemen?'

He looks to his colleagues for agreement, and most nod, though a few could easily be asleep, and some possibly don't understand English.

We sit down, he introduces his colleagues while coffee is served, and then the formal part begins.

Much of it is standard stuff. While I never really thought I'd be in this kind of situation, I'm a fast learner and I quickly identify their hot buttons. One key point is that they want me to tell them how they are perceived in the market. They are seeking a candid opinion, so I nod gravely and pause to reflect before replying. This stuff is so easy, just like pitching to a client. I've been doing it for years and even in my sleep I could lie for England.

'A sleeping giant.' In other words, fat, dumb and happy. 'Grossbank is hugely well capitalised, the only triple-A rated bank left in Germany.' Let me loose here and I'll soon change that. 'But it's never realised its full potential. It's never stretched itself outside its domestic market.' It's just stuck to solid, profitable business that it knows and understands. We'll soon change that as well. 'To the outside world, it's incredible that a bank of this size, of this historic importance, should be a lion at home and frankly a mouse overseas, especially when international markets represent the best growth potential going forward. Standing still is not an option. We have to take this firm forward.' Forward and downward in the next great recycling operation of dumb foreign money in the City of London.

'But can we succeed?' It's one of the grey men, and I need to be careful because I actually thought he was asleep.

'With respect, that's the wrong question. We must succeed. It's not *if*, but *how*. Failure is not a possibility!' I bang my fist down on the table as I say this, and right on cue my face starts twitching. They all perk up and pay attention, and several of them, including Schwartz himself, start nodding their heads vigorously. I sometimes feel sorry for the older generation of Germans. It's hard for them to show true aggression without feeling guilty about their country's past and coming over all anxious that people will think they're going off to invade small nations again. But as a foreigner, albeit a potentially soon-to-be-hired gun, I have no such inhibitions. 'Gentlemen – the bank already has a presence in the London market, but it's neither one thing nor the other. Too big to be a niche player, and too small to go head-to-head with the big boys. It's forwards or die. I have a clear vision for what can be achieved in the London market. The only question is whether we have the will to deliver!'

I go off into a rant about how I've identified the ten major business areas that the bank should focus on, and how we will become a top three player in all of them within three years. We will swoop on other firms, hiring their best teams, paying premium rates for the best people in each business area, then let them loose with the full balance-sheet of the bank behind them. We'll take bigger positions, place bigger bets, and unleash the full unrealised potential of the most talented people in the market. Resistance is futile. Victory is inevitable.

Quite whether I could actually do any of this is another thing. As a mid-ranking, relatively low-flying MD at Bartons, no one ever trusted me to try. And why should they? Only arch politicians like Rory got to play with the full train-set.

'What would you need in order to succeed?' This from Herman the German. All eyes are on me now.

'Carte blanche to hire and fire in your London operation as I see fit. Overall authority for running the investment banking business globally, including those parts of it that are located here in Frankfurt. In principle, agreement on the broad thrust of the product by product approach that I've just described and direct budgetary authority to implement it – and gentlemen, I'm assuming we'll invest a billion euros in the first year, and we'll be underwater for the first three years of operations. That's how long we'll need before the full potential of the huge money machine we're building can be released.' And I'll have left by then, having passed Go three times and collected the kind of money that would make Rory turn green.

'And what would you seek personally, always assuming you were successful?' This comes from one of the oldest board members present, someone not yet carried along by Herman's enthusiasm.

'Do you mean my own package?' He nods and glances at some of his colleagues. 'My own package would be huge.' He gives them an 'I told you so' look. 'It has to be. None of the top professionals we'd be looking to hire would take the career risk of joining a relatively unknown name without significant upside. And in investment banking, you lead from the top. People expect their bosses to be high earners.' I briefly catch Herman's eye. This is clearly music to his ears, not that he would ever put his personal interests before those of the bank, obviously. I shrug carelessly. 'I don't care about the detail, only the big picture. It has to be convincing, gentlemen – the going rate and then some.' For once I'm relieved that my cheek doesn't start twitching.

MY FIRST CHRISTMAS alone since I got married passes in an alcohol and drug fuelled haze of heaving, panting, naked bodies. Did I say drugs? What I meant to say is that there were a lot of parties where certain people were doing drugs. I admit I occasionally have a glass too many of falling over juice, and I have from time to time been partial to the fairer sex, but drugs are not my scene. Honestly.

As a newly single man, with a bank balance freshly fattened for Christmas by Rory's generosity – I got him up to three million, to the amazement of Bartons' HR department – and Wendy still camping out in Buckinghamshire with Samantha, I had a ball. In fact, several balls, often on the same night.

Wendy doesn't know about the settlement with Bartons, for which I opened a new bank account, and I have to be careful not to create the wrong impression, but recklessly I decided to send Samantha a last minute surprise: half the toy department at Harrods, knowing that Wendy's mother lives in a tiny cottage where it would be impossible to unpack, let alone play with, a full-sized Wendy house, a Cinderella castle, giant-sized cuddly toys of all the Disney characters, nine different dressing-up outfits, and two new tricycles.

I sent Wendy nothing.

She called on Christmas morning, but I cut her off before she could say a word. 'Don't say a thing. Don't expect me to apologise, don't expect any regrets. Anything I may have done I did because you drove me to it. You pushed me over the edge, and now here we are. Before you complain, before you accuse, think about it.'

Then I hung up dramatically and ignored it when the phone kept ringing, partly because I thought it was the right thing to do, and partly because I was too busy with Tygra, nineteen, from Estonia, and Charlotte, twenty-one, from Lithuania, for whom I had bought presents.

Like all good things, it came to an end, and in the first week of January I started work at Grossbank, on a package of 'three by five' – a five-million pound a year bonus, guaranteed for three years – with the same again in employee stock, plus a million sign-on (i.e., they pay me a million pounds just for turning up on the first day) and a further ten-million pound package of stock that vests in five years if I'm still around and achieve certain pretty astronomical revenue targets (I very cleverly hung out for this, because it made them think I might be here for the long term – as if...) I'm counting on Wendy not reading the financial press, because there are some inconvenient reports that I wouldn't want her to see:

> Grossbank are rumoured to be paying top dollar for City hard man and former Bartons investment banker Dave Hart, who last year hit the headlines when he took on Yardie gangsters in Jamaica, killing their leader and rescuing British toddler Toby Mills.
>
> Hart, who still sports a prominent scar from a machete wound, was unavailable for comment...

That's it, I have my label now. I'm 'City hard man' – me! I've been defined. In any event, I need a disguise to wear to work at the new firm, and City hard man seems fair enough, at least for people who don't know me. So I summon up my full chameleon-like capabilities and morph into a City hard man – or at least what I think a real City hard man might be like, if ever there were such a thing.

It doesn't help that it's January, when most of the City goes dry. After the pre-Christmas excesses, bodies saturated with alcohol are drying out. This is when people briefly start going to the gym, try to lose a few pounds, and generally get serious. Where before they might have gone out at lunchtime, now they stay at their work-stations. Where before they met for drinks after work, now they return home, miserable, unfulfilled, full of suppressed rage.

And the markets roar. Analysts talk about the January effect in the stock market, referring to the way in which share prices soar – and sometimes plunge – amid heavy volumes of aggressive trading. Theses have been written about why it happens, but behind closed doors we know. Fifty thousand market makers, traders, sales traders, dealers and brokers are drying out. And they're like a whole herd of buffalo with sore heads.

That's the backdrop when I arrive at the Grossbank London office on my first Monday morning.

GROSSBANK ARE in a small building off Threadneedle Street, not far from the Bank of England, but a million miles from the giant concrete and glass palaces of Bartons and the other major firms. A few hundred people work here, but until now I've never even met someone from Grossbank London, let alone known anyone – they were just too far down the food chain.

Sometimes new bosses like to make an impression by arriving at the crack of dawn, catching everyone unprepared, and then proceed to install a new regime of early morning meetings to show how macho they are. For their first month, they don't leave the office until late into the evening, forcing everyone else to stay at their workstations. And they appear in the office at weekends, checking on who's working.

As a fundamentally lazy person, I think that's all bullshit.

I arrive just before ten, by which time they are wondering if something's happened to me. I have a newly prepared corner office made by combining the offices of the head of equities and the head of research – who are now sitting in much smaller offices next to the trading floor, scowling at me. I make a note to fire them.

I have been given a long-serving secretary, mid-forties, half-German, unmarried, and built like a barn door. Her name is Maria, and she has been with Grossbank in London and Frankfurt for nearly twenty years. She's definitely a spy, put here to keep an eye on me, and I immediately decide I have to keep her.

That's right, I'm going to keep her. Keep her, and use her. She'll be my back door communication channel to the board. I spend the first day going through formalities, getting my photograph taken, signing endless papers, and meeting the faceless, one-dimensional people who served the old regime.

By four o'clock, having eaten nothing more than a sandwich at my desk, feeling the desperate need for alcohol, and with my face twitching at a medium fast rate, I'm overcome by the desire to do something. You know what they say. Lonely? Bored? Depressed? Call a meeting! I call a meeting.

My meeting takes place in the conference room next to my office. Maria summons for me the heads of equities, fixed income, treasury, foreign exchange and structured finance. I ask where the head of corporate finance is, but am reminded that we don't actually do corporate finance. Oh.

I find myself staring around the table at a group of nervous, defensive verging on hostile, fifty-something men. So this is where they all go when they get moved on from proper firms. At Bartons only the Chairman and the people actually running the firm were over fifty. I realise then that the Grossbank London office was a sayonara job.

I get them each to give me five minutes on their business area, its achievements, strengths, weaknesses, and finally ask them to say who on their team they would rate as their star performer. I make notes, nod, twitch, but don't smile. When the last of them has finished, I pass a note to Maria, then while away the minutes in small talk, asking them how long they've all been at Grossbank, where they were before, do they have kids – or even grandchildren – and so on.

The London head of HR is in my office, summoned by Maria, and in another glass-sided conference room, visible to the heads of business areas sitting with me, another group is assembling – the individuals they named as their star performers, or at any rate the people in their departments who were the least bad.

'Excuse me, gentlemen – I'll be right back.' I leave the conference room and return to my office. The head of HR looks no different to the men I've just left – mid-fifties, tired, ragged round the edges, on the downward slope of a City career.

'I'm Dave Hart – what's your name?'

'Charles Butler, Mister Hart.'

'Call me Dave.' I point to the conference room I've just left. 'Charles, do you see those men in there?'

'Yes, Dave.'

'You know who they are?'

'Of course.'

'Good, because I'm firing everyone in the room. Call Security, have them send some people up to walk them out of the building. Tell your people to draw up severance papers.' I pat him on the arm and return to the conference room, where there is a sweaty odour of fear and a deathly hush.

I stand at the end of the table. 'Gentlemen, this place is a joke.' One or two of them frown and cross their arms, and there are a couple of muttered 'Steady on's'. I pause and stare around the table, waiting for absolute silence. 'I don't feel like I've come into an investment bank at all. I feel like I've walked onto the set of "Carry On Banking". Well let me assure you, there's a new era dawning at Grossbank.' They nod, trying to summon some enthusiasm, though probably feeling sick to their stomachs. 'An era of high performance, high ambition...' I hesitate before allowing myself to smile. '...and high pay.'

'Hear, hear!' It's the head of treasury, Norman something or other.

I pause and stare at him. 'Be quiet, you obsequious little shit.' My face is twitching, right on cue, and I stare at him.

'I... I'm sorry.'

'Quiet!' I slam my hand down hard on the table, then look slowly around the room. On the trading floor beyond the glass walls of the conference room people are looking at us, wondering what's going on. They know the men in this room. The men in this room run Grossbank London. They are Grossbank London. And now, as they look at me, they are truly frightened. This man kills. This Dave Hart, a man they'd never heard of until last year, a man who took

195

out a gangster with his bare hands, now seems barely under control. They are fascinated by my twitching face, the scar, the manic spittle that flies whilst I talk.

'A new era is dawning, and you, gentlemen, will not be part of it.' I point at them each in turn. 'You, and you, and you, and you, and you, have failed. All of you. You had one of the greatest opportunities in investment banking in the City of London, and you blew it.' I look up to see several security guards standing outside with Charles Butler and a couple of his assistants. All activity has come to a stop on the trading floor. All eyes are on me, standing in this glass bubble with five – five – petrified victims in front of me. For years I took this shit. Now I'm dishing it out. Awesome. My voice is a hoarse whisper. 'You had the opportunity to build something great, with the strength, the muscle, of one of the world's most powerful financial institutions behind you. And you didn't even know it. You're all fired. Now get out of here!'

This job rocks.

As if one meeting in an afternoon isn't enough, I then walk over to the second conference room. The group sitting here are about ten to fifteen years younger than their bosses, one or two look quite keen and bright, but in general they strike me as classic big fishes in small, sleepy ponds. Only now there's a shark loose in their pond.

Once again, I position myself at the end of the table, standing looking down at them. 'Gentlemen, good afternoon. We haven't actually met, and if you'll excuse me, I'm not proposing to go through the usual round of introductions.' I look around the table with a sort of twisted half smile on my face. 'You see that room over there?' They nod and glance over to where I've come from, where a group of bitter, broken men are being led away to collect their personal belongings. 'I've just fired everyone in that room.' This brings a sharp intake of breath, tempered by a venal, self-interested glint in the eyes of one or two who think they see an opportunity. 'Some of you won't be around long enough to make it worthwhile investing the time in getting to know you. Those who make it will soon get to know me anyway. I'm placing each of you in temporary charge of your departments. If I don't see a material improvement in results over the next month, you'll be replaced. If you deliver, you can expect great things. Each of you will have a five minute slot with me each day to report how well you've done. Don't send me paper, don't send me e-mail – talk to me. And each day I'll be spending at least an hour walking round the office, dropping in from time to time, just to keep my finger on the pulse. You'll get used to it.'

I actually have no idea what their results are like. For all I know they might be stellar, though from the look of the previous heads of businesses I doubt it. Anyway, it was my first Monday. I was bored, and I hate January.

Two meetings in one day is quite enough. When I get back to my office I tell Maria to get me Herman on the phone.

'Herman? Hi, it's Dave. Great. First day's been terrific. We're making very significant progress already. I've just fired everyone.'

By five thirty I'm out of there, in a cab home, calling up Ilyana from Kiev and Natalia from Bucharest.

TUESDAY'S FINANCIAL press carries some interesting stories. The best headline reads *Bloodbath at Grossbank*. I wonder what Rory will make of that one. They're all running the line that 'City hard man' Dave Hart marked his first day in his new job by firing all the heads of department in what was clearly a carefully orchestrated plan. The tiny quarter page devoted to business news in the *Daily Post* is the one I like best: *Hart by Name, Hard by Nature*.

But now the heat's on and I need to move fast.

When I get to the office, somewhere around nine-thirty, I call another meeting. Maria's already finding it hard to get people to come to meetings with me, but I insist that they drop whatever they were doing and attend. The first meeting is with Bill Foreman, who is nominally in charge of marketing and PR for the London operation. I say 'nominally', because before I came here, people had barely heard of Grossbank London.

He's a lean, nervous type in his mid-thirties, wearing a collarless shirt buttoned up to the top and no tie. Probably thinks it's media-cool. He worked for a succession of minor PR agencies before winding up at Grossbank five years ago.

When he first enters my office, I'm sitting in my big leather power-chair, staring out the window. He stands awkwardly, coughs, and then falls silent, waiting for me to acknowledge him. He probably thinks it's a power game, but the reality is that Ilyana and Natalia gave me simply the best time ever last night. I don't know what we were all on – well, I do, but I'm not telling you – but we carried on until four, and I'm honestly feeling pretty shagged out, as well as hung over – and yes, I know it's January, but anyone can slip momentarily. I've got shadows under my eyes and I feel as if I'm labouring just that little bit harder against gravity today – it's a 2G day. With a monumental effort I swing my chair around and stare at him. I have only a mild twitch, probably due to tiredness rather than stress. He remains standing, awkwardly, and I don't signal him to sit down.

'Bill, our PR is crap.'

'I – I agree.'

'You agree?' I'm taken aback by his candour.

'Of course. It's all directed from Frankfurt, and they have no idea how the British press works. Their marketing campaigns are crass and heavy-handed, and they never want to spend any money.'

'Oh.' I gesture to the chair beside him, the strategically low, deep chair that leaves even the tallest visitor looking up at me, either hunched forward with their feet on the ground, or sitting right back with their legs dangling. He chooses to hunch, cravenly I feel, probably anticipating a summary execution.

Perhaps he senses my hesitation, and like a Death Row inmate holding out for a governor's pardon, he'll say anything to secure a delay in the sentence. 'Have you ever seen the posters they wanted us to put up? The huge ones to go on billboards in the City, and as full page ads in the financial press? *If size matters to you, choose Grossbank* – can you imagine? We'd have been a laughing stock. Then they had *Grossbankers make sure our clients come first and we come second* – they'd commissioned all this from a German agency that had never done any work in the UK. It was all I could do not to use this stuff.'

Remarkable. A head of marketing and PR, who spends his time avoiding marketing. But I can see what he means.

'Bill – which is the most expensive, trendy, high profile PR firm in the UK?'

'Ball Taittinger.'

'Get them in here. I want to meet them to discuss a marketing campaign for Grossbank London.'

'You bet. Fantastic. It's what I've wanted to do for years.' He looks as if a huge weight has been lifted from his shoulders.

'Bill?'

'Yes, Mister Hart?'

'Call me Dave. Bill – congratulations!'

'Wh... what do you mean?'

'You've just survived a meeting with me. You see, it is possible.'

He laughs, thinking I'm joking, but when I don't respond he dries up.

'Thank you, Bill.'

He tries to stutter something, nods and exits.

Next on is Charles Butler, the head of HR. I've got in front of me the bonus list for last year.

'Charles, these bonuses were a disgrace.'

'Wh – what do you mean, Dave?'

'I mean how can people live, when they get paid like this, let alone perform out there in the market?'

'I – I don't see your point. Last year was a pretty reasonable year by Grossbank standards.'

'But the biggest bonus paid, presumably to one of our "star performers", was three hundred and fifty thousand pounds. Charles, how can a man live on that sort of money? Don't our people have wives and children and homes and yachts and fast cars? Don't they have dreams and aspirations, mistresses and drug habits?'

He's not sure how to take this last point, and smiles and nods – just the way I did with Rory! – as if he's getting used to my slightly zany sense of humour. 'But Dave – the firm can only pay what it produces. We're not very profitable.'

It's true. The whole London office produced less last year than the worst performing business area at Bartons – mine, as it happens – so they couldn't pay out.

'Charles, all this is going to change. We're going to implement Plan Alpha.'

'Plan Alpha?'

I nod. 'Plan Alpha. It's what I discussed with the board in Frankfurt.' They didn't actually know it as Plan Alpha, and neither did I until a few seconds ago, but it's all I can manage when I feel like this. I get up and walk over to a flip chart. 'Charles – you know the management structure we've employed in the past in London?'

'Of course. Matrix reporting. Business heads reported in functionally to Frankfurt, and each region had its "champion" on the board, with geographic responsibility.'

I pause. I didn't know that. It sounds pretty sensible to me. But it's such an effort to stand here concealing my hangover, that I press on anyway.

'We're going to adopt a new structure.' I pick up a red marker pen and draw a square box on the flip chart. Inside the box I write 'Me'. 'Okay, Charles, let's take this slowly. Here I am. Are you with me so far?'

He nods, giving me an uncertain, sideways look. I then

draw two diagonal lines stretching downwards and outwards from the first box. I draw two more boxes and write in one, 'Head of Markets', and in the other 'Head of Corporate'. I turn back to Charles.

'This is the new structure. Simple, lean, streamlined, easy to understand and manage.' I point at the two boxes. 'The head of markets runs equities, fixed income, treasury, foreign exchange, and the head of corporate runs all the corporate client facing businesses – structured finance, corporate lending, project finance, new business areas we don't yet have a presence in, like mergers and acquisitions, leasing and capital raising. The underlying businesses report in to them. They make a whole raft of strategic hires, bring in complete teams from other firms, and take responsibility for their businesses and their results.'

'So what do you do?'

'I'm in charge of the two of them.'

He seems puzzled, as if he doesn't quite get it. 'But I thought you…'

I cut him off. I don't have time to waste. 'Charles, I'm going to need the best headhunters in the business ready and raring to go when these people come on board. We'll be hiring people like they're going out of fashion.'

He points to the two boxes I've just drawn. 'B – but do you know who these people are?'

'Sure. I'm planning to recruit both of them this week.'

IT'S FRIDAY MORNING, and I'm having breakfast at Claridge's with Paul Ryan, the Chief Operating Officer at Hardman Stoney. A few weeks ago, Paul wouldn't even have taken my call, but now he's positively deferential.

In fact they all are. Just in the past few days I've had breakfasts, lunches and dinners with a bunch of people who would never previously have given me the time of day. Some of them tell me they checked me out with Rory, who was unusually reticent and if he did say anything, limited his advice to telling them to 'be careful'. The kind of people I'm talking about are all in the 'three million and over' club – that's annual bonus, in case you were wondering. They're successful, wealthy people accustomed to dealing at the top table.

And I wouldn't hire any of them.

The reason I'm having breakfast with Paul is that he's different. The others I wanted to meet because I needed a crash course in top table manners and conduct – the way they speak, the way they relate to one another, the things they think about. Pretty soon I'll find myself in a situation outside the safe haven of Grossbank's London office, and I'll have to act the part. The Emperor might be stark naked, but there's nothing to be gained from advertising the fact.

And if I'm honest, I got an ever so tiny thrill from having Maria call these people up and invite them out, at very short notice, so I could listen to what they had to say while scarcely opening my mouth, and then not offer them a job. It spooks them, when nothing happens, and it creases me up.

Paul on the other hand is quiet, serious, understated, and very practical. He's six-foot three, with a lean, athletic build, wavy dark hair, film star good looks, a neat, perfectly trimmed appearance, and a penchant for wearing sunglasses throughout the year. Naturally, being so good looking and well turned out, he's gay. The reason he's COO of one of the biggest and most aggressive US firms is that he gets things done. Senior investment bankers can generally talk a good story – at least by the time they reach board level – but they're not good at doing things.

Paul knows his business inside out. He designed the software programmes that the firm runs on, and he's a master of the detail that sends me to sleep but keeps a business running: information and reporting systems, risk management, IT.

'Don't you get sick of being COO?'

'Why should I? I'm irreplaceable, no one wants my job, and I get very well paid. I keep my head down, stay out of the politics, and don't get hurt when the market falls out of bed or rates go haywire.'

'But is this it? Is this as far as you go?'

'What else is there?'

'How old are you?'

'Forty-one.'

'Forty-one? That's crazy. You can't stop now. You can't just... hang up your ambition and say "that's it, I'm going to sit here and get fat and happy".' Everyone needs a new challenge.'

'What sort of challenge?'

I lean forward across the table and try to put on my energised, enthusiastic, messianic look – though not too close, in case he gets a hint of my stale alcohol breath. I came here directly from an all night session with Barbara from Estonia and Nina from Columbia.

'Head of Markets at Grossbank.' I hold up my hand and start counting off businesses. 'Let me see – running equities, fixed income, treasury, FX, derivatives, commodities and precious metals…'

'But Grossbank isn't in half those businesses, and the ones you are in you come nowhere. You're talking fantasy investment banking.'

I lean back triumphantly. 'Exactly. Fantasy is the word. You inherit a bit here and a bit there – the legacy businesses – but in most areas you have a blank canvas. Build your own firm, in your own style, with your own ethos, your own systems, your own infrastructure. You've got three years and a billion euros to do it. Hire whoever you want. Hell, if you really want to, you could buy the opposition. It would still be small change for Grossbank. The only rule is that you must succeed.'

The thing about Paul is that he could really do this. He'd have the credibility, the experience, the technical expertise, to pull together a world class business. In fact he has everything that I don't have, which is why, like all good bosses, I want to delegate the real work to someone far brighter and more competent than myself. I want to say that the Panzer divisions are on the march, and you are either with us, or you can be crushed beneath our tracks, but Paul is too thoughtful for that kind of rhetoric. 'How many times in your one unrepeatable life is someone going to make you an offer like that?' I pass him a napkin. 'Here – write down what you want by way of a package.'

With my right hand taken care of, I need to sort out my left hand. Whoever I hire to be Head of Corporates needs to have a natural top table manner, great connections, smoothness, charm, but also steel. Of all the people I've come across, 'Two Livers' MacKay is the most outstanding candidate, different in a way that I find exciting, but which some find hard to take. Two Livers has a reputation as one of the hardest drinking corporate coverage officers in the City of London. Starting at Bartons, then moving on to Schleppenheim, and finally Berkmann Schliebowitz, Two Livers outdrank the Russians at vodka to win some of the great Russian privatisation mandates, out-Scotched the Koreans and Japanese to refinance both countries' heavy industries after their markets crashed, and out-Schnappsed the Germans to pull off the first hostile takeovers in what had been a closed corporate world. A lot of people are jealous of Two Livers – mostly people who missed out on mandates they thought were in the bag – and a lot, myself included, admire the ruthlessness, the single-minded determination, and the dedication of a true corporate stormtrooper. And there's one other thing about Two Livers. She's beautiful.

Two Livers MacKay is one of the new breed of women in the City who are good for something other than typing or shagging. She's thirty-six, single, blonde, with a great figure and an Olympic athlete of a liver. She needs very little sleep, works like a dog and looks like a goddess. I haven't spoken to her in almost ten years. In her early days at Bartons, we were pretty close for a moment – a brief coming together on a business trip to Madrid. But she sussed pretty quickly that I was a shallow, vacuous low-flyer who wasn't to be trusted and would never commit.

Now things are different. Now a random spin of the wheel on the great roulette table of the Square Mile means that I can offer her even more millions than she's getting at Berkmann Schliebowitz. Suddenly she wants to have dinner again.

I'm meeting her at Gordon Ramsay tonight, but first I have a chore to deal with – Wendy wants to meet me. She wants to know 'what it is that I want'. Typical woman's question – hell, I don't even know what I want, other than money and success and fine malt whisky and willing, nubile young things in my bed at night. I may be a hero in some people's eyes, a big swinging dick in others, but at heart I'm just a guy.

I go back to the flat and change into my oldest suit, undo my top button, loosen my tie and splash some whisky on my face like after-shave. Then I wander round the corner to the coffee bar – 'neutral ground' – where we've agreed to meet.

The first thing I notice is that she's made an effort. Starting with the shoes – Manolo Blahnik – up through the legs – freshly waxed, with a silky sheen and a tan – to the skirt and jacket – Chanel – and the yellow and white gold necklace and matching bracelet – Bulgari. She's at her elegant best. She looks like the kind of woman who would be an asset to any greedy, vain, ambitious investment banker.

Except that's not what I am any more.

I explain that I'm in bad shape. In desperation after being shafted by Rory in the bonus round at Bartons, I've taken my sayonara job at Grossbank. She knows as well as I do that Grossbank are a joke. It's not how I ever imagined I'd end up, but needs must, and now I have to do whatever I can to make ends meet. I fear that we've grown too far apart for a reconciliation, and besides, I never saw her with a loser. She deserves better, and she's still young enough and good-looking enough to try. Whatever we decide should be friendly, civilised, and involve as few lawyers as possible. Samantha should be the priority and we should put her interests first. And anyway, I'm having so much fun shagging hookers and snorting nose candy that I'd have to be an idiot to get back together with her.

Just kidding about that last bit.

The trouble is, Wendy's nobody's fool. She tells me she's heard from Gloria Finkelstein – wife of Matt Finkelstein, who runs the swaps desk at Hardman Stoney – that Grossbank have actually given me a real job, with power and authority and that I'm doing things like firing people and offering big packages to new hires. She wants to know what I'm earning because as the woman who stood by me all through the tough years of my early career, she surely has a right to some of the benefits now that I've re-launched myself?

I take her hand across the table and look her earnestly in the eye. I'm good at this. I assure her that I would never, ever wish to deceive her about any aspect of my career, my finances or my life. We've been together too long and know each other too well for that. I promise to get her a copy of my contract of employment from Grossbank to settle things between us once and for all. We agree to meet again in a few weeks' time. She asks if I'd like to see Samantha this weekend and I explain that I'd love to, but I've got urgent business to attend to in Lithuania and Estonia, and she gives me a parting peck on the cheek, wrinkling her nose when she realises that it's ten a.m. and I've already been on the whisky.

After she leaves, I head back to the flat again, wash and change, and take a cab to the office. I ask Maria to call Charles Butler in.

He appears about thirty seconds later, looking nervous, as if his time might finally have come.

'Good morning, Charles.' I don't look up and I don't smile, but my cheek is twitching.

'Good morning, Dave.'

I toss Paul Ryan's napkin across the desk. He stares at it, uncomprehending.

'Paul Ryan's leaving Hardman Stoney.'

'Really?' Charles looks as if he doesn't understand the significance of this. I wait a few seconds, and finally he asks, 'Where's he going?'

'He's coming here.'

'Here?' Charles almost laughs. 'Paul Ryan is coming here? What's he going to do?'

'This job.' Without looking over my shoulder I raise one hand to point to the right hand side of the flip chart behind me.

'What job?' Charles is looking puzzled.

I turn and see that my 'org chart' is gone, presumably removed by the cleaners – or maybe Maria, to be sent secretly to the board? - and I'm pointing at a blank sheet of paper. 'Plan Alpha. Head of Markets.'

'Oh.' Another pause. 'You mean *the* Paul Ryan?'

'No. I'm talking about the other Paul Ryan. The one who works in the mailroom at Hardman Stoney as a messenger. That's the one we're hiring.'

For an instant his eyes widen, but then he realises it's just my little joke and he finally rises to the occasion.

'Congratulations! That's amazing. People won't believe it. I can hardly believe it myself. It will finally give us credibility. I mean – even more credibility than we already have since you joined.'

I indicate the napkin on the desk. 'We worked his package out on a napkin, and shook hands on it over breakfast. Draw up an offer letter, would you?'

He picks up the napkin and examines it, frowning. 'What exactly am I looking for?'

I grab it back and look at it, turning it over several times in frustration. Damn, I've picked up the wrong one. That's what comes from doing important meetings when you've been shagging all night and you're still half cut.

'Maria!'

She appears at the door. 'Yes, Mister Hart?'

'Call Claridge's. See if they can find the other napkin from our table. Paul wrote some numbers on it. It's quite important.'

'Yes, Mister Hart.'

I no longer have any idea what numbers he wrote, other than that they were impressively large. Damn. I look at Charles and tap the side of my head.

'Need to fix my head. Sometimes think I'm going crazy.'

'Really?'

I don't reply, but rub my chin pensively. 'Charles, there's one other thing.'

'What's that, Dave?' He's watching me intently, and I think I can spot a nervous tic in his cheek too. I wonder if eventually everyone at Grossbank will have one.

'Charles, I don't know quite how to put this, so I'll tell it to you straight. I'm having to let you go.'

'G – go? G – go where?' He knows exactly what I mean, but is in denial.

'I didn't know how to do this, and to be frank, I'm not really sure how to fire the head of HR. After all, you're supposed to be the one who handles all the firings. And you can't exactly fire yourself, can you?' I smile benevolently and walk around the desk to stand behind him, a friendly hand on his shoulder.

'W – why?'

'Why? Well it's obvious, isn't it? You don't fit in.'

He half turns to face me. 'H – how?'

'You have no sense of humour. You don't laugh. You don't fit in.'

'But I try to. I really do.'

'Okay. Let me give you an example.' I start pacing round the room, so that he has to squirm and wriggle in the low chair to follow me. 'I'm planning a practical joke to play on some friends of mine. People I've known for a long time, and who have a great sense of fun. I want to show them a contract of employment, on official Grossbank letterhead, that shows me earning, oh... let's just say a preposterously small amount of money. At Bartons, I'd have gone to the head of HR, who would have run me off a contract in a flash, and would have asked me afterwards how it went. But you're distant, you have no sense of fun, you don't join in.'

He's nodding now, frantically, and almost trips over the words in his haste. 'I c-c-can do that. I think that would be terribly funny. A scream. You w-want a prop for a practical joke? Of course, no problem, we're great practical jokers here.'

'Really? I must have misjudged you. Okay, let's put it to the test.' I look at my watch. 'It's quarter to twelve. I have an important recruitment dinner tonight, and my back's been giving me such gyp that I'm seeing my acupuncturist at twelve-thirty, which means I'll probably work from home for the rest of the day. Let's see what you can do before I leave the office in, say twenty minutes, shall we?'

He nearly sprints from the room. What a good man. I can see that we're going to get along fine. My acupuncturist is nineteen years old, blonde and comes from Belarus. And after that I'll probably be so tired that I'll have to sleep until dinner.

THE GORDON RAMSAY restaurant in Royal Hospital Road, Chelsea, provides the ultimate dining experience: sublime food served in perfect surroundings with exceptional wines and service that is attentive without being intrusive. There could be no better place to meet Laura 'Two Livers' MacKay. I get there ten minutes early, still feeling tired after extending my acupuncture session by three hours – some of these nineteen-year-olds have incredible stamina. I'm worried that I might fall asleep. The trouble is that Viagra extends my ability to perform way beyond what my body can naturally sustain. I'm not a marathon runner, just a regular guy who eats too much rich food, drinks too much and never exercises. I need to slow down. At this rate I could kill myself.

There are a smattering of diners at other tables, chatting

quietly to the occasional tinkle of cutlery on plates and the chinking of glasses. It's peaceful, discreet, luxurious.

And then there's a hush.

I look up to see a vision of beauty drifting serenely across the room. She's wearing an elegant, pale yellow mid-length dress and matching shawl by Loro Piana. The dress is not particularly low-cut – too sophisticated for that – but it clings to her body as if she was sewn into it. She's got amber and gold earrings, beautifully crafted, and to my shame I can't place them. Around her neck she has a matching amber pendant. No rings on either hand, which is a relief.

I stand to greet her, beaming like a kid in a candy store. 'Two Livers – how the hell are you? It's been a while.'

She dazzles me with her perfect white smile, ignores my outstretched hand and leans close to kiss me on the cheek – not a formal peck, but a softly lingering kiss that allows me to soak in her perfume – *Un Bois Vanille* by Serge Lutens. As her cheek gently caresses mine, she whispers in my ear, 'Yes.'

YES? A voice in my head is screaming at me. What does she mean – yes? The maitre d' pulls the chair out for her and she sits down, leaving me feeling like an awkward teenager, way out of my depth and struggling for words. I sit down and bury myself in the formalities of what would she like to drink – a large Screwdriver made with Uluvka vodka – and does she prefer still or sparkling – neither – and would she like to look at the menu – no, she already knows what she wants.

'Yes.' She's leaning forward across the table, smiling, running her fingers up and down the tall cocktail glass that's just been placed in front of her. Her eyes are fixed on mine.

Damn. At my time of life, there aren't many women who can do this to me. I put down the menu, trying not to appear flustered. 'Yes?'

'Yes, I want to work for Grossbank – I'll need three by four sterling with a million sign-on and a buyout of my unvested paper – and yes, I'll have sex with you.' Her voice is low, husky and clear. And she definitely said she'd have sex with me.

I put the menu down. 'Great.' I look around to see if anyone else has heard our conversation. 'How hungry are you?'

She lifts her glass and I watch while she downs it in one. 'Not hungry at all. Shall we go?'

THE PROBLEM with having sex with four different women in twenty-four hours, not getting any sleep, rushing around London in taxis to attend high impact recruitment meetings, seeing your soon-to-be-ex-wife, having to lie convincingly to her about the true state of your finances, and having to threaten your head of HR to get him to produce a bogus contract of employment that you can use to deceive said soon-to-be-ex-wife, is that the toll eventually catches up with you.

Just as Two Livers and I collapse naked onto the bed in my apartment, our clothes scattered on the carpet where we have pulled them off, I pass out. I wish it were otherwise, but the cumulative effect of all that's been going on finally hits me. When I eventually wake up, around six the next morning, she's gone. I wonder if any of it really happened, until I wander into the bathroom, and see written on the mirror in red lipstick: 'Yes. 3 x £4 + £1 sign-on + buyout. + sex.'

THINGS ARE going well. We've fired a lot of people, mostly second-rate, and we've hired a bunch of first-rate people, all very expensive, and hardly any of them available to start for several months, because their spiteful firms are enforcing the gardening leave provisions in their contracts. Grossbank's London business has actually picked up slightly, as people make a real effort to avoid what they fear might be a campaign of ethnic cleansing once the new people start.

So why have I been summoned to Frankfurt? I call Herman and he sounds almost apologetic. 'It's Doktor Biedermann. He's one of the old guard. He doesn't like what he hears about the London operation. He used to be responsible for the London office on the board. He personally knew most of the former business heads. In fact he was responsible for hiring them.'

'So what does he want?'

'He wants to trip you up. He wants you to come to Frankfurt far too soon, before any of your efforts have born fruit, and be humiliated. It's the old way. It's his way.'

'And what do you suggest I do?'

'Come here and face him. You of all people are not a man to run away from confrontation.'

Damn. 'You bet, Herman. Let me know just as soon as I can come over.'

'Next Tuesday would be good. The regional managers from all over Germany will be here. You could address them first, and then talk to those board members who are... most concerned about our investment banking strategy.'

'Next Tuesday? Really? Great. That's... five days away. Wonderful – I'll see you Tuesday morning.'

Double damn. All investment bankers live in fear of being found out. This really could be it. This could be the moment when they say it was all a joke. Did I seriously think they'd put me in charge of anything, let alone running the entire London office? Being in charge is all about faking it. I like to think I can fake it with the best of them. But if you so much as blink you're dead. I could already feel the onset of rigor mortis.

'Maria!'

'Yes, Mister Hart?'

'Maria – get me the smartest associate in the firm. I need a presentation prepared on our global strategy – a complete business plan in fact. Budgets, revenue forecasts, the lot. And a speech. A killer speech for Frankfurt.'

She hesitates. I look at her, irritated. 'What's the problem?'

'Where will he get the information? I don't think we have any budgets or forecasts or plans.'

'Really?' She's right, of course. So far, I've been winging it. 'Well, tell him to write them. It's a great opportunity.' What do we pay these guys for anyway?

The next few days are hell. A weasel-faced kid called Jan Hagelmann, a trainee on loan from Frankfurt, sits outside my office working on a laptop, poring over figures, producing draft after draft of numbers, graphs and charts.

I can barely understand half of what he gives me, and several times fly into a rage, tearing up presentations and throwing them across the room at him.

What really pisses me off is that he never really reacts. The kids at Bartons used to tremble if a MD let rip at them – they could be fired in a heartbeat, and often were. But Jan has a German employment contract and he's bullet proof. The only thing I can do to him is make him work, and I go for it with a vengeance, making him stay late every night and work through the weekend, biking round revised drafts to me at home, which I return, unread, with comments like 'Hopeless' and 'No – start again. More detail!' or 'Bin this and do it properly – be more concise!' On Sunday night I call him in the office around ten o'clock.

'Still there, Jan?'

'Yes, Mister Hart.'

'And you haven't finished?'

'No, Mister Hart.'

'Really, Jan – you can't be very good, can you?'

By Monday night he's exhausted. I stop by his desk, confirm that he's e-mailed the latest version of the presentation to me and to Frankfurt, and tell him I think he's useless, unimaginative, bone-idle, and has no future in investment banking.

Christ, I love my job. Nowhere else in the civilised world could you treat another human being like this and get away with it.

IT'S TUESDAY morning, and I'm flying to Frankfurt with Paul and Two Livers. He looks like a male model, tall, sleek, not a hair out of place. He's wearing a conservative, pale blue suit from Brooks Brothers, a white shirt and a dark blue tie from Salvatore Ferragamo. Two Livers looks like Miss World with a brain – pale grey trouser suit from Armani, white collarless blouse that buttons up to the top, with a small gold crucifix around her neck and – get this – no earrings and very little make-up. She's sipping a bloody Mary, and looks earnest, studious, the kind of woman you'd definitely take seriously, and yet at the same time you'd want to rip her panties off. At least I would. In fact the other night I did, but that's another story.

Technically they are both still on 'gardening leave' from their old firms, but everyone knows that certain rules are there to be broken, and they've already been out hiring people, dealing with head-hunters, ordering new systems and infrastructure, and generally planning the move to a much larger new building in Docklands – our European flagship headquarters, which we've labelled the Pleasure Palace, and which will recycle the kind of money that even Frankfurt will notice. They're energised and excited.

By comparison I'm dull, grey and depressed. I feel like a condemned man. It's as if I've already been found out, and now I'm going to have to own up that I really shouldn't be these guys' boss, more like their bag carrier. They each have more talent and experience in their little finger than I have in my entire body. Gloom and depression start to set in, the black dogs are circling, and I can feel myself sliding into danger.

In the nick of time, like a life preserver that inflates automatically on hitting the water, my investment banker's self preservation instinct kicks in. I remind myself that it really doesn't matter who runs an investment bank, as long as they vaguely look the part. You could pick more or less anyone at random from most trading floors, tell them they're in charge, and for as long as they didn't blink, everything would be fine. Achievement doesn't so much come from effort by management, as the state of the markets, the amount of corporate activity, and whether your firm happens to be around at the right time. This is normal, so don't panic. I start to feel better.

We're sitting in Club Class, which means nothing on these short-haul Euro- pean flights. Every seat is taken by businessmen, bankers, lawyers, accountants, management consultants, the faceless grey masses swarming all over the world's business centres. The overhead lockers are full, so my briefcase is shoved under the seat in front of me, the hot breakfast smells nauseating, and I know I'm going to get off the flight at the other end looking and feeling sweaty, crumpled and tired. I make a mental note that next on my shopping list has to be a smoker – a private jet like Rory's. If I survive.

In Frankfurt we're met at the airport, whisked into town in a Grossbank limo, and greeted at the bank by Herman and some of his team. They show us into a large auditorium, where after ten minutes or so a couple of hundred middle-aged Germans file in and sit down to stare at us as if we are some kind of exhibit. These are the regional managers, the men who manage the lifeblood of Grossbank, its access to all the hard-working, wealthy citizens who are paying my bonus. They look sceptical, unconvinced, as if they are here on sufferance.

I take my place on the podium, flanked by Paul and Two Livers. Herman has disappeared – apparently he's too senior in the German hierarchy to attend this sort of meeting, which makes me even more nervous. One of Herman's flunkies stands up and starts talking in German, which I don't understand, except for a reference to 'Doktor Hart'.

'Doktor Hart'? It's well known that Germans are a highly educated people, spending far longer than the rest of us at university, and have great reverence for titles – they apparently call it *Titelfreude*, the joy of titles. It says something about our two nations that in England we have the joy of sex, in Germany the joy of titles. I have no idea if Herman's flunky knows I don't have a doctorate, but I make a note for future reference. Over here, this stuff counts.

The flunky finishes, and indicates that I should step forward to the lectern. There's a clear plastic idiot board in front of me for me to read my presentation from – or Jan's presentation, since he wrote it – and a laptop to advance the Powerpoint slides. I went through it all last night: lots of numbers, charts, graphs, organograms, enough to bore the most heavyweight investment banking anorak rigid.

'Gentlemen, good morning.' A few heads incline in my direction, but otherwise no reaction. I click on the laptop, and the introductory slide appears: 'Grossbank's future in investment banking'. I look at the idiot board and read off it. 'My name is Dave Hart.' Thanks, Jan – I probably could have managed that one myself. 'I'm an investment banker. I'm here today to tell you about Grossbank's

exciting plans to go forward into the twenty-first century.'
This is pretty banal, dumb stuff. I don't recall it from the
previous versions. If you don't grab an audience like this
in the first thirty seconds, you're toast. Click to slide two
– 'One key message'. I read off the idiot board again. 'I
have one key message for you today. If you take away
nothing else from this presentation, remember this.' Click
to slide three: 'You're on your own, pal.' I read off the
idiot board: 'You're on your own, pal.'

Shit! I click on rapidly, but all the other pages are blank,
and nothing's coming up on the idiot board. I glance
across to Paul, but he shrugs his shoulders helplessly. That
dumb, fucking kid Jan Hagelmann just committed career
suicide. Doesn't he know I kill people? I'll wring his
fucking neck. I look out at the audience. They are
frowning, trying to work out where I'm coming from,
what this is leading up to.

'We all are. Every one of us. We come into this world
alone and we leave it alone. It's what we do along the way
that defines us.' I pause and stare out into the middle
distance, wondering what the hell to say next. 'That's why
I'm not going to give you a formal presentation this
morning.' I can't. I don't have one. 'I could tell you how
we are going to unleash a tiger in the world's markets,
how this firm's enormous financial resources are going to
be put to work behind the best teams, the finest people in
the industry, and how we are going to come from
nowhere and sweep the board with our competition. I
could bore you endlessly about the business streams we've
already identified where this firm will be a top-three player
within three years. I could show you projections for the

obscene profits that will be thrown off by the great financial engine that we will create.' I need to change tack fast, because some of them are whispering to each other, probably wondering what I am going to tell them. Maybe if they have any ideas, they could share them with me. 'I could tell you all of that, and it's all true.' Yes, honestly. 'But it won't happen overnight. It will require patience and forbearance and enormous investment, and still it won't be easy. But life isn't meant to be easy. Life is about challenges, and you face those challenges best with friends and comrades alongside you.' I could add that there is no comradeship quite like that created by millions of pounds of guaranteed bonuses, but these people get paid peanuts, so I don't. 'So I'm going to talk to you instead about people. Our people. The real people inside these suits.' What the hell can I say next? That the 'real' us are driven by shallow, materialistic greed and alcohol and drug-fuelled lust? That we'd sell our soul for a bigger package, say 4 x 4?

I point to Two Livers. 'You will come to know my colleague, Doktor MacKay, over the coming years as someone who is constantly pressing you for introductions to corporate clients in your regions for potential investment banking business. You'll think her a dragon, a demon in woman's clothing, who is constantly demanding more.' Though not quite the way she was demanding more from me the other night. 'But on Sunday mornings you would see a very different Doktor MacKay. On Sunday mornings you'd find her on her knees...' Preferably kneeling at my feet, and you can guess what she'd be doing. '...Doktor MacKay is a lay preacher.' She can certainly get preachy after she gets laid, especially on the subject of senior management incentives.

I glance to my right. Bang on cue, Two Livers touches her crucifix, then looks down modestly at the desk in front of her and tilts her head to one side. She looks like an angel. I could kiss her... at least.

'Paul...' I gesture towards Paul, sitting behind me on the other side. '...Paul is gay.' I pause meaningfully for this news to be absorbed around the room. The great thing about Germans is that they are on the whole very liberal-minded – they have this huge tolerance thing, which has come to be an article of faith among the educated classes. 'Paul knows what it's like to be alone. He knows what it's like to suffer because you're different. During the week, Paul will be a demon of the markets, but at weekends he spends his time counselling young men.' Generally after he's shagged them. 'He doesn't talk about what he does at weekends.' You wouldn't, would you? 'But he's as driven by what he does out of hours as what he does during the working day.' A fucking sex maniac, from what I've heard.

I can feel a change in the room. This isn't what they expected. Weakness, vulnerability, concern for one's fellow man, coming from investment bankers? Nah, get out of here. But I can sense that I've got them.

'Some of you may have heard wildly exaggerated rumours, tittle-tattle really, about my alleged salary and bonus package. I'm not going to dignify those rumours with a comment.' Mainly because they fall well short of the truth. 'But let me assure you of one thing. Half of everything I actually do earn goes to good causes. Not ten per cent, as some religions require, certainly not the few per cent that many of you voluntarily pay in church taxes. Half goes to good causes.' Fucking good causes. Like women's causes in Eastern Europe and Latin America. In fact I'm spending so much of my after tax income on these good causes that even on my enormous package I'll soon have to slow down.

'Remember the words of that truly great philanthropist, Andrew Carnegie, that he who dies rich, dies disgraced. It's who we are that matters, and how we live our lives. That's what I wanted to talk to you about today.' I search for something really fatuous to wind up with. 'Gentlemen, we're not alone. We're all in this together with our values and our beliefs – one dream, one team, one firm.' I clench my fist and wave it in the air. 'Grossbank rocks! Thank you.'

Phew, now I can go and kill Hagelmann. I pause, waiting for some polite applause. But then the strangest thing happens. The guys in the audience start banging the tables in front of them. What is this, a riot? Are they going to start throwing things? I turn to Two Livers and Paul. 'Let's get out of here.'

We rush to the exit, trying to ignore the ever louder banging behind us, and Herman's flunky hurries after us. When we get outside, I turn on him, furious. 'Do you have their names?'

'Y – yes, of course.'

'Good. Fire everyone in the room.'

'Wh – why? They liked you. They loved you. That's why you got this response. I've never known it before.'

'You mean...' I do an impression of a fist banging a table.

'Yes.'

'Good. That's what I thought. So what I want you to do is fire everyone off a message from me, saying how much I enjoyed meeting them, but this is only the beginning. I want me and my team to spend much more time really getting to know all of them. Fire them all off something like that straight away.'

As Paul and Two Livers fall in behind me to take the lift to the fifty-fourth floor, both of them goose me. I grin. The A-Team.

DOKTOR BIEDERMANN looks like the villain Blofeld in the Bond movies. Bald, bespectacled rather than wearing a monocle, but with the same slow, deliberate movements. All he lacks is a cat sitting in his lap to stroke.

I'm sitting in his office with Herman, around a coffee table well away from his huge power desk. Paul and Two Livers have had to wait outside – some sort of German hierarchy thing. The wall to one side is what the Americans call a 'Me Wall'. I didn't know the Germans went in for this, but since I'm meant to look at it, I do. There are photographs of Biedermann with the German Chancellor and President, and various dignitaries that I'm sure I should recognise, but don't. There's a set of shelves with various Lucite deal tombstones, family photos, and some interesting *objets* – highly appropriate fossils, which presumably he's collected himself, and some spectacular quartz crystals. I check out the family photos and do a double take when I see a shot of a family group and spot a familiar face. I turn to Biedermann.

'Isn't this...?'

'Yes. My nephew, Jan Hagelmann. I understand he helped you prepare your presentation today, which was so successful.'

Fuck. Jan the dead man. I was already fantasising about the torture I would put him through before setting him up for an exit that even a German employment contract couldn't stop. 'Yes. He's brilliant. Wasted in London, but brilliant, nonetheless.' It's bad enough having Maria reporting back to Frankfurt on me, without Biedermann's personal spy as well.

'Wasted in London? Surely not. I thought London was where the action is.' Biedermann looks across to Herman, who for once seems less sure of his ground.

'Doktor Biedermann, we need bright people everywhere, and most of all here in Germany, where our franchise is strongest. Someone with Jan's talent should be here, at the sharp end, showing by example what can be achieved.'

Herman looks briefly grateful. 'How would you use him here in Germany?'

'Leave that to me. I've had it in mind from the outset to put really bright, sharp young Germans into the field, somewhere relatively small, but where they can have a big impact.'

Biedermann and Herman are both nodding. 'Good. We'll follow this with interest.'

We are briefly interrupted by the arrival of two more fossils in the room. Both come in, shake hands, mutter their names, which I instantly forget – apparently they are members of the supervisory board, which sits above the management board, and is even more fossilised.

Biedermann leans back in his chair and forms a bridge with his hands, savouring the moment. 'So, Mister Hart.' It's that *Titelfreude* thing again. 'I know it's still early in your time at Grossbank, but some of us...' He looks at the two fossils, who nod their heads wisely, avoiding eye contact with Herman and me. '...some of us feel that it is important to take stock of the direction in which the London operation is heading. To us it seems that so far, all we have achieved is to fire our existing people – people of long service and great loyalty – spend vast sums hiring expensive people from other firms, announce grandiose schemes for a new building, which will cost us further millions, and we have yet to see a concrete business plan for the board to approve.' He leans forward, fixing first Herman, and then me, with a stare. 'Or am I wrong?'

There's clearly a power play going on here between the old guard and the new. The old guard probably liked the bank the way it was: rich, successful and secure. If it isn't broken, don't fix it. The new guard are bored, greedy, and envious of their British and American peers. They want a new train set. It's clear whose side I'm on.

When Herman doesn't respond, I take it as my cue.

'Gentlemen, the reason I haven't presented a detailed business plan is obvious.'

They all look at me, and even Herman seems puzzled.

'We don't have one.'

Herman looks horrified, and the others sit back smugly, an ugly grin spreading over Biedermann's twisted features.

'If we did have one, I'd have to ask you to fire me.'

'What?' Now they're really puzzled.

'If at this juncture, I was tying the bank's future to a

specific, single plan, no matter how well devised, I'd be dumb and you'd have to fire me.'

Biedermann is nodding. He's looking forward to firing me. Didn't think it would happen quite this soon, but he's relishing the prospect.

'Gentlemen, there's a saying in English that goes back to the early dawn of warfare: no general's plan ever survived the first shot of battle. We could come up with a plan, sure we could. We could hire management consultants and have long navel-gazing sessions, playing games of fantasy investment banking until the cows come home. But we'd get nowhere. Analysis paralysis. Or we can be like the Special Forces. Parachute into the jungle with a crack team, an unbeatable team and win! Someone far older and wiser than me once said of strategy in investment banking that the only point in having one is so that at year-end you know what you've departed from. I can't tell you what markets are going to do, or rates, or what sort of corporate activity will occur over the next twelve months. We can guess, we can speculate, we can make predictions, but ultimately we have to create a team, a business, that is flexible, responsive, pragmatic. They say elephants don't sprint, but this elephant will dance and sprint!' I tap the table top with my finger. 'Gentlemen, our plan is not to have a plan! We'll assemble the best of the best, equip them with state of the art systems, put the weight of the bank's capital behind them, and then sound the bugles and charge.'

I make my voice drop to a whisper. 'And we will win. That will be the legacy of the investment banking initiative in years to come. In years to come, when people take it for granted that Grossbank is a major force in global investment banking. That, gentlemen, will be your legacy to future generations.'

Silence. Then, from Biedermann, who looks to be seething, a slow hand clap. The fossils glance at him, irritated. My little speech may actually have got their pulse going again briefly. He can see they are not with him. Herman pulls out a handkerchief and mops his brow. Dumb move, Herman. Don't ever play poker.

'Mister Hart. You make a very good case for not planning. But in this bank we are accustomed to doing things after we have thought them through, not before. You have shown you can destroy what the bank built over many decades in the London office. You have shown you know how to spend money. But you have not won any new clients, Mister Hart. That is what I would like to see. Where are the clients? Gentlemen, I propose we meet again in one month's time to review progress. And I will be expecting news of clients.'

Herman's visibly relieved. He's off the hook, at least for now. The fossils nod their agreement, and a few minutes later I'm standing in the anteroom to Biedermann's office, where Two Livers and Paul are waiting.

'How did it go?'

'Great, we've got one month to make it work.'

They both smile. They know when I'm joking. I wink at Two Livers. 'Better have fun while we can.'

JAN HAGELMANN is finally crying.

He's standing in my office, in front of my desk, while I lounge in my chair, feet on the table, staring out of the window.

'Y – you really agreed this with my uncle?'

'Yes. And Doktor Schwartz. It'll be good for you. And good for the bank too. I'm told that Gruenkraut is very picturesque. It may be a quiet sort of place, with an ageing population, and not quite the night life of London, but it's only an hour-and-a-half from Munich.' I swing my chair around and give him an enthusiastic smile. 'And it's a challenge. If you can show the people at our branch offices that even the dullest, sleepiest, most boring village in Germany can produce the goods if it's tackled properly – why, the sky's the limit.'

'But... why three years?'

'Three years? Why because that's how long it takes to get to know a place, find your way around, identify the key people in the local business community, cultivate them, and eventually... bite them in the neck. The way investment bankers do. Now get out of here.'

I know I shouldn't enjoy this, but I do. The same way I enjoyed sitting at my computer and ordering nine-hundred dollars' worth of postgraduate degrees and diplomas from American universities first thing this morning. They'll be going up all over the back wall of the office. And Maria has the presentations team working their Adobe Photoshop image editing software to produce a whole new set of shots of me. They all think it's another one of my little eccentricities, or some practical joke.

How wrong they are.

Right now, I need to find clients. So I do what all investment bankers do when they need to justify their existence at team meetings or in front of their bosses: I read the paper. Some would call it ambulance chasing, because by the time a deal reaches the newspapers, the firms that are working on it have long since been appointed. If it's a piece of business requiring a group of banks to be formed – a syndicated loan, say, or a share sale or bond issue – then there might still be a chance to squeeze a few crumbs from someone else's table. For the price of a newspaper, you at least get the chance to say, 'Sadly this time we only had a co-management position in MegaCorp's issue, because our terms were a few basis points away from Hardman Stoney's, but next time we'll be more aggressive.' Never underestimate the importance of the press.

On the inside pages, there's a feature on the private security companies working in the Gulf. They're employing thousands of armed guards, mostly ex-military, to protect government employees and companies engaged in rebuilding Iraq. They've got people in Afghanistan too, on private contracts, doing close protection and armed escort work. The editorial slant of the article is that it's a bad business, with poorly organised, greedy companies sending ex-squaddies into harm's way without proper training or preparation. Hell, I bet some of them don't even have business plans.

The biggest firm out there, with multi-million dollar contracts, is called Military Overseas Security Solutions, or MOSS for short. They have nearly five thousand pairs of boots on the ground, huge contracts from the British and American governments, friendly Middle-Eastern regimes, and blue chip corporate names. They are the only firm in the region that the paper gives the thumbs up to, run properly and efficiently by a former trooper in the Special Air Service, called Mike Moss – hence the name.

These companies are private, because they probably think they could never float on the stock market. Too difficult a business, lots of legal problems, duty of care to their employees, nature of their work, too little transparency, I can see all the reasons why investment bankers would put them in the too difficult tray.

But we're not most bankers. We're Grossbank, and we're desperate.

The only thing against MOSS in the article is that some of their guys on the ground have put bumper stickers on their vehicles saying things like 'MOSS – no messing' and 'MOSS – peace through superior firepower.' It's the sort of thing that most banks' new business committees would get twitchy about. Luckily it doesn't bother my new business committee, because I'm it.

'Maria!'

I tell Maria to track down Mike Moss and get me a meeting.

One swallow doesn't make a spring. I need more firepower behind me if I'm to survive another month. I've got an idea – something Two Livers mentioned on the flight back from Frankfurt. She's arranging a meeting with the European Chief Investment Officer of Boston International Group, the London arm of one of the world's largest fund management firms. In the old days, he would never have given Dave Hart the time of day, but now, with Two Livers vouching for me, his door is open.

Irritatingly, in the midst of all this activity, I have to see Wendy. She's had my letter of employment for a few weeks now, and we need to resolve things between us. She doesn't want to stay out in Buckinghamshire, she wants to come back to Chelsea. And if we are going to split, then she agrees – or rather her lawyer does – that we should make it as amicable as possible – i.e., she'll take legal advice, but hopes that I won't. Based on my stated income of seventy-five thousand a year plus a season ticket loan, with uncertain bonus prospects, no savings, accumulating debts, and the need to finance Samantha through her education, they are proposing an out of court lump-sum settlement. She's sent me papers that are ready to sign. She wants a 'clean break', that would leave me free for the future – probably because her lawyer's told her that an MD picking up seventy-five thousand a year at a sayonara place like Grossbank is clearly going down the toilet. She knows it's an onerous sum for me to raise, and imagines that I would have to take on considerable borrowings, but perhaps Grossbank would advance me the money?

She wants two million pounds. I nearly laughed when I heard. The first rule of a City marriage has to be: tell your wife nothing.

We meet again in the coffee bar.

'Two million? How on earth can I raise that kind of money? Are you trying to kill me, or what?'

My face starts twitching, and she reaches out to touch it, a spontaneous, natural gesture of affection that twists an unexpected dagger of guilt in my gut.

I pull away. 'Don't. We're not close any more. It can never be the same and you know it.' Our eyes meet across the table, and I can see that hers are full of tears. 'I've moved on. It's only fair that you should know that there's someone else in my life now. It's hard work, but I'm making an effort.' And what an effort! There are actually dozens of people in my life now: Lithuanians, Estonians, Romanians, Ukrainians, Argentinians, Brazilians, Columbians; it feels like half the United Nations. What they have in common is that they are all under twenty-five, have great bodies and if the money's right, they are insatiable. And I love them all. Honestly. And then of course there's Two Livers, an exceptional perk for any man.

WENDY APPEARS shocked and terribly upset. I don't know what she was thinking. Maybe two million would be an impossible sum for me to raise. For 'old' Dave Hart that would have been true. But 'new' Dave Hart could write her a cheque tomorrow. Or maybe it's the fact that she thinks I've found someone else dumb enough to take on a loser like me. Maybe it was me she was hoping for. Nah! I look at the document lying on the table between us.

'I don't know how I'm going to finance this.' I shake my head theatrically. 'But if this means we can draw a line and move on, and can still be friends, and do the best for Samantha, then I'll sign.' I slowly, reluctantly, get my Mont Blanc pen from my in-breast jacket pocket and carefully unscrew the top. I look up at Wendy, who still seems stunned by the turn of events. I can imagine the conversation with her lawyer – 'You're perfectly safe. It's win – win. There's no way he can sign this, but if he does, you should celebrate.' But they underestimated Dave Hart. As if forcing myself to be decisive, I sign the paper in a flourish, put the pen away, wipe my eyes with my handkerchief and leave without saying another word.

Outside, I hail a cab to the office, and glance back briefly to see Wendy sitting, shaking her head, crying her eyes out, mascara staining her cheeks as she stares at the papers I've just signed.

Christ, I'm good.

TIM TURNER is one of the most powerful fund managers in the City of London. Boston International Group – 'BIG by name, BIG by nature' – runs mutual funds, pension funds, unit and investment trusts, high net worth portfolios, hedge funds – you name it, they have it. They are a top three commission payer to every investment bank and broker in town. When they say 'jump', the investment banks ask 'How high?'

Turner himself is tall, very overweight, inclined to sweat profusely from even minor effort – like getting up from his desk to shake hands – and oozes arrogance from every pore. His jacket is slung over the back of his chair, his shirt sleeves are rolled up, his tie loosened, and he has bright red braces with black dollar signs and the initials BIG monogrammed on them.

His nickname in the markets is 'Tripod Turner', because apparently he's the biggest swinging dick of them all. In the cab on the way over I ask Two Livers if she wants to comment on that, but she smiles and stares enigmatically out the window.

We sit down in his huge corner office – even larger than mine – get the pleasantries over with and the coffee poured, and I start to explain why we've come.

'Mister Turner, you may have heard that Grossbank is

intending to become a major force in global investment banking over the next few years.'

'Yeah, I heard the Germans have decided it's their turn to step up to the plate and pour money down the drain. Someone has to keep house prices rising in London.'

I smile, as if in appreciation of his little joke. Wanker!

'Grossbank doesn't yet have a presence in asset management outside Germany.'

'You don't have anything at all outside Germany – apart from yourself and Two Livers and Paul Ryan, plus a few hired guns I hear you're taking on.'

'What the market hasn't yet realised is how serious we are. We're following a two-pronged strategy: build, and buy.'

'Buy? What are you going to buy? Do you want to buy BIG?' He laughs, a sort of snorting noise that makes his vast bulk shake.

'That's why we're here.'

He laughs properly this time, a great thigh slapping roar. We sit patiently, not reacting. Eventually he subsides, and looks at us speculatively.

'Are you serious? BIG would be a stretch even for Grossbank. And you guys aren't exactly players.'

At this moment, with immaculate timing, Maria calls on his secretary's number. From the corner of my eye I see his secretary get up from her desk, approach the big glass-walled office, and knock discreetly before entering.

'I'm sorry, Tim, but Mister Hart's secretary is on the phone.' She turns to me. 'You have an urgent call from George Soros. She wants to put him through now.'

'Later.' I wave my hand dismissively. I look at Tripod Turner. 'Of course we're serious.'

For the first time, he looks flustered, as his secretary shrugs and returns, muttering, to her desk to explain to Maria that I can't take Mister Soros's call right now.

Turner points out to where his secretary is sitting. 'Was that *the* George Soros?'

'No.' I shake my head emphatically.

'No?' Now he's really confused. In fact it was Maria, my secretary, following the instructions I gave her before we left.

I turn to Two Livers. 'Go for it.'

She nods, crosses one beautifully tanned and streamlined leg over the other, and starts reading from her notes.

'Let's talk about BIG. You're currently capitalised at around eleven billion dollars, and closed last night in New York at eighty-five dollars a share. Employees own forty-three per cent of the company, and your own stake is close to seven per cent.'

He nods and says nothing. At least we have his attention.

'You also have employee options to buy shares at ninety dollars. Ten million options for yourself alone, and a lot more are held by your colleagues. These were issued a few years ago when the company was in trouble. There was a management crisis, and the board felt it had to lock in key personnel. But the shares have never traded that high – the market seems to know that ninety dollars could trigger the exercise of a raft of options and the release of a lot of shares into the market, and it acts as a kind of ceiling on the share price.'

Again he nods.

'These employee options are about to expire in six

weeks' time – worthless, unless the stock goes through ninety bucks.'

'You don't need to rub my nose in it.'

I take over. 'We're not. We're going to make you a happy man, Mister Turner. Tomorrow morning, Grossbank is going to announce that it's going into the market to acquire a strategic stake in the company, and that we don't rule out eventually making a bid for the entire firm.'

'Are you crazy? Tomorrow? The whole firm?'

Funny how even the biggest swinging dicks are only human.

Two Livers takes over again. 'We're not really planning to go through with it. BIG really would be too much, even for Grossbank to swallow.' Funny how we both look at her when she says the word 'swallow'. She could add that our board in Frankfurt don't actually know about this yet, but that's detail, and I like to think I'm a big picture man. 'Tomorrow morning we'll acquire a small stake in your company, which we are sure will be a good long-term bet for our shareholders. We won't actually commit ourselves firmly to bidding for the entire company, but we'll say enough to make sure your stock goes through the roof. If it doesn't hit a hundred dollars by the New York close, I'll give up drinking.' She reaches down to her handbag and takes out a small bottle of Evian water. At least it says on the bottle that it's Evian water. She unscrews the top and takes a long drink while we both watch. Then she looks down at her notes and adds, as if as an afterthought, 'Oh, and your ten million ninety-dollar options, currently worthless, will look quite attractive again. If you exercised them at ninety dollars with the share price at a hundred, you could make ten dollars a share times ten million... that's a hundred million dollars.' She turns to me. 'Not bad for a day's work.'

I nod. 'Not bad.'

He jabs his finger at us. 'Why are you doing this? What's in it for you?'

Two Livers smiles. 'We're in the happiness business. We want to make you happy.'

'Bullshit.'

I take over again. 'Let me put it this way, Mister Turner. We're not going to lose money on this transaction. It's good business. And Grossbank doesn't have many friends in the City of London.'

'So what?'

'So we want to be your friend.'

AFTER ANOTHER night of relentless drugs, booze and hookers, even my stamina's being tested. Today is a 3G day – I feel I'm labouring under three times the force of gravity. Worse yet, I'm actually starting to get bored. Really!

Did I say drugs? Okay, I am getting into drugs in a minor way, and probably have been for a little while now, but only coke, and not every night. It's far more common than you might think, and it's pretty harmless really. It gives me a buzz, keeps me flying. The girls bring it with them – it's a way for them to earn a little extra pocket money on top of what I give them.

The shadows round my eyes are getting darker now, and my face seems more lined – more distinguished – and there are more grey hairs. I suppose I'm growing into my role, looking the part more, getting more miles on the clock.

Speaking of which, I perk up as I remember that today I get to pick up my new toy, a silver grey Bentley Azure convertible. An awesome, throbbing power machine, rather like her owner. I take a cab to the garage, have a half-hour briefing on how she performs – shame they don't offer this with women – then cruise round to Two Livers' flat in Mayfair, to collect her and take her down to Sussex, to a disused airfield that serves as the UK headquarters of MOSS.

Mike Moss looks like a wiry prop forward. He has wavy dark hair, broad shoulders and exceptionally large hands. He speaks in an almost unnaturally soft voice, and is quiet and deferential in the way that you can only ever hope to be if you enjoy complete confidence in your ability to kill any human being on the planet.

His office is spartan, as I half expected, with posters of weapons on the walls and photographs of convoys crossing deserts. The coffee is instant, from a jar by a kettle in the corner, and he makes it himself. It's a remarkably low overhead operation, even though it's picked up contracts worth eighty-million dollars in the last twelve months alone.

He's googled me, and starts by congratulating me on what I did to the 'bad guys' in Jamaica. We have the sort of conversation that you can only have between men who have faced the ultimate challenge and won.

'How was it?'

'Tough.'

'Did you think about it much afterwards?'

'Sure.'

'You always do the first time. I shouldn't say this, but it gets easier.'

Lots of things left unsaid, and probably best so in my case.

He's also checked out Grossbank, and in the nicest possible way, doesn't know what we can do for him. Under normal circumstances, he'd be right, but he doesn't know how desperate we are. I let Two Livers do the talking.

'Mike, this company needs additional financial resources to expand.'

'No, we don't. We're a cash machine. Completely flexible. Bring people in as we need them. Keep the overheads low. Look at this place. Costs nothing.'

'But you could certainly use additional funds.'

'No. We'd waste it. Right now, we're really well organised, tightly run and efficient. We don't hire officers. We let the lads get on with it. And it works.'

'But you personally could use some extra cash. It's not as if you haven't earned it.'

'No, I couldn't. I've already put aside more than enough to look after the family. And besides, the beauty of this place is that if the contracts come to an end, I can lock the door and go off and do something else.'

'But you've created considerable value in the company. A stock market listing would allow you to unlock that value. It would reflect the full extent of your achievement.'

'Who cares? Like I said, I don't need to.'

Exasperated, Two Livers takes a swig of Evian and throws in the towel. 'Mike, has anyone ever told you about greed?'

He smiles and rubs his chin. We're obviously not from quite the same planet after all. My turn.

'Mike, have you ever wanted to make a real difference?'

241

He shrugs. 'Sure. We all do.'

'Have you ever seen something that really makes your blood boil?' Like a Hardman Stoney MD with a bigger apartment than you?

'Sure. When we're in country, in both Iraq and Afghanistan, there's a huge amount of poverty, deprivation, local people whose lives are going nowhere. We support local projects where we can, with funds or supplies.'

Gotcha! 'Exactly, Mike – and that's what this is all about. You support local projects where you can. Mike, you could list this company on the Stock Exchange, sell shares for tens of millions of pounds, and put the funds into a charitable foundation that could really make a difference on a grand scale. Tens of millions, Mike. Think about the effect that would have at the sharp end.' He says nothing, but I can see I've got him. 'Come on, Mike. How can you just shrug your shoulders and walk away from that?'

On the way back we put the top down. I light a large Cohiba, which I feel is in keeping with the image of the car. It's a surprisingly warm late February day, with the first hint of an early spring. Better yet, as we drive through Horsham a loser in a BMW Z3 pulls alongside me at the traffic lights, looking across at me and revving his engine. I wait for the amber light to appear, then put my foot down and smile as the silver grey beast hurls itself forward, leaving him behind. He catches up at the next lights, and the same thing happens again. At the third set of lights he winds his window down and leans across.

'I think you're a sad git.'

I look at him and smile, take a puff on my cigar and nod. 'You're probably right.' Then I put my foot down again and leave him in the dust. Fucking hairdresser!

We get back to the office at two o'clock London time, half-an-hour before the New York opening. Paul has briefed our dealers, and all eyes are on the screens. We're going on an elephant shoot today – Grossbank will be acquiring a stake in the Boston International Group.

There's a lot of tension in the dealing room. Grossbank has never done anything like this before. Neither have I, but everyone has to start somewhere. As soon as the stock opens, our announcement goes across the wire and we're in there buying. This being the New York Stock Exchange, the reaction is instantaneous, and BIG shares go haywire. We pick up some in the high eighties, but within minutes they are in the mid nineties, before racing through a hundred dollars a share and settling at a hundred and five. We've managed to spend about four hundred million dollars acquiring a stake at the lower levels, before backing off and keeping our remaining powder dry.

It takes a little while for Frankfurt to realise something is going on, but when they do, Maria comes rushing over.

'Mister Hart – I've got Doktor Schwartz and several members of the board on the line insisting they speak to you urgently.'

I wander back to my office, flop down on my chair and put my feet on the desk. 'What line are they on?'

'Line three.'

'Okay, tell them to start talking. I'll pick up in a minute.'

She stops and gives me a strange look.

I grin at her and wink. I flick the phone to speaker.

'Dave Hart here. Good afternoon, gentlemen.'

For once, they ignore the formalities.

'What is happening? What are you doing? Are you mad?'

I try to be patient, talking in a mild, matter of fact tone. 'If you're talking about BIG, which I assume you are, it's a normal investment banking transaction, well within our remit. Gentlemen, I'm surprised that you're surprised. If I bothered you with every little thing, we'd never get anything done.'

'Every little thing? You have just announced that we are buying an eleven billion dollar company.'

'Actually, it's worth a lot more than that, since we started buying their shares. But let's not split hairs. We are not buying the company.'

'So why did you release this press statement?'

'Gentlemen, if you read the press statement carefully, you'll see it says simply that we are acquiring a strategic stake, and may decide to move to a full acquisition in the future. Well guess what? We just decided not to. If the stock stabilises around these levels we'll unload our position in a few weeks' time. BIG was trading at a discount to other comparable quoted fund management groups, because of a perceived overhang in the market caused by a large block of employee share options priced at ninety dollars. The upside was capped. Well, we just blew that cap away. Now the stock's free to trade at a higher level, and we'll cash in our chips as soon as we can. We'll tell the market we couldn't get a big enough stake and so we're selling.'

A long pause at the other end, then: 'We still don't like it. Why didn't you tell us?'

'We sent a full presentation by e-mail last night, for the attention of all management board members, the head of Frankfurt PR, and the supervisory board.' It's true. I told Paul to prepare it, and make sure it ran to at least a hundred pages, including appendices. 'You were told everything.' Silence. These guys probably can't even open e-mail. They rely on their secretaries to do it for them, and anything that runs to more than a couple of pages can't be important.

'Gentlemen – imagine it's 1939, and the tanks are rolling. They're five kilometres into Poland and you decide you don't like it. What are you going to do? Call them back?'

The line goes dead.

I AM FAST becoming a legend.

Tripod Turner thinks I'm a genius and wants to buy me dinner. Herman the German is looking at a hundred and fifty million dollar profit on our BIG stake – now trading around a hundred and twenty dollars a share, actually ahead of other comparable companies, and Biedermann is so desperate to pick a hole in what I'm doing, he's coming to London with Herman and the fossils to have our next review meeting.

Maria is starting to like me, despite herself, and has thrown herself into the creation of my 'Me Wall', getting my various doctorates and diplomas from American universities framed along with the doctored photos from the presentations team. Whereas once I joked about her leaving her broomstick outside the office on hover, now I find I'm warming to her.

Best of all, I'm going to have a meeting with my – sorry, our – possible new PR advisers, Ball Taittinger. Bill Foreman, our London office PR director, has got them in to pitch their services to me – sorry, us.

They say that perception is king in the Square Mile. Get the smoke and mirrors right, and the substance will fall into line. So today we're going to talk about... me!

The team from Ball Taittinger are everything you would expect from a top PR firm – a grey-haired, craggy-faced, seen it all, knows everyone, goes to all the best places senior partner, who is slick, seasoned, ultra-smooth, and could be a senior investment banker, except for the pale pink tie; a much younger, mid-ranking adviser, who looks like he spends his out of hours time partying even harder than I do, and actually it's quite a privilege that he's struggled in to attend this meeting; and not one but two lots of eye candy – blonde and brunette – who surprisingly seem to have brains, probably did most of the background work for today's meeting, and get major speaking parts in the presentation, possibly because the number two on the team is too shagged out to talk.

The presentation is called 'The Hart Enigma'. The moment the slide goes up, they've got the business. They really don't need to say anything else. But the girls go on to say how Grossbank needs to be associated in the public mind with me, my courageous action in Jamaica, my tough-guy, firm management style, and my vision for the future. Out with the old Grossbank, in with Dave Hart, modern day hero.

I try to appear detached. 'Isn't there a danger in creating a cult of personality around one man?'

The senior partner – in my mind, I've nicknamed him the Silver Fox – takes this one. 'An investment bank is no different from any other business. It has to deploy its assets efficiently and dispassionately, to best effect, regardless of the individuals involved. This is not about you. It's about the bank, and what's in the bank's best interest. In the case of Grossbank, the principal asset here in London is you. I know it's difficult to discuss people in this hard-nosed way, but you're effectively a device to be deployed with the media. People look at you and they see someone who is young, handsome, hugely successful, decisive, highly intelligent and yet willing to risk it all to save a little boy. All of that will play brilliantly with the media. It already has. We can use it to build a huge campaign around you – and completely re-invent Grossbank's image in the process.'

This is better than sex. Well, almost. 'Go on.'

'People see you as someone who has it all, yet still takes huge risks – a physically courageous individual in an age of selfishness. You're a maverick, charismatic, a natural leader, someone the best and brightest in the City of London will look to for leadership. Someone they'll follow into the unknown, with an exciting new venture that will revolutionise world markets.'

This is awesome. I could sit here all day. 'I see. What else?'

He pauses for a second, takes a breath, and goes on, speaking more quickly now. 'You'll go where others fear to tread. You left the security of a well-established firm – Bartons, a top UK name – and went into the unknown, into virgin territory, to shape your own destiny. You're a pioneer, and you're not afraid. You don't have to be. You've faced real danger and won. A man like you isn't afraid of anything that can happen in the stock market, or in some boardroom. You're Dave Hart!' He's standing now, clenching his fist with passion.

'Excellent. I'm convinced. Let Bill know what your fees are and we'll get started straight away. Maybe some profile pieces in the weekend papers? Anyway, I'll leave the detail to you.'

OUR NEWLY FORMED equity capital markets team are working on Grossbank's first UK flotation, of the security company Military Overseas Security Solutions. The press coverage has been mixed. There are suggestions in the left-wing press that the MOSS Foundation is a cynical ploy to legitimise a dirty business. In the financial press there are questions about Grossbank's ability to get the deal done. Will we be able to put together a syndicate of banks for a potentially controversial deal? If we don't, will institutional investors buy shares in a company that may not be followed by other firms' research analysts, or traded by other firms' market-makers? Grossbank may be spending money to hire heavy-hitters, but one firm can't do it all.

I decide to make some calls. First I call Mike Moss. I explain that we're making good progress, the deal is shaping up well, and we're at the stage where we need to bring in a syndicate of other banks.

'Mike, this is a controversial deal. People don't know if it'll work, and so they're keeping their heads down. It's the first deal of this type led by Grossbank, and the oppo aren't exactly queuing up to help a new competitor get established. If we have to do it alone, we will. You know that. But I want to try another route first. I need your help.'

'Anything I can do, Dave.'

'Do you know the US military attaché at their Embassy in London?'

'Of course. Bill Fraser. Former Green Beret. Some of the boys from the Regiment worked with him in Gulf War One.'

'Is he well-connected in Washington?'

'Are you kidding? He's got a direct line to the Joint Chiefs of Staff.'

I mentally tick one box. 'Another question. Of the top four or five corporate clients that you work for in the Gulf, who's most dependent on you to keep their operations going?'

'Has to be Anglo Petroleum. They're rebuilding the main pipeline south. We keep it from getting blown up.'

Bingo! I tell him what I want him to do, then I call Tripod Turner. I need some weight behind this deal, and he's just the man to help.

Maria comes in to run through my diary. Wendy called – do I want Samantha this weekend? No, but I get Maria to send some presents round. The property search agent wants to show me a house in Holland Park. We fix a time. Am I still intending to see my chiropractor about my back this afternoon? Yes, and I'll probably work from home afterwards. And finally, a lady phoned who claims she knew me in Jamaica – Sally Mills.

Sally Mills? Yes, I'll definitely see her. My jaded appetite is rekindled by the thought of finding a way into her perfectly clean, practical white cotton panties. She's free tomorrow morning, and there's just time to squeeze her in before Herman and Biedermann and the fossils arrive.

Life is looking up. I might be tired most of the time, I might feel as if I'm racing just to keep up with myself, I might even wonder in odd moments if this is really happening to me, but I'm having fun! Every day is different, and I'm starting to enjoy myself.

I put my feet on my desk, light a cigar, and blow smoke rings at the freshly installed 'No Smoking' sign.

SALLY LOOKS as great as ever, in an innocent, wholesome, well-scrubbed way. Spring is definitely in the air, and she's wearing a pretty floral dress with a white cardigan and practical, flat brown sandals. We meet in a coffee bar not far from my office.

Things start badly. I lean forward to give her a friendly peck on the cheek, but instead she holds out her hand for me to shake. On closer inspection, she looks tired.

I'm at my solicitous best. If only I behaved like this all the time, and actually meant it, I'd be a really nice person. I ask after her, after Toby, whether he had any after-effects from that awful experience, and how about Jasper and Monty, and of course Trevor the teacher. I'm half hoping that she's going to break down at this point, cry on my shoulder, and say they're finished and she doesn't know what to do any more, and can I please hold her tightly and tell her everything's going to be okay? That way I'd definitely get into her panties.

But instead, she says how Trevor has shown her occasional press articles about me from the finance pages. How Grossbank seems huge and very powerful, and so much seems to have happened in my life in a very short time and I must be very important now, and she feels guilty for not having kept more closely in touch.

She asks about Samantha, and I explain that no, sadly it's as I feared, and I haven't had the chance to spend time with her. I could explain that I have a photograph of Samantha on my desk, and another in the apartment, and a small one in my wallet, so I don't actually need to see her. But I don't think Sally would like that.

The conversation goes on, and it gets more apparent that she's skirting round whatever the real issue is. My investment banker's bullshit-ometer is on overload. Time is short, and I cut to the chase.

'What's really on your mind, Sally?'

She takes a breath, obviously summoning up courage, and plunges in. 'It's Harry.'

'Harry?' Who the hell is Harry? Does she have a lover? Has someone got there before me?

'My brother Harry. He's Chief Executive of Hastings BioScience.'

My news filter generally blocks out items that aren't in some way relevant to my own well-being, so I have to dredge quite deep to remember.

Ouch. I can see why she's worried. HBS provide animal testing services for pharmaceutical and healthcare companies. It's a vital service to test new drugs that will one day save people like me from an early grave. HBS are interesting because they set out to do controversial work in an ethical, transparent way. They don't get involved in animal testing for cosmetics companies, and they limit their experiments to dread diseases and other dire medical conditions that contribute to the sum of human misery. So naturally the eco-terrorists are after them.

'Is he the one who was attacked? By the Animal Freedom Front? Didn't they beat him with baseball bats or something?'

She nods and gets a tissue out to wipe her eyes.

'Here – take this.' I hand her a new silk handkerchief from Harrods men's department. She wipes her eyes and goes to pass it back to me.

'No. Hang on to it. You can let me have it back next time.' Yes – next time! Hart, you're a pro. But she's still upset, so I tilt my head to one side, empathising with her as she summons up the courage to talk about this painful subject.

'They beat him about the head. He could have been killed.'

'Cowardly bastards.'

'He's very brave. He won't give up. I told him about you. He said he wishes he could be as brave as you.'

I look down at the table modestly. 'I did what anyone would have done.'

'But anyone didn't do it. You did. That's why I'm here today.'

Christ. I get a sudden nervous twinge. I hope she doesn't expect me to be brave twice in the same lifetime.

'Harry's firm are close to bankruptcy. Their building's like a prison camp, with barbed wire and police and security guards. Anyone going in and out is heckled by a mob of demonstrators. It's been going on for over a year now.

The staff have to be escorted in and out of the premises, and even then they get followed home. They've been sent horrible things through the post – human excrement, hate mail – and now the bastards are targeting their shareholders and bankers. Anyone who owns shares in HBS has their name and address put up on a website, and has to live in fear of being attacked by these nutcases. Their bank has given notice that it can't carry on lending them money. Apparently they're in fear of what might happen to their own employees if they carry on – they say they have a 'duty of care' to their own people, which means Harry and his company just get ditched.'

'Awful.' I shake my head. 'Poor Harry must be at his wits' end.'

'He is. That's why I said I'd come to you.'

'Me? What can I do?'

'You can step in and finance them. Not you personally, but Grossbank.'

Is she mad? I can't really tell her that ever since Jamaica the mere sight of a black man with dreadlocks makes me nearly wet myself. Now she wants me to take on the eco-nutters as well. No woman, no matter how wholesome she might be, no matter how great the challenge of the chase, can really be worth dying for.

'Sally, I hate to say this, but I can't help.'

'Why? It's so... so important. HBS will go bust in a matter of weeks if no one helps. They're on the brink already. And if they go under, lots of important medical research will go with them. People will suffer, Dave, real people, who deserve not to be bullied by thugs.'

'I know... and if it were my decision alone, you know I'd be with you in a heartbeat. But I have to carry my colleagues along with me. If Grossbank were to step in now, we'd be putting ourselves into exactly the position that HBS's existing bankers are in. We have a duty of care to our people too. We're not paid to take risks.'

'Yes, you are.' Her reply is abrupt, her manner almost contemptuous. 'You're all paid millions. If anyone's not paid to take risks, it's the policemen who stand guard around the HBS building, who get in the way when the bricks are being thrown. Or the soldiers you see on the television. Soldiers don't get a fraction of what you earn, and look at the risks they take, or firemen, or lifeboat men...'

'Sally, please. Don't go on.' It's too fucking painful. 'You're right.' Her eyes suddenly brighten. 'I'll see what I can do. I have to warn you that it's very unlikely we'll be able to do anything at all, but I'll try. I'll give it my best shot.'

'Oh, thank you, thank you.' She throws her arms around my neck and gives me a wonderful, fresh, moist kiss on my cheek. It's a beautiful moment, and so of course I have to blow it. I glance at my watch, and it's two minutes before I'm due to be meeting Biedermann and the Inquisition. Damn, there's no time to mess around. And so instead of putting my hands gently on her shoulders, staring into her eyes and saying, 'Sally, I'd do anything for you, because the truth is that I've loved you since the day I first saw you', there's a terrible grinding of gears in my head and I find myself reverting to my nocturnal default mode and saying, 'I want you, Sally Mills. I want you in my bed tonight'.

Even as I say the words, I know I've blown it.

She recoils, blushes to her ears, picks up her handbag and virtually sprints out of the coffee bar.

I look at my watch. I'm due right now with Herman and Biedermann. Fool, Hart, fool. I peel off a tenner, drop it on the table and scoot.

WHEN I GET back to the office, I find Biedermann looking at my 'Me Wall', studying it with intense curiosity.

'Gentlemen, my apologies – an urgent new business development meeting.' I shake hands with everyone and take a seat at the small conference table with Herman and the fossils.

Biedermann carries on looking at the exhibits lovingly hung by Maria and the presentations team.

'Did you really go to all these universities?' He looks at the various certificates and diplomas. 'Six different universities, all in America? Three doctorates?'

I'm not sure quite how to play this one, so I grunt something incomprehensible and busy myself with serving coffee. Herman seems amused.

'And is this really you?' Biedermann is staring at a photograph of me sitting between Putin and Bush at a dinner. It's next to one of me kneeling in front of The Queen at Buckingham Palace, obviously receiving some form of award, and another of me with Charles and Camilla at the reception that followed their wedding. His eyes follow the line of photographs along the wall: me shaking hands with Nelson Mandela; me on a podium with Bill Gates, addressing an audience; me playing golf with Tiger Woods. At least the face is me, and the girls have done a great job.

'You've obviously had a very full and varied life.' Germans aren't necessarily great on irony, so I'm still not sure how to respond to Biedermann, and instead I clear my throat and pull out a chair. Lucky for me I rejected the girls' less plausible efforts: me planting a Union flag at the top of Everest; me collecting a gold medal at the Olympics; me in a codpiece and tights holding aloft the prima ballerina of the Royal Ballet. I sent one of me singing on stage with Madonna to Samantha, wondering what Wendy would make of it.

'Doktor Biedermann – please take a seat. If you gentlemen are ready, I'll give you an update on where we are.'

'Before we do that...' Biedermann is giving me one of those *For you, Tommy, the war is over* stares. '...could we talk about my nephew Jan... in Gruenkraut?'

Herman is hiding his face in a handkerchief, and even the fossils are looking for something to stop them laughing. They probably haven't had this much fun since they were alive.

'Gruenkraut?'

'Gruenkraut. When you said you were thinking of sending him 'into the field', I didn't think you literally meant a field!'

'Well, Gruenkraut is a very beautiful place, quiet, but full of challenges and opportunities. Or so I'm told. And a good man will always create opportunities, wherever he goes.' Biedermann is seething, and his cheek is twitching. Perhaps it's infectious. Perhaps everyone who gets to work with me ends up with their cheek twitching. I decide to twist the knife. 'And besides, it's only for three years.'

Herman dissolves into a muffled sneeze, and Biedermann stares at him, not bothering to hide the full extent of his loathing for the younger man.

Maria enters and hands out some papers that Paul Ryan has prepared.

'Shall we go on to the business report?' By way of response, Biedermann turns and stares at the picture of me with The Queen. I ignore him and plough on. 'Gentlemen, these show our summary operating results. You'll see that the first quarter of this year significantly exceeds our entire contribution for the whole of last year.'

'That's because of your little adventure in America, with Boston International Group.' Biedermann has stopped even a pretence at civility.

'It's true that we have made more money on that one trade than on everything else the London operation has been doing, but most of the rest is what I call legacy business. It's what we inherited from... your time, Doktor Biedermann.'

'What do you mean, "from my time"? This is still my time. I am still a board member of this bank, or had you forgotten?'

'Quite right, Doktor Biedermann. Forgive me – a slip of the tongue.'

Herman is studying the figures. 'But even the old businesses are doing better now. Why is that?'

'Fear and greed. You spill a bit of blood, you dangle a carrot.' I look again at Biedermann. 'Never happened in the old days.'

I can see the old man is seething. The fossils seem content, and Herman obviously has his tail up. Biedermann tries one last gambit. 'What about clients? I said last time that I wanted to see progress with clients.'

'Our first corporate client transaction is underway as we speak. We are starting to market shares in Military Overseas Security Solutions, a UK-based security company, which is our first London Stock Exchange flotation.'

'And how is the transaction going? Have you formed a syndicate of banks underneath Grossbank to help distribute the shares? Are other brokerage firms going to follow the shares with their research analysts? Are they going to commit their capital to trade the shares?'

Bastard. He's just that little bit too on the nail with his questions.

'Why don't we hear from Paul Ryan, our Head of Markets?'

Biedermann has a twinkle in his eye. He thinks I've suggested Paul talks us through the deal so I can distance myself from it and set someone else up as the fall guy. As if.

Paul is summoned and introduced.

'Paul – Doktor Biedermann is concerned about our ability to form a syndicate of banks for the MOSS deal. Could you update us on where things stand?'

'Sure. I don't mind admitting we've been struggling.' Biedermann smiles smugly and nods an 'I told you so' to the fossils as Paul continues. 'It's been one of the hardest deals I've ever worked on.' Now Biedermann's grinning broadly. 'No one wanted to know. It's seen as a controversial deal, tough to sell, tough to syndicate.'

'Exactly. I knew this would happen.' Biedermann can't contain himself. Herman is fidgeting uncomfortably and the fossils are staring ahead inscrutably. 'We should never have accepted this business. I knew it would fail. Gentlemen, Grossbank's investment banking efforts have failed before they even began!'

Paul smiles deferentially at Biedermann. 'Well, that's not strictly true, Doktor Biedermann. You see, this morning, there seems to have been a change of sentiment in the market.'

'Oh? What are you saying?'

'Bartons called our syndicate desk and asked to be allowed into the deal. Said they'd like to support it, and that they'd like to welcome us as a newcomer to the UK market.'

'Bartons? Why?'

Because the Chairman of Anglo Petroleum, MOSS's biggest client, called Sir Oliver Barton and told him to, you idiot. And Sir Oliver wants Bartons to lead the project financing for their pipeline. I intervene. 'Paul's probably too modest to say this himself, but he does have a certain reputation in the market. Pulling power.'

Paul smiles modestly. 'And Hardman Stoney, Berkmann Schliebowitz and Schleppenheim have all called up as well. They're all looking for a piece of the action.'

'Really? All of them want a place in our deal?'

Sure, arsehole! Because the Chairman of Hardman Stoney in New York wants to be the next US Secretary of

Defence, the American head of Schleppenheim's UK operation sees himself as a future US Ambassador to the Court of St James, and Berkmann Schliebowitz were told by Tripod Turner that he'd send them on a three-month commission holiday if they didn't fall into line.

'Will all of them commit to research and market-making?'

'Already have. And so have a number of other firms who are not in the syndicate. Boston International Group gave us a lead order for ten per cent of the deal first thing this morning. They're making it a core holding in their flagship Omega Fund, and have put the word around that anyone dealing with the Omega Fund has to cover MOSS, the way they do all the core holdings.'

'So this will be a great success?'

Paul looks at me and we both shrug. 'Should be. You don't often get a following like that for a first-time deal by a new player.'

Biedermann gets to his feet and paces to the end of the office. He's staring at the photo of me with Nelson Mandela.

'The difficulty I have with this deal, gentlemen, is that it is a deal without soul.' He waves his hand dismissively. 'Soldiers for hire – call them whatever you like, but they are mercenaries.' He looks at Paul and me. 'Hired guns. Grossbank made its name and reputation historically as a bank that was grounded in principles. We stood for what was right, even if it hurt our profits. Many powerful German companies have experienced difficulties over the years. But we stood by them. Other banks – investment banks – would have disappeared. Not Grossbank.

'And because we stayed with our clients, because we stuck to our principles, we prospered.' He positions himself strategically standing behind the fossils and points at Paul and me. 'Where are your principles, gentlemen?'

Fuck it. It's him or me. This place isn't big enough for both of us. 'Doktor Biedermann, if you want principles, I'll give you principles. Not abstract concepts, but real, down-to-earth, here and now principles. Grossbank is going to do some- thing no other firm in the City of London is prepared to do.'

I certainly have their attention. Even Paul is wondering what I'm on.

'We are going to refinance Hastings BioScience.'

Beside me, Paul takes a sharp breath. The Germans seem nonplussed. They haven't heard of Hastings BioScience. Why would they?

'HBS is a British company that assists pharmaceutical and healthcare companies from all over the world to test pioneering medical advances for dread diseases – cancer, Parkinson's, Alzheimer's, HIV-AIDS, you name it. All of us may one day have reason to be grateful for their work. They're world leaders in what they do, and I believe we should support them.'

The Germans are nodding. Herman speaks first. 'In principle I don't see any reason not to.'

'That's the thing – it's a high risk business. Right now, they're on the brink of going bust. They're struggling with huge uncertainty over the future, workforce issues, corporate clients who can take their business overseas, the kind of thing that could make some management teams throw in the towel. But these people are different. They have a vision, a mission and a great future, if only someone will stand by them. I want that firm to be Grossbank – in the finest traditions of the firm.'

Biedermann is puzzled. 'In principle, subject to confirmation of the numbers and the appropriate credit checks being carried out, I cannot argue with you. Do you know the company well?'

'The Chief Executive is waiting for my call. With your agreement, gentlemen?'

They look at each other, shrug their shoulders and nod. Paul rolls his eyes towards the ceiling and gives me one of those 'What the fuck are you doing now?' looks.

I slap him on the shoulder and wink. 'Come on, Paul – nobody wants to live forever.' Except me. I want to live forever so that I can carry on shagging.

THE OFFICES of HBS are rather like I imagine Fort Knox to be. Barbed wire fences, windows with metal shutters, and security cameras everywhere. Two Livers and I arrive in the Bentley, which is now bearing my new personalised number-plate: H1 PAY. I chuckle at what Wendy will make of it when she hears.

A crowd of low-lifers are hanging around outside the gates. Kids in dirty combat jackets and new age beads and earrings, with beards and funny hairstyles, holding placards and chanting and maintaining an uneasy truce with a row of policemen in bright yellow jackets. The drill at the gates is obviously well rehearsed. As we swing into the entrance, whoever is monitoring the security cameras presses a button so that the gates swing open and we can glide in past the crowd. The shouting picks up as they realise we are visiting HBS, and I slow down and open the window of the Azure.

'Why don't you all go home, have a shower and see if you can get a job?'

I put my foot down and swing inside to safety as the gates close behind us and the crowd surges forward to battle with the policemen.

Harry Peters looks remarkably like his sister, except that he definitely isn't shaggable. He's late thirties – probably around my age – and has the frazzled look of a man who's been pushed to the limit. Dark shadows around the eyes, the first grey hairs, shoulders that default into a slumped position, and lines on his face that have nothing to do with laughter.

I wonder briefly if he spends all his nights shagging hookers and doing whisky and drugs, but he's not an investment banker or a hedge fund manager, so how could he afford it?

He greets us in the lobby and looks past us to the crowd outside, where a full scale battle is underway. As we watch, two more vanloads of police arrive.

'I don't know what's got into them. They aren't usually that bad. Perhaps it was the car – they probably see you as capitalists or something.'

'Something like that,' agrees Two Livers, giving me the sort of dirty look that doesn't turn me on.

He shows us into his office and goes into an excruciating hero worship speech about everything Sally's told him. How his nephew doesn't seem to have had any after-effects from Jamaica, and even mentions how they are testing a new synthetic skin for burn victims that might be useful if I ever considered surgery for the scar on my forehead.

Is he kidding? This scar and I are old buddies now. This scar's my meal ticket.

Eventually he dries up, and looks rather helplessly at us. He reaches over to a photograph of a smiling red-haired woman – probably seven out of ten, certainly shaggable. She's holding a baby. I guess she's his wife. 'We're calling in the receivers in two weeks' time.'

There's a long, poignant silence. I can hear the crowd shouting outside, more police sirens, and in the office, a clock on the wall ticking. I turn to Two Livers.

'Your call.'

Two Livers has spent the whole journey down here telling me I'm wrong on this one. I need to think again, I really am going too far, we're not paid to do stuff like this, and why the hell have I involved her?

But now she turns to Harry and sighs.

'Two weeks?'

'We've got no choice. The board decided we have no alternative. Those people...' He nods towards the sound of the crowd. 'They've won. We're throwing in the towel.'

She shakes her head. 'No, you're not. The cavalry's arrived.'

THE JOURNEY BACK from HBS is mixed. We get out of the gates under a flurry of stones, bottles, eggs and rotten fruit. There's a major riot underway, more protesters are arriving and being matched with huge numbers of police. TV crews are recording what has clearly become a major incident. A police car is lying on its side, its windows smashed. As we speed away a Molotov cocktail flies through the air and explodes in the road behind us. We pass rows of police vans unloading officers in riot gear.

'Fucking parasites. Who do they think they are?'

Two Livers is sulking, swigging from a bottle of Evian. 'Why did you make it my call?'

'Because when you start getting hate mail at home, or parcels of human excrement through the letter box, or your name gets registered on paedophile websites, I don't want you to ask me for more money. It was your call.'

'But you're the hero. I don't want to be a hero. Just rich.'

We lapse into an uneasy silence, until the mobile goes and it's Paul Ryan.

'We just priced the MOSS deal. Top of the range and it's trading at a premium. Mike Moss says you're a hero.'

Two Livers looks at me. 'See what I mean?'

It gets worse. Some selfish bastard has had an accident up ahead and the traffic comes to a standstill. We're hemmed in by VW Golfs and white vans and everyone seems to have their windows open and the radio thumping out Thick FM. The sooner we get road pricing and the chance to clear these people off the road, the better.

When we get back to the office I call a team meeting to prepare for the next steps with HBS. They can't quite believe we're doing this. Neither can I. Every- one seems to be taking comfort from the fact that I'm so certain about what we're doing. If this is leadership, it's damned scary.

The whole thing needs to be perfectly stage-managed, so Bill gets in the PR team from Ball Taittinger.

In the middle of all this, Wendy calls, angry and suspicious. She was watching the television news about the riots at Hastings BioScience and saw footage of me leaving the premises in a Bentley with the number plate H1 PAY and a blonde beside me. What's going on? Before I have a chance to lie to her, she says she's already spoken to her solicitor, and she wants the flat as well.

Can you believe this? The bitch, the greedy cow wants to take away my home, my refuge, my beloved shag-pad. I tell her to fuck off and hang up, making a note to send Samantha some more presents.

Then I get another call. It's Sally Mills. She's crying on the phone. Harry's called her and told her what we're going to do. What I'm going to do. She's so grateful. I seize the moment.

'Sally – what I said last time, it was unforgivable. I want to apologise. I have to apologise. When can I see you again so I can put things right?' She hesitates at the other end. She doesn't want to piss me off, because Grossbank haven't actually done anything yet. On the other hand, the prospect of us getting anything straight between us – as it were – may not be exactly what she has in mind.

'Dave, I'd love to, but...'

'No buts, Sally. I need to talk to you. The next few days will be hard. I'm putting everything on the line to do what's right. When are you free? Tell me, and I'll be there.'

How can you refuse a hero? We fix a date and she hangs up. There's still time for her to change her mind, but after tomorrow? Nah. After tomorrow she'll be gagging for it.

THE SILVER FOX and his team from Ball Taittinger have done a fabulous job. The main conference room at Grossbank's London office is standing room only. Wall to wall media – not just the dailies and the broadsheets, but TV and radio, and of course the financial press, and the women's magazines too. They're here for me. Don't you just love it when a plan comes together?

I mount the podium with Harry Peters, and Two Livers and Paul Ryan sit on either side of us.

The Silver Fox has prepped some of the media already. There's a buzz that even I find quite intoxicating. And I know all about intoxication.

The press conference has been scheduled for twelve noon, in time for the lunchtime news bulletins, after the morning's news and announcements have been absorbed, and in plenty of time for tomorrow's papers.

'Ladies and gentlemen, thank you for coming here this morning. Some of you know me already, but for those of you who don't, I'm Dave Hart, global head of investment banking at Grossbank. Seated on my left is a man who has sadly become familiar to all of you over the last two years, Harry Peters, the Chief Executive of Hastings BioScience.' I go on to explain how Harry and the people at HBS have been threatened, physically assaulted, persecuted and slandered, and all by extremists of the worst kind, who refuse to work inside democratic processes, but ride roughshod over the rest of us in their single-minded quest to impose their will on the majority. I pay tribute to his stamina, his determination, and his courage, and I underline the vital contribution to medical research of controlled, properly managed animal testing.

Yes, it's a horrible practice, but dread diseases are even worse. If we have to choose, then until there's some better alternative, it's clear where Grossbank stands.

There's a round of applause as he stands to speak.

'Ladies and gentlemen, I wasn't expecting to be standing here today.' He pauses, and it's not an act. The emotion is almost too much for him. He reaches down to the desk and takes a swig from Two Livers Evian bottle. His eyes light up and he's back again.

'I was expecting to be announcing the calling in of the receivers. It was almost over for HBS, and with us would have gone dozens of vital medical research programmes, hundreds of research jobs, and a good chunk of the future for the British pharmaceutical industry.

'The reason? Finance. No one was prepared to stand by us. No bank, no finance house, no institutional investor would support us. Not because they disagreed with what we were doing. But because they were afraid. Well, one bank wasn't afraid. Grossbank has agreed to refinance all of our debt, giving us a fresh chance for the future, and granting a reprieve to all of the vital medical research that would otherwise have ceased. It took guts to stand up and be counted, and it won't surprise you that the man who did so was Dave Hart!'

A round of applause goes up. It's pretty unusual for journalists anywhere to applaud anything, and I get the feeling that half of them are thinking I've lost my marbles, but what do they know?

I lost my marbles long ago.

'Thank you, Harry. Ladies and gentlemen, you've been given copies of the press releases from both Grossbank and HBS outlining the transaction. If there are any questions we'll be glad to answer them.'

A reporter in the front row sticks his hand up. 'Eddie Strange, *Daily Post*. Mister Hart – you've got a reputation as a hard man, but aren't you concerned for your own safety and that of your staff in taking on the Animal Freedom Front?'

My staff? Nah – they're expendable. 'Naturally. But this decision comes from the highest level within Grossbank. I'm the man on the spot, and I'll do what I have to do. As a firm we'll take whatever steps are necessary to protect our people. We already have enhanced security in place, and this will be increased following today's announcement.'

'Mister Hart – I'd assumed you were the man behind this financing. Are you saying the decision came from higher up?'

'I'm proud the bank is taking the stand it is, but the real credit should go to this man…' I turn and point to the screen, and right on cue, an enormous photograph of Biedermann appears. 'Doktor Biedermann personally instructed us on this transaction. He's the man who should get the credit at Grossbank. He's a board member of long standing. You'll find his photograph and bio in your packs.'

'Dick Harper, *Wall Street News*. Why is Grossbank, a German bank, taking a stand like this for a British company? Is it your fight?' Awesome. I make a mental note to double the Silver Fox's fees.

'Thank you, Dick. This is everyone's fight. All of us are affected by this, whether we choose to walk by on the other side of the road or not. We've made this our fight, and we hope that others will join us. We're a new boy in town, but it doesn't mean we can't stand up and be counted.'

'Ralph Clark, *Evening Echo*. Isn't this just a cynical ploy by Grossbank to squeeze huge fees out of a company that's on the ropes?'

'Thank you, Ralph. I'm grateful that you asked that question.' And even more grateful to the Silver Fox for planting it. 'I have here a summary of Grossbank's earnings in this transaction.' A slide appears behind me, headed 'HBS re-financing: summary of earnings'. It's blank. 'And for those from the financial press, who want more detail, here's how that breaks down.' Another slide appears: 'HBS re-financing: detailed earnings analysis.' It's also blank. Some of the journos start tittering.

'Er... Dave, those slides you just showed us were blank.' More giggling. A few of them are looking at the Silver Fox, to see if he's embarrassed. They love it when a dog and pony show goes wrong.

'I know.' I look around the room, savouring the moment. 'We're waiving our fees on this transaction, and we're not charging any loan interest either. We're doing this one for love.'

LATER, WHEN it's all over, and I'm sitting in my office, Mike Moss calls to congratulate me. 'Dave, I always knew you were different. I've met a few bankers in my time, but never anyone like you.' Luckily, I feel I know him well enough to be sure he's not taking the piss. Everyone else is. Everyone else thinks I'm mad.

'But Dave – watch your back. I worry for you. These

Animal Freedom Front people are nutters, and even you need to sleep sometime.'

If he only knew. This weekend I went for thirty-six hours without sleep with Clarisse, a black girl from the Congo, and Breathless Beth, a twenty-one year old blonde from Texas. I'm starting to think I'm super-human, though I notice that Maria looks concerned whenever I come back refreshed from a visit to the gents'.

The Grossbank refinancing of HBS is lead item in the day's television and radio news, the switchboard have already received threatening phone calls from the AFF, and a few low-life's have gathered at the entrance to the Grossbank building, where police and private security guards are watching them.

On the other hand, we've had a dozen incoming calls from chairmen and chief executives of large companies wanting to meet us. Two Livers is following them up – all the principled individuals who would 'love to do something', but don't. Giving business to Grossbank could just become the next corporate fad.

Maria calls through to me. 'I have Doktor Biedermann's office on the phone.'

'Put him through.'

He's apoplectic, and I'm glad we don't have video-phones, so he can't see me fighting to control myself. No one had ever heard of HBS in Germany, but now there's an angry crowd outside the Grossbank Tower, he's had threatening phone calls, the Greens are calling for an inquiry, and already posters are being put up around town by anarchists showing a caricature of him dissecting a kitten. The bank's security department have decided that he's going to be chauffeured around in an armoured limousine with a couple of bodyguards, and his wife has been advised to leave town. As if this wasn't enough, the media are all over him, and he's got to give a press conference in half-an-hour. What the hell do I suggest he says?

'Stick to your guns! Tell it to them the way you told it to me, here in London. You inspired me, so inspire them. It's all about principles, Doktor Biedermann, that's why we've done this.' It takes me a few seconds to realise he's hung up.

Maria brings me a sandwich at my desk.

'How's Two Livers doing?'

'Miss MacKay left a message to say 'five out of seven so far' – she said you'd know what it meant.'

Damned right I do. We're aiming to get the chairmen, chief executives, or finance directors of the largest UK-based pharmaceutical companies in here tomorrow, for an urgent meeting. It's payback time.

Right now, it's time for my osteopath. I tell Maria I'll be working from home after my treatment.

LAST NIGHT I had my first threatening phone call. The phone rang, around three a.m., just after the girls had left. Like a fool, I picked it up, and a scratchy, hate-filled voice, said 'We know where you live. Best look over your shoulder, Hart.'

I'd had most of a bottle of Scotch, a couple of amazing tablets that the girls brought, and I thought it was a joke.

'Dan Harriman, you wanker. Come on over, it's only

three o'clock. I've just sent the girls away, but I can call and get them back.'

Silence at the other end, then the scratchy voice again: 'Dave Hart, we know where you live.'

'Stop being a wanker. How many hookers do you want? Have you got any drugs?'

Click. 'Brrr...'

I put down the phone.

'Wanker!'

When I get to the office, the day's papers are laid out on my desk. It was a quiet news day, and we've made a splash. The *Post* once again has the best headline: *Bankers with Balls take on AFF*. They have pictures of Biedermann and me. 'City hard man Dave Hart yesterday sent a message to the Animal Freedom Front: up yours!' The cartoon in *The Times* shows Biedermann and me on top of a tank with black crosses on it. A group of City suits in pin-stripes and bowlers on one side are cowering from a bunch of skinheads on the other. The caption reads, 'Got a problem, chaps?'

It's only ten o'clock, and Two Livers is hitting the Evian already. She has one of her biggest days ahead of her since joining Grossbank, and she's spooked because last night someone called in the early hours and told her they know where she lives.

'That was Dan Harriman. He's a wanker!'

She looks at me with pity. I don't like it when she looks at me that way. 'It wasn't Dan Harriman. I was with Dan Harriman.'

'You... were with... Dan Harriman?'

'Why not? Who were you with?'

'That's different. I'm the boss.'

'Oh sure, boss, I forgot.'

And then I start to think.

'Maria!'

'Yes, Mister Hart?'

'How long would it take someone to find my home address?'

'Five minutes, perhaps less. If they had access to the internet. Do you want me to show you?'

'No. What about my phone number?'

'Are you in the book?'

I've no idea if I'm 'in the book' – Wendy always dealt with that sort of thing.

'Possibly.'

'Then about thirty seconds.'

'What if I'm not?'

'Harder. They'd have to get inventive. Probably not impossible though. Do you want me to find out?'

'No. But I tell you what – call my lawyers, tell them Wendy can have the flat after all, but I need signed papers by this afternoon, because this is definitely it. My final, final offer. Then call my real estate agent and tell him to raise the bid on the house in Holland Park, but I'm going to want to buy it through an overseas holding company.'

Now I'm spooked too. It's great to play these games, but nothing's actually supposed to happen. Not to people like us, anyway.

A succession of visitors are arriving downstairs, and Two Livers goes down to greet them. Six out of the UK's seven largest pharmaceutical and healthcare companies are meeting today at Grossbank's offices. The exception is

Eastern Pharma. Their management are on a roadshow in the States, but their Chairman is getting up early to join us by video-conference.

When Two Livers shows them into the large conference room, I'm stuck on the phone in the corner and shrug apologetically.

'Yes, Secretary of State, yes.' I look at them as they take their places. 'They're here now. We just need to get Eastern Pharma on the video-link, then we'll kick off. I'll pass that on. Thank you, Secretary of State.'

I hang up. 'Gentlemen I'm sorry – politicians do rather like the sound of their own voices.'

I can see they're curious, but don't elaborate. I told Maria before the call that she shouldn't get used to being addressed that way, because I didn't intend to make a habit of it. Two Livers does the intros and organises coffee for everyone else and a large bottle of Perrier – brought in by her rather nervous assistant – for herself. Finally we call up California and get a bleary-eyed, elderly suit on the video-link, who is apparently Sir Crispin Monk, Chairman of Eastern Pharma.

'Gentlemen, thank you for coming here today, and a special thank you to you, Sir Crispin, for joining us so early in your morning. We're here to discuss follow-up to yesterday's announcement concerning Hastings BioScience, which I know everyone on this side of the Atlantic has read about in today's newspapers.'

'And over here too.' The face on the screen is slightly out of sync with the voice, but Sir Crispin is holding up a copy of the *Wall Street News*, pointing to a small piece on the front page. 'Grossbank has been very courageous. I didn't think the Germans had it in them, but I suppose it's down to you. Our chaps have been pretty hopeless on this, and the Yanks haven't been seen for dust.'

Music to my ears. Two Livers is smiling smugly.

'Thank you, Sir Crispin. Your kind words are greatly appreciated. But words sadly are not enough. Grossbank has put its neck on the line to maintain a world class testing facility here in the UK that is vital to all of your businesses, both now and in the future. We're taking a risk not just corporately, but personally as well – because we believe in this. But we can't do it alone. If everyone else says, "Great, Grossbank have got us off the hook, we're in the clear", and the AFF come after us and our staff the way they went after HBS, it will only be a matter of time before Frankfurt loses its nerve. We need to send Frankfurt a signal – a clear and unequivocal signal – that we're not alone here, that others appreciate what we're doing and will support us.'

One of the men sitting around the table interrupts at this point. 'So what are you looking for from us? A public statement?'

'No. Like I said, words are cheap.' I point to the telephone. 'I have it on good authority that the British government is going to be behind us all the way on this. Government support doesn't necessarily count for much in some sectors, but healthcare is different. We have a lot of goodwill there, and when it comes to things like accelerating approvals for new drugs, or getting the National Health Service to adopt a new product, we'll be well placed to help the companies we're working with.'

The suits around the table sit back, pondering what I'm

saying, and wondering if that really was Joanna Harriet, the Secretary of State for Health, on the phone.

'The trouble is, we're not working with any at the moment.'

'So you want our business?'

'Investment banks always want your business, and we're no different. But what we want – what we need – is your endorsement of Grossbank, and what we're doing. And the best endorsement, the one that speaks volumes to the world, is when you appoint us to lead, or participate in, major transactions on your behalf. If HBS means anything at all to you, at least give us a shot.'

'You're right.' It's Sir Crispin, his lips still out of sync with his voice. I wonder if it's the video-link, or something he's on. Maybe I could get like that, if I keep playing every night. 'Eastern Pharma is floating its US subsidiary on the New York Stock Exchange. We're over here roadshowing the company to investors right now. Hardman Stoney are leading the deal for us. I'm going to tell them I'm appointing Grossbank alongside them. I don't care if you perform in the deal or not. It's about making a statement.'

Bingo! Two Livers is smiling to herself. Was it really me who swung him? She avoids my eye. And takes another sip of Perrier.

I'm about to thank Sir Crispin, when I realise he's saying something else. 'Eric? Is that you sitting there?'

One of the suits nods and says yes.

'Well, you should put Grossbank into the project financing for your new Turkish manufacturing plant. You're using Bartons, aren't you? Where were they when the chips were down?'

And so it goes on. Sir Crispin is unstoppable. He goes around the table, pinning them down one after the other. A lease financing here, a bond issue there, some of them significant, others more symbolic. By the end, when I'm showing them out, and assuring them that I'll give the Secretary of State a full briefing, we've created the basis for launching Grossbank as a major force in global health- care investment banking.

Christ, I'm good.

When the last of them has gone, I nudge Two Livers and grin. 'I don't know what Sir Crispin was on, but he was flying today – what a star. We should form a global healthcare advisory board, make him chair of it, and hold meetings twice a year in the Bahamas and Zermatt. Just as a reward for today.'

She waves her hand dismissively. 'No need.'

'No need? Why not?'

She winks at me. 'Sir Crispin and I go back a long way.'

Damn, this girl's an operator.

I report in to Herman to give him ammunition in the continuing war against Biedermann, which has taken a turn for the worse with several bank employees hurt in a demonstration outside the Grossbank Tower by eco protesters, anti-capitalists and other radical groups.

'Look at it this way, Herman – at least everyone's heard of us now.'

He doesn't see the funny side.

I return to my desk for an interview with a cute female reporter for *Her* magazine. She asks me a bunch of dumb questions about what it's like to be a hero, and can I sleep at night, worrying about what AFF extremists might do to me. Honey, I never sleep at night. Why waste time? I've got far better things to do. She asks me if finance is boring.

'Finance is the sex of the twenty-first century.'

'Really? Can I quote you on that?'

Sure, if you want to, but everyone will know it's not true. Sex is the sex of the twenty-first century, and if you don't believe me, ask Ilyana, and Nina, and Carla, and Breathless Beth...

TONIGHT IS DIFFERENT. Tonight I'm not going to shag hookers, or if I do, it won't be until much later. Tonight I have a date. I'm meeting Sally Mills, and I intend to give her every opportunity to show me just how grateful she is for saving her brother's bacon.

When I leave the office at around six-thirty there are a small group of animal rights protesters standing behind a barrier with several policemen and some of Grossbank's private security guards preventing them from interfering with employees. I'm tempted to follow the example of some of our traders and wave a fistful of fifty pound notes at them, but apparently it's considered provocative. I collect H1 PAY from the underground car-park next to the building – similarly protected by police and private security guards – and head south and then west along the Embankment. I'm meeting Sally at the Savoy, on the grounds that some of my most successful seductions have started with drinks in the American Bar.

She's as beautiful as ever, in fact even more so. I realise I've never really seen her like this, when she's made a special effort. She's wearing a simple black mid-length dress, strapless, with a pearl necklace and earrings, and she's put her hair up. The effect is simple, designer-free and elegant. I don't ask where Trevor is.

She starts by thanking me again for all I've done for Harry. He's apparently like a new man. His whole team have been re-energised. No one believed that a firm like Grossbank would come to the rescue.

Neither did I, but I don't say that.

We have a couple of cocktails in the bar, then wander through to the restaurant for dinner. Conversation is remarkably easy, but I feel like there's an elephant in the drawing room, and we're both pretending it's not there.

By the end of dinner I'm feeling completely relaxed – always a dangerous state – she's slightly flushed from what for her is probably an unusual amount of alcohol, and as we sip our coffee it seems to me the time has come to find out where I stand. Will I rip her panties off or not?

'Sally – it's been wonderful tonight. All that I hoped for.' Except a blow-job. At least so far. 'But there's something I need to ask you. You know my feelings for you. I've got you in my head and I can't let go. I want you. I don't want to scare you, and I don't want you not to see me again, but all I can do is be honest with you. It's the truth, Sally – I'm in love with you.'

She puts her napkin to her eyes and starts sobbing. 'Oh, Dave, don't. Please don't.' She looks at me helplessly. 'I can't. It would be wrong. For me, for you, for Trevor, for the boys. It's not that I don't have strong feelings for you – what woman wouldn't?' Quite. 'But I can't. I'm sorry.'

Before I can start the line about it sometimes being right to go with your feelings, to trust your instincts, even if only for a single night, the maitre d' appears and asks if the young lady is all right. Then someone at another table points at me and says, 'Isn't that Dave Hart, the banker who's taking on the Animal Freedom Front?' and all heads are turning our way, some discreetly, some not caring, and a couple of schmucks from another table come over to shake my hand and ask if they can buy us a drink. Damnation. The moment is gone. Furious, I decide to call it a day.

The doorman drives H1 PAY round to the front of the hotel, holds the door for Sally, while I let myself in, and I slip him a fiver for his trouble. It's gone midnight, it's been raining, and we drive in silence through the dark, almost empty streets. Sally's staying with her cousin, who lives in Bermondsey, so I head south to drop her off, inwardly seething that this means still more delay before I can call Nina and Beth and get the evening properly underway.

There aren't many cars around as we head into a part of London that I'm not familiar with. The Bentley has a satnav that keeps me on the right route, but a couple of times when I'm stopped at traffic lights I imagine I see a car some way behind me slowing down, keeping its distance.

Snap out of it, Hart – you'll be seeing greens under the bed next. We drive on, until we reach another set of lights.

That's when everything goes pear-shaped. As I'm slowing for the lights, an anonymous, battered white van comes up fast behind us. I see its lights in the mirror, and assume it's going to slow down. But it doesn't, and I brace myself as it smashes into the back of the Bentley, pushing us forward across the road and into a wall. The front hits the wall and crumples, while the air bags explode in front of us.

I'm not sure exactly what happens next, but I remember looking at Sally, who's lying against the passenger door, her eyes shut, as my door opens, someone reaches over to undo my seatbelt, and I'm yanked out of the car. Part of me thinks I'm being helped, but as I stand unsteadily beside the car a fist smashes into my stomach, winding me so that I crumple slowly to the floor.

I'm lying on the wet road, my cheek resting on the ground, looking at a pair of Doc Martens. A voice says, 'Look at the City's not-so-hard man now.' I look up and count six of them, standing around me. Five men and what is theoretically a woman, though she barely qualifies. Combat jackets and jeans, shaven heads or long, dyed hair, boots and gloves. One of them has a baseball bat, and another has a long length of chain. The one standing nearest to me pulls out a flick knife and clicks it open. He grins, a dirty-toothed, bad breath grin. 'Say night-night, big Dave – it's lights out time.' I groan and try to push myself to my feet. I hear another voice.

'We goin' to do her, too?'

'Yeah.'

'NO!' I surprise myself as I leap to my feet, nearly overbalance, and swing my right fist – straight into the wall. A fierce pain shoots through my arm as I stagger back, stung as much by the scornful laughter that greets my attempt at heroics. I run at the nearest one, grab his jacket, and find myself spinning round as he twists and throws me to the ground. I lash out and my left fist smashes into the road surface. One of them kicks me in the stomach, and I groan and choke back tears.

They are hysterical with laughter now as I desperately fish for my mobile phone in my jacket pocket and start dialling.

The leader squats beside me and watches me dial. 'Go ahead, big Dave – call the police. Average response time, this part of town? I'd say about ten minutes. They don't really want to get here any sooner, see?'

I can hear a voice at the other end, and I start repeating over and over the name on the street sign on the corner. I'm still half dazed, still in shock.

That's why I'm not too clear what happened next.

A powerful engine, tyres screeching, doors opening, and I roll over to see a dark coloured car, a Range Rover, stopped in the middle of the road. Four men get out, average height, slim build, short hair, probably late twenties to mid-thirties, wearing anonymous dark suits and ties. They're not rushing, but they don't hesitate.

One of them approaches the thug with the baseball bat, who raises it and steps forward to take a swing at him. The man in the suit parries and sweeps the bat away, then brings his other hand into the thug's ribs. He does a one, two, three burst of rib-cracking punches, a swift karate chop to the neck, so that the thug goes down, all without breaking step, speaking or catching his breath. Then he's on to the woman, who yells at him and swings her fist, but he parries again, gives her a stiff-finger jab to the throat which leaves her clutching her neck, gasping and making horrible suffocating sounds, then doubles her up with a punch to the stomach, and as she falls to her knees steps around her and gives a one, two, three to the kidneys. She collapses to the ground, heaving for breath and making horrible, unnatural sounds. Four against six takes about fifteen seconds, though time isn't working for me the way it usually does. There are no dramatic kung fu kicks or thuggish head-butts, as far as I can see no blood, not even any words exchanged. One of the eco's screams something at them, but he's cut off mid-shout by a karate chop. And then there are only crumpled bodies on the ground.

One of the men from the Range Rover kneels beside me. 'Mister Hart, are you all right?'

I nod yes, and he helps me to my feet. 'Check her. In the car...'

One of them opens the passenger door, leans in and then calls across. 'Fine. Bump on the head.'

They turn as we hear a police siren faintly in the distance. The one who's holding me pats me on the shoulder. 'Mister Hart, Mike Moss sent us. He said you might need looking after. You'll be fine now. But we need to go. We don't work in the UK, only overseas.'

They walk – do these people ever run? – to the Range Rover, climb in and start the engine. One window slides down. 'You'll be fine – just don't mention us.'

The Range Rover roars off around the corner as I stand, unsteady on my feet, and look at the crumpled bodies all around me. I stagger over to check on Sally, who is unconscious, but still breathing. The minutes tick slowly past while the distant sirens get closer. One of the eco's starts moaning on the ground a few yards away, lifts his head and starts coughing up blood. With all the strength I can muster, fuelled by fear and pain and humiliation, I kick him in the head, just as a police car pulls up beside me, its flashing blue light casting a surreal effect all around. The doors open, and two policemen step out, one of them talking on a handheld radio.

'Roger, control, a silver grey Bentley Azure, registration Hotel One Papa Alpha Yankee. I recognise the driver from the papers. It's that Dave Hart, the bloke who's taking on the AFF. Looks like he took 'em on tonight, all right. You're not going to believe this...'

ANOTHER DAY, another dollar. Or in my case, another great heroic deed. If Sally Mills doesn't have sex with me after this, I may join a monastery.

I'm not pressing charges against the AFF, although the police are still considering their own position on charging them, and the AFF members are sticking to their code of omerta.

Which may be just as well, because it would ruin a great story.

With the police and the ambulances last night came the usual press pack, tipped off by chums on the inside. The *Post* has a front page picture of me standing by an ambulance, having my knuckles bandaged by a paramedic, next to a line of unconscious bodies on stretchers: *Chopper Hart Nails AFF*. I'm 'Chopper' now – another label! I hope people understand it's because of the incident in Jamaica, and nothing to do with whatever might happen late at night between consenting adults. It was too late for all but the last editions, but I'm the lead story on the radio and TV news.

That's the good part. The bad part is Trevor the teacher. Sally has mild concussion and so I get to call him from the hospital, dialling 'Home' from the mobile phone in her handbag. He thought she was at her cousin's. I explain that she wanted to tell me more about Harry and HBS, that we overran so decided to eat and then I was driving her back to her cousin's when it all happened. It's hard to tell if he believes me. When he arrives he stares around the ward, never having seen one before.

I'm too exhilarated to sleep, having just had a terrifying near death experience, so after calling the AA to remove my badly injured H1 PAY, around three a.m. I take a cab to the flat that Nina and Beth share in South Ken and have a party.

By the time I get into the office, around ten-thirty, everyone wants to speak to me. Even the ones who don't want to speak to me want to glance surreptitiously at my bandaged knuckles.

I call Mike Moss and thank him, and say how awkward it is having everyone think that was my work last night. He chuckles and says it's a double whammy – it got me off the hook, and people might think twice about having a go at me in future.

The Silver Fox has gone into overdrive. He has a whole series of interviews lined up for profile pieces, the TV people want me on the *Dick and Sally* show, and will I appear on *Finance Today*?

Everyone is calling. Even Herman congratulates me. 'Dave, you are astonishing. How did you do this? Are you all right? I thought this sort of super-hero action only happened in the movies.' It does. The conversation drags on. I know last night was impressive, but I can sense there's something more on his mind.

In the end he can't resist telling me. 'Have you heard about Doktor Bieder- mann? He heard what happened to you, and he's gone into hiding. Just for the moment. It's on the advice of the bank's security department.' There's one particularly juicy item that he just has to pass on. 'Oh, and he has changed his office too, with all of his photographs and mementos, since his visit to London. In fact a number of board members have. Word seems to have spread fast in Frankfurt about your ironic pastiche. So self-deprecating. So typically British. Such humour.'

Ironic? Self-deprecating? Me? I glance at my 'Me Wall'. Damn, I'll have to change it now. Maybe I'll ask Samantha to give me back the photo of me with Madonna.

Wendy calls, but I tell Maria to take a message. Tripod Turner sends a huge novelty condom filled with helium to float around my office – 'For the biggest swinging dick in town'. Dan Harriman is apparently indisposed, but sends two hookers to the office dressed as policewomen, but security don't let them through, and I send flowers to Sally in hospital, with a message saying I will never, ever let anyone hurt her. Realising she's concussed and may not remember what actually happened, I enclose a short letter in a sealed envelope as well, ambiguously stating how what happened last night will be forever etched in my memory. It's true, after all. And if she misunderstands and thinks we might have already had sex, it might not be such a struggle second time around.

After a night like last night, some people might take a day off. But in the fast moving world of investment banking, you go forward or die. And anyway, I'd only spend it with my chiropractor or my acupuncturist, and I'm tired enough already. After another meeting with the police, signing more statements, and a couple of press interviews, it's back to business.

I have a meeting scheduled, with Two Livers, at three o'clock at the Meridien Hotel on Piccadilly. Biedermann has told people in Frankfurt that we still haven't won any 'real' corporate clients. He told Herman that MOSS was a one-off, and doesn't count because no other firm would take it on. HBS doesn't count either, because it was a basket case, and no other firm had management suicidal enough to want it. So now Two Livers and I are going to win a piece of real business.

The Old Orinoco Trading and Investment Company is straight out of a time warp. It's a Columbian company, state-owned, and for years was run as a private fiefdom for successive Presidents and their friends and families. But now, in a sign of the times, they are looking at a partial privatisation by way of listing their shares on an overseas stock exchange. Their senior management are in London for a beauty parade of investment banks. They own vast amounts of agricultural land, timber and mineral rights. With the right strategy, this company could be worth billions. Every major investment bank in town is after them, and quite why they'd ever give us the business is beyond me.

But that won't stop us trying.

We arrive to find the meeting schedule is already running late, and a team from Schleppenheim are in the anteroom waiting to go on. They are sitting around drinking coffee and chatting, looking buttoned-up and preppy. The conversation stops as soon as I show up.

'Aren't you Dave Hart?' The team leader, an early forties MD, puts down the paper he was reading about my adventures last night. I nod. My hands are starting to ache, my stomach is hurting from where I was punched and kicked, and I'm feeling very tired and short-tempered.

He obviously wants to make conversation, probably so he can tell his buddies that he was chatting to Dave Hart today. Isn't that something? Six months ago, he'd probably never heard of Dave Hart, or if he had, thought Dave Hart was some anonymous, middle-ranking turkey in Rory's team at Bartons.

I sit on one of the couches with Two Livers, and slowly – and rather painfully – start unwrapping the bandages around my left hand. This fascinates everyone in the room, and they even start wincing in sympathy as I have to tug to pull them free from the scabs that have formed on my knuckles.

The team leader approaches again. 'Painful?'

I wince as the scab on my forefinger splits open and starts bleeding. 'No.'

He turns to Two Livers, perhaps wondering if she might be easier conversation. 'So it's just the two of you?'

She glances across at his team of five. 'That's about equal.'

He grins and nods, and I want to give her a high five, but I'm too absorbed in what I'm doing.

Two Livers ignores him and turns to me.

'So Dan wanted anal sex again last night.'

'Really?' I barely raise an eyebrow. The schmuck from Schleppenheim is standing by us, clearly taken aback by the turn in the conversation, not sure if he should join in or move away. His team are looking at him standing there like a dork, wondering what he'll do.

'I've lost count of the number of times I told him I think it's disgusting. He comes up with all these lines about how everyone does it, you use lots of gel, it might be painful at first, but you get used to it.' She looks round suddenly, and the team from Schleppenheim instantly do very poor impressions of reading newspapers, glancing through their pitch books and staring out of the window. The schmuck self-consciously ambles back and sits down on a couch.

'So I got Claude round.'

'Claude?'

'My friend from Haiti. Male model. Six-foot ten, black guy. Swinger.'

'What for?'

'I told Dan okay, we'd do it, but first I wanted to play some new games. I handcuffed him to the bed. Face down. Wrists and ankles.'

You can hear a pin drop. When one of the Schleppenheim team turns over a page in his newspaper, the rest glare at him.

'Handcuffs? Really?' I'm still picking at my scabs. 'Face down? What did he think was going to happen?'

'Massage.'

'So did you oil him up?'

'Sure. Then I let Claude in. Claude's huge. Dan got a shock. Went mad. Started screaming.'

'Really? I'm not surprised.'

'I told Dan not to worry, Claude would use lots of gel, everyone does it, it might be painful at first, but he'd get used to it.'

'Did he?'

'Not the first couple of times.'

'Will you see him again?'

'Don't think so.'

The door to the meeting room opens and a pretty receptionist type comes out. We all stand and the Schleppenheim team start to get their pitch books together.

'Excuse me.' I wander over to the receptionist, dumping my soiled bandages in a bin. 'Dave Hart, Grossbank. You may have heard, I had a rather eventful night last night. I'm not feeling my best. Would you mind if we went in next?'

The schmuck is about to protest, when Two Livers gives him a beaming smile. 'Hey come on, loosen up. You wouldn't say no to a lady, would you?'

No. He wouldn't say no to her. Nor to me. His whole team stare at us, then he shakes his head and we go through into the conference room.

Shock and awe. Moral superiority over the enemy. That's what we just achieved. Have you read *The Prince*, or *The Art of War*? Neither have I, but at least I own them.

We go through a reception room, where the girl sits,

then into a large conference room with a broad oval table. We meet Oscar Rodriguez, the chairman, a short, fat, shiny-headed bald man with a big grin and the sort of suit worn by drug dealers in *Miami Vice*. He has with him his weasel-featured finance director and a couple of 'advisers', one of whom sits on his board, from the Orinoco Banking and Finance Corporation. They will work jointly on the deal with whichever bank is appointed, and Oscar has complete faith in them, partly because he also sits on their board.

Oscar has on the table in front of him several newspapers, showing photographs of last night. He begins by congratulating me, saying how I must be part-Columbian, because that is how they would deal with these people – I manage not to say that I thought they just shot them – and once again everyone is fascinated by my knuckles.

After the introductions I explain that Two Livers will give them an outline of the main issues we see facing them as they think about listing their shares, and will run through our capabilities and what we see ourselves bringing to the party. She starts talking and they stare at her breasts, her neck, her ear-lobes, her lips, her eyes, and her surprisingly strong fingers – she can do one of the best handshakes of any woman I've ever known, and I have known one or two. They take no notes, and she sits and purrs at them, unaided by any slides or handouts that might distract them.

After fifteen minutes, she's done and I ask for any questions. While they're thinking, I ask if they mind if I smoke. Oscar actually seems relieved to have met the first non-PC banker in London.

I take out a large Cohiba and put it on the table in front of Two Livers. Without blinking, she picks it up, sniffs it, rolls it between her fingers, nods that it's okay and fishes out a cigar cutter from her handbag. She places the end of the cigar in the mouth of the cutter, and looks up to catch Oscar's eye as she snaps the end off. He winces and sits up in his seat. Then she puts it in her mouth, moistening it with her lips, rolling it gently around so that the whole of the end is wet, and lights it with a lighter from her handbag. After a few puffs, she looks again at Oscar and blows a perfect smoke ring across the table at him. Then she hands me the cigar, all the while without making eye contact with me or saying a word.

'Thank you.'

'Yes,' Oscar sighs. 'Thank you.'

He motions me to get up and step over to the coffee pot on the sideboard at the end of the room. His finance director starts asking inane finance director questions of Two Livers, like how did we come to our valuation, what fees would we charge, what financial statements we'd require for the prospectus, and other such bullshit.

Oscar puts his arm around my shoulder and leans in confidentially so that we can talk.

'Are the two of you...?'

I gesture innocently towards Two Livers. 'Married? No. But we're... close.'

'Oh?'

'Yes. I'm close to all of my female employees.' I smile knowingly and wink, with a man-to-man look on my face.

He laughs and slaps me on the shoulder. 'Hombre. You

are truly a man. I thought this sort of conduct was not permitted between colleagues in this country?'

'Grossbank is different. I set the rules. Any woman employee wanting to make managing director has to sleep with me at least three times. Just so I know she's good enough.'

He looks at me as if he thinks I might be joking. I stare back, dead pan.

'Hombre.' Another slap on the arm.

We take our places again, and I put another cigar on the table. 'Miss MacKay, I think Mister Rodriguez would like a cigar.'

When he shows us out, ten minutes or so later, amid much back-slapping and laughter, the Schleppenheim team get up from their seats and prepare to go in. As she passes the most junior member of their team, a nervous looking kid in his early twenties, Two Livers opens her handbag and passes him a small tin of Vaseline.

'Here – when you get inside, pass this to your boss. Tell him it might help.'

WEEKS HAVE passed. Busy, hectic weeks.

Our new people are arriving in droves now, scooped from the most successful firms on the street, and paid the sort of money that creates a feeling of obligation to deliver in even the most hard-nosed cynic. Everyone has heard of us – at least, they've heard of me – and we're starting to do business, and not just in the pharma sector. It all feels remarkably like it might actually work, and when it does, people won't resent it too much, because we showed we had balls, and we did something they didn't dare to do.

As far as regular business goes, my most spectacular coup so far was a block trade. The French government decided it was going to sell its last remaining twenty per cent shareholding in Société Financière du Sud, an industrial conglomerate and holding company previously under state control.

Rather than trying to place their shares in an orderly manner, hiring a group of banks to market them carefully to institutional investors around the world, they decided to follow the latest market fad and conduct a sudden death blind auction, whereby all the large investment banks are told the deal's coming and they should prepare a bid – in strictest confidence – so that after the market closes they can compete to commit commercial suicide by buying the entire shareholding and then selling it on the next day.

The only investment bank likely to make money out of a trade like this is the one advising the government, because they're running the auction and so can't be a bidder. The others ought to laugh and give a short answer ending in 'off', but instead they work themselves up into a lather of excitement, desperate to see if they can 'win' this 'prestigious' piece of business.

The banks have discreet conversations with large institutional investors, especially hedge funds, giving them inside information about the forthcoming sale on a strictly confidential, 'no dealings' basis, to establish what investor appetite there is for the shares.

These investors, who have to be among the few people in the world even more unscrupulous than investment bankers, knowing there is a large block of shares about to hit the market, instantly start selling, knowing the price is about to fall. Hold on, you say, they just said they wouldn't deal. As if. If they don't already own the shares, they borrow them, selling something that they don't actually own but expect to be able to buy back more cheaply very soon – 'closing their short position' in the jargon of the market. Sell it for a hundred and buy it back for ninety, and you've made a ten euro turn.

When eventually the bids go in, and one lucky bank 'wins' the auction, everyone knows that the crazy idiot is going to have to scramble to unload the position, and the lucky losers also join the hedge funds in selling the stock, putting further pressure on the price, to rubbish the competition and make a little money along the way. It's a horrible situation to be in. The investment bank that wins generally loses a ton of money, the company in question sees its shares get a hammering, and only the government is happy, because it got its money. And the block trade business? As someone once said, it's a great way for investment bankers to show who has the biggest dick and the smallest brain on the block – at least until now.

What's different this time, is that Grossbank is on the list of bidders. Paul Ryan has called in a favour from an old buddy at Financial Solutions, the small advisory firm running the auction. The idea is that if people think we're bidding on a trade like this, they'll start to take us seriously. No one expects us to win, including my own team.

Unlike the other firms bidding for the block, we aren't really in a position to talk to many hedge funds, because we hardly know any. Unlike the other firms, we don't yet have a proper sales force of brokers. Tripod Turner tells me not to touch it with a barge pole. I call Herman the German and he asks if I'm sure I know what I'm doing, and I say of course not, I hardly ever know what I'm doing, which makes him laugh. The shares close at sixty-two euros ninety, and I suggest we put in a really aggressive bid at sixty-three euros a share.

'The government holding's been overhanging the share price for months. As soon as it's gone, the price will rise. Come on – let's win this sucker. We're Grossbank – Grossbank rocks!'

It's only then that I recall that at Bartons, no one ever took any notice of my views on bidding for blocks, or much else for that matter, so it really didn't matter what I thought. The problem is, now I'm in charge, and despite the obvious misgivings of the team, the bid goes in, to the amazement of Paul's old buddy at Financial Solutions. Since anyone with a brain is bidding at least a small discount to the closing price, we win.

Paul Ryan looks sick. 'What do we do now? We own twenty per cent of the company. First thing tomorrow everyone's going to be shorting the hell out of it, the price will go into free-fall, and if we manage to get rid of half of it, even at a huge loss, we'll be lucky. What's the plan, boss?'

I like it when he calls me boss. It's late, and I have a rendezvous with Fluffy and Thumper from the Pussy-Cat Club – beautiful Thai twins, who do an extraordinary double act guaranteed to whet even the most jaded appetite – so instead of saying how the hell should I know, I've never bid on a block trade before and I didn't expect to win, I look confident, wink and tell him we'll think about it in the morning.

He thinks I've got nerves of steel, and carries on looking sick. The reality is that I still haven't fully fathomed out exactly what I've got us into.

In the morning, the shares do indeed go into free-fall. I'm scared shitless, a rabbit caught in the headlights, everyone looks to me for a lead, and on my instructions, we do... nothing.

'Sit tight – don't lose your nerve.' No trader ever sits tight. But I'm desperately tired, it's a 3G day. I feel like I've got alcohol oozing from every pore, my whole system saturated from a night of truly excessive excess with Fluffy and Thumper, and there's a brass band marching up and down in my head. When the stock hits fifty euros a share, I panic and tell our traders to go into the market and buy a shed load more. If we own some at sixty-three euros a share, and some at fifty, our average price will be a lot lower than it was. At least that's why I keep telling myself it's a good move.

By noon, we're up to thirty per cent of the company. Herman wants to know what's going on. So does Paul. So do I.

'Let's just say it's a reverse block trade. We're not selling these shares, we're buying them.' It's a vague attempt at humour by a condemned man, as I face the imminent prospect of the whole pack of cards collapsing around me.

I say it to Paul in the middle of the trading floor, and word spreads like wildfire. Since no investment banker can ever keep a secret, and everyone on the trading floor has at least one telephone, the word soon gets around the market.

'Grossbank isn't selling Société Financière du Sud – it's buying it!'

A couple of minutes later, reports are going across the wire that there is speculation in the market that Grossbank may be buying SFS, either acting on behalf of a potential acquirer – various names are mentioned – or possibly for its own account, as part of a foray into merchant banking-type principal investment. Herman calls.

'Are we buying SFS?'

'I don't know. Are we?'

The price is no longer in free-fall, but rising rapidly as the market gets wind of the fact that not only has the government overhang been removed, but there's a predator on the loose, hoovering up shares with a view to launching a bid. An official announcement is expected imminently. Now all the short sellers are rushing to buy shares, closing out their short positions. Sell something at sixty euros a share, and buy it back at seventy, and the trade doesn't look quite so clever, does it sucker? The institutions which actually owned SFS shares and sold them on news of the block trade are out there buying them back, not wishing to miss out on the action now that something's happening. On the trading floor at Grossbank, the traders cheer every time the price goes up another euro. At sixty-five euros, we start unloading shares, and carry on selling them as the price reaches seventy, finally losing the last of our position at seventy-three. When the French Trésor call up to ask what the hell's going on, I don't even need to lie. We've sold the whole position, and no, we have no idea where the takeover speculation came from.

Amongst our own traders, my stature and prowess have reached previously unimaginable heights. When all around were panicking, I stood there, saying nothing, doing nothing, while the stock went through the floor. Balls the size of melons, and made of steel. No wonder, because I'm Dave Hart – or Chopper as they call me now. For the first time, I hear two of my own employees saying 'Grossbank rocks' and giving each other a high five. Truly, I am a legend.

I'M FLYING TO the Fatherland again, but this time things are different. Tom, my new driver, has taken me to Northolt in the armoured, S-class Mercedes the firm is insisting I use for my own security and their well-being – I'm a key man, after all. Tom is well over six feet tall, strongly built, and if he wasn't working for Grossbank, could probably get a job with Mike Moss. I'm flying from Northolt because I'm taking a smoker – a private jet – so as to avoid the pressures and delays of public transport, and because it affords me the privacy to work on sensitive things during the flight. The sensitive thing I'll be working on during this flight is twenty-two years old and used to be an air hostess with one of the major airlines, before switching to private aviation. The bank pays a thousand pounds a trip for her to take care of me. She serves drinks and snacks during the flight, and makes sure my newspapers are on board. Anything else is a private matter between consenting adults. Honestly.

Today I'm feeling particularly pleased with myself, even

by my standards. Last night I had a major coup. Wendy and I are hardly speaking since I moved out of the flat in Sloane Square and she moved in. I'm living in a large house in Holland Park, which is still in chaos while an interior designer gives it a total revamp, chooses furniture, art, books, sculptures, etc – everything a tasteful, cultured, well-rounded, successful investment banker would wish for at a certain stage in his life, but couldn't possibly find time to buy for himself.

In the meantime Wendy is getting hate mail, packages of human excrement, and even a pretend bomb from the AFF and associated nutters – all addressed to me, and all arriving at the flat. She thinks I did it on purpose. At the same time, the flat is bursting with presents I've sent round for Samantha, and Wendy is seething that my financial fortunes have improved so dramatically since joining Grossbank – and only after we signed our final settlement.

The only cloud on the horizon is Sally Mills. How any woman could be saved by a hero in single combat, taken by him to hospital, sent flowers by him, and then simply disappear off the radar screen, after he had put his neck on the line to save her brother's business, is quite beyond me. When I make enquiries, I'm astonished to learn that Trevor the teacher has quit East Hampton Comprehensive and the family have moved – not even waiting till the end of term – to Scotland. What's going on? I have visions of flying in to a lonely Scottish farm in my Grossbank corporate helicopter, playing the *Ride of the Valkyries* over loudspeakers, and rescuing my beloved from imprisonment in the cold and clammy North.

In the meantime, and just so you know I'm not pining too hard, I'm getting through hookers at the rate of one or two a night.

So back to my coup. I haven't seen Samantha all year, but it's Easter and her new school in Belgravia has organised an Easter play, where we can all sit and coo at our little beloveds as they scamper around on stage in fancy dress and fluff their lines.

When it comes to parenting, mine is the ultimate outsourcing generation. We hire private obstetricians to make neat little cuts in our wives to take the pain out of pushing, maternity nurses to take away the sleepless nights, nannies and maids to take away the everyday drudge, kindergartens and private tutors so we don't have to read or spell or do adding up with our kids, and instructors to teach them everything from swimming and sport to dancing and drawing, all of which is terribly important, and none of which we could possibly do ourselves.

But the one thing we can't delegate is attending school functions. We fight to get our kids places at the most exclusive schools – because it shows how much we love them – and once we get them in, there's major kudos to be had from showing up at events. The bigger the swinging dick of a husband, the greater the New Age brownie points to be had from showing up to gaze adoringly as little Nathan and little Susie play two of the six snowflakes present at the birth of Christ in the school Nativity play, or in my case, Samantha plays an Easter bunny.

The problem is, school functions are an intense form of

competitive sport, and without a team – in my case a wife – you can't win. It all begins way ahead of the official start time for the event, when the pushiest mothers – the fathers are always still at work – show up to claim the best seats, right at the front, so that they can show little Nathan how much they adore him by swooning from the front row. They mark their territory with coats and bags and then disappear to form a gossipy cabal in some trendy wine bar round the corner. Naturally, they are all fully war-painted, dressed to kill, finest jewellery, hair freshly done, mani/pedi and waxing taken care of, and they scrutinise each other for the slightest flaw or weakness. The guys show up much later, stressed out with whatever they've escaped from at work, no time to shave or freshen up, still in their work clothes, and usually still on the mobile when they arrive to take the places their wives have saved for them.

Wendy and I used to be a great team, but I know she won't have kept me a seat, and it's not my style to sit at the back and look like a loser.

Fortunately, I have Tom. Tom's a fixer, a multi-talented man who can deal equally well with weirdos and nutters from the AFF or the PTA. Tom visits the school the night before the play, slips the caretaker a lazy fifty, and gives him a pile of coats, jackets, hats and gloves, all freshly acquired from the hospice shop on Sloane Avenue. When the ÜberMums appear on the night, two hours before the play is due to start, they are shocked to discover the entire front row taken.

The best is yet to come. I arrive bang on time, with the hall full, walk to the front, ignoring Wendy, who's in row three, lift a coat from one of the front seats and drop it on the floor in front of me. Then I sit down, lean back, cross my legs and relax, ignoring the tutting and muttering from behind me, the nudges and whispered comments that they hope there won't be a scene when the owner of the coat arrives.

It gets even better. Just as the play is about to start, there's a buzz of conversation from the back of the hall, and heads start turning. It's Two Livers and the turbo-babes. Two Livers has been hoovering up all the talent she can find from any of the major investment banks, to form the first female-dominated corporate finance department in the City. She arrives looking like a million dollars – courtesy of Manolo Blahnik, Prada and Versace, followed by dark-haired Nicky from Toronto – twenty-nine years old, Harvard MBA, wearing Dolce and Gabbana with jewellery by Bulgari; fair-haired Sabine – twenty-eight years old from Italy, INSEAD MBA wearing Donna Karan with accessories by Mappin and Webb and a two-tone gold pendant from Kiki McDonough; Connie from Cologne – twenty-six years old, Chicago MBA wearing Armani with jewellery by Van Cleef and Arpels; and Marie-France from Nice – twenty-eight years old, Price Waterhouse trained accountant, wearing Dolce and Gabbana, with diamonds by Graff.

I could have brought hookers, but these girls are even better. In the City they're starting to be known as 'Hart's Angels'. If you think it's amazing what a thousand pounds can buy by way of female company, try a million. Or two.

Two Livers has told them I'm going to be hung out to dry tonight by the ex-wife, and I'm too good a man for that, so here they all are. Every woman in the hall is wondering who the hell they are, and wishing they would die, but only after they first get fat. The turbo-babes ignore the women in the hall, and the only acknowledgement any of the men get is when Nicky nods to a corporate lawyer she recognises, who then has to explain to his wife sitting beside him that they work on merger and acquisition deals together.

Two Livers and the babes greet me, paying homage with a kiss on both cheeks while I remain seated and acknowledge them with a nod, godfather-like, and then they similarly discard the clothing from their seats and join me in the front row.

The very best of all happens half way through the performance. The girls and I are clapping Samantha, ensuring that anything she does is greeted with even more flashes from digital cameras than anyone else, when the Chairwoman of the PTA starts coughing. She's seething in the second row, fuming that for the first time she doesn't have an uninterrupted view of darling Abigail, when she has a serious coughing fit. Without asking, she grabs the small bottle of Evian that Two Livers has placed discreetly under her chair, and takes a long swig. Then she really starts coughing, goes red, starts gasping, eyes watering, mascara running, pointing to her throat, unable to speak, and is helped from the hall mid-performance by her unfortunate husband.

There are drinks afterwards, at which I am surrounded by some of the most beautiful, glamorous women in London, all of whom have brains the size of planets. This is so far outside the normal social order, that most of the mothers retreat hissing to the corners, while the more adventurous husbands try to engage the babes in chit-chat, rapidly backing off when they find themselves interrogated about why they haven't made partner yet, or when their firm's stock is going to start trading in line with their competitors. Nicky takes a call from New York, and Two Livers and Sabine are discussing a proposal for a Japanese private placement, and it's all just so intimidating that Wendy leaves with Samantha without stopping by to say hello.

MY TRIP TO Frankfurt coincides with Doktor Biedermann's emergence from hiding, after what can only be described as a sustained campaign of terror and intimidation by the extreme wing of the German radical movement. They flour-bombed him when he was giving a talk to university students, threw paint bombs at his house in the suburbs of Frankfurt, and tipped pig swill over him on a visit to the opera. He has born it all stoically, living with police protection in a constant state of nervousness, reminded by his security advisers that he has to be lucky all the time, the bad guys only need to get lucky once.

And what is it that kept him going when another man would have caved in to the pressure, resigned from the board and gone into hiding on a South Sea island?

Me. Dave Hart. The man he loathes above all others. The man behind Grossbank's extraordinary success – yes, success – in investment banking. As I take the elevator to the fifty-fourth floor, I wonder if the doors will open and he'll be waiting for me with a machine-gun.

Things would be going well for me if only I didn't feel so constantly tired. I've been running on empty for so long that my brain feels permanently fuzzy. I've twice fallen asleep in meetings, and worse still, I've started falling asleep in bed, when I had quite different things in mind. My eyes seem to be shrinking back into the dark circles that surround them, I have a permanent cold and runny nose – probably because I am so run down – and nothing seems capable of lifting me for long.

I feel desperately in need of a buzz, of something to raise my spirits and boost my energy levels again. Instead, I meet Doktor Biedermann in the corridor, muttering quietly to the fossils, while an uncomfortable Herman looks on, obviously the outsider.

'Dave – how are you? Welcome to Frankfurt.' At least he's pleased to see me. Biedermann just scowls.

I hand my coat to one of the All Germany Ladies Piano Throwing Team and we go into Biedermann's office. His 'Me Wall' is gone, and instead there are vivid splashes of red paint all over the wall and the back of the door.

'Doktor Biedermann, did you commission this?'

One of the fossils chokes back a laugh. Probably the most excitement he's had in decades. No wonder they like coming to my meetings.

'No. One of our junior employees did this. Someone who was... unduly influenced by things he read in the media.' Oh. But there's more. 'I suppose you've heard the news from Gruenkraut?'

Now both the fossils are trying not to laugh, but their shoulders are shaking and Biedermann has a nervous tic in his cheek. Herman is studying his fingernails.

'Gruenkraut? You mean from…' I search for the name, without success.

'Jan Hagelmann, my nephew.'

I snap my fingers. 'Exactly. Jan – a great kid. No, I haven't. How's he doing?'

'Very well. Your theory was correct. He has been very successful.'

I feel sure it's a wind-up, because there is no way that an arrogant little shit like Hagelmann could have found any new business opportunities in a village of seven hundred people.

'Have you heard of a computer game called *Spectres of the Night?*'

I start to wonder if the pressure has finally got to him. 'Should I?'

Well, you will, Mister Hart, believe me, you will.'

'May I ask why?'

'Because it was designed by a computer programmer in Gruenkraut. It's a live, real-time fantasy computer game played each night by millions of people all over the world, and managed from a farmhouse in Gruenkraut. My nephew met the founder and creator on his first night there, and now they are charging the players ten Euros each month by subscription, and my nephew is to be Chief Executive with twenty-five per cent of the company, and they will float on the stock exchange in a few months' time.'

This has to be a wind-up. 'Well, you must be very pleased.'

'No! I am not pleased. My nephew is planning to leave the bank.'

Well you would, wouldn't you? 'I see. But Jan will become very rich. And floating a high tech entertainment company like that is great business for the bank.'

'Money is not everything, Mister Hart.' He looks at me. 'Too much money too soon can be bad for you. Especially for such a young man. And the bank will not be floating the company.'

'Really? Who's he using?'

'Hardman Stoney. They have been waiting to break into the German market for years.' He turns and stares out of the window, his head bowed in shame. If only I had a revolver with one bullet in it, I'd pass it to him now.

'Is it something I did? When he was working for me?'

Biedermann sighs. 'No. He always wanted to rebel. Now he can. His mother – my sister – is heartbroken. He has grown very pale, he does not shave or cut his hair, he only plays computer games night after night. And it is making him very rich.'

Isn't life a bitch? I don't know where the conversation can go after this, unless I offer to send round some hookers to bring him back to reality. Knowing Biedermann just a little, I decide instead to move on to the business report. But his heart isn't in it any more.

When I tell him we've been appointed to float the Old Orinoco Trading and Investment Company, beating off competition from the likes of Schleppenheim to do it, he simply nods and says 'Congratulations'. When I say that their partner bank, Orinoco Banking and Finance, have started doing huge volumes of share trading through us, he doesn't react. Even Herman looks sad. If this is victory, it sucks.

MORE WEEKS PASS, weeks that turn into months, more success, greater profits, not dozens but hundreds of new faces, and amazingly, in such a short time, Grossbank is turning into a winner. Our people walk into pitch meetings expecting to win the business. The competition actually take us seriously now. It's amazing what happens if you hire hundreds of talented people and turn them loose to do their thing. Or at least, if you're lucky enough to hire the people who hire hundreds of talented other people. I'm surrounded by so much talent now that I no longer have anything to do. Except be in charge, which is of course important – I keep telling myself I'm still the most important man in the firm. Early next year, the new building will be ready and we'll all move down to Canary Wharf. It's an extraordinary success story.

And inevitably, I'm bored. These days I take it for granted that people know who I am, that I have to live in a secure bubble, insulated both from specific hatred directed towards me, and from the more mundane realities of everyday life. I have monthly meetings with Scotland Yard to review security, both at the bank and at home – not just the AFF, apparently the Yardies might still be a concern too. I no longer have problems with restaurant bookings, or the need to use public transport, or getting my expense claims signed off. I've arrived.

And I can't tell you how dull life is. The only person who might have livened it up, Sally perfectly-white-panties Mills, is in Scotland, refusing all contact with me, living with the appalling Trevor the non-achiever. I could offer her millions, and instead all she wants is a fucking schoolteacher.

Paul Ryan is sitting in my office, going through risk positions after the market close. Orinoco Banking and Finance have turned out to be a huge client of the Equities and Fixed Income businesses, taking massive positions, placing hugely aggressive bets that markets will go in one direction or another. More recently, they've introduced us to a clutch of Middle Eastern banking institutions that they work with, most of whom we'd never heard of before, and who have turned out to be almost as big. Paul calls them the Dodgy Dozen, and he worries that if they were to lose serious money they might default, but in the meantime, the profit we're making from them is huge. Right now, they are all lining up to short the market, betting that the current bull run is going to come to an abrupt halt and the market will fall. They're bucking the trend, betting against everyone else in huge size. I call Tripod Turner and ask what he thinks.

'Anyone shorting this market needs his head examined. We're in a bull cycle and there's a good ten per cent still to run, maybe more. The only thing that could stop it is a bomb going off.'

That's when the bomb goes off.

It's quite a large bomb, enough to bring down half the newly refurbished Department of Trade and Industry building in Whitehall. Luckily – or maybe not – it's after six o'clock, and the building is empty.

The effect on world markets is instantaneous. New York goes briefly into freefall, as terrorist alerts go off all around the world. The Prime Minister is taken to a secure bunker, although sadly he's released the next day, armed police are everywhere on the streets of London and other major capitals, and markets are in a tail-spin.

The Dodgy Dozen are about the only people around with smiles on their faces.

When I get together with Paul the following morning, they have booked paper profits of over a billion euros. He's not a happy man.

'This sucks. Everyone else has taken a bath. Including our own traders.'

The giant news screens on the trading floor are showing a video tape released to a Middle Eastern news agency of a guy with a beard in Arab dress sitting in a cave somewhere saying they did it, and there's more to come. What is it with these people? Why spoil things? Why can't they just be happy with drugs and booze and hookers like the rest of us?

'What do we really know about the Orinoco Banking and Finance Corporation?'

Paul shrugs. 'They're very big in Columbia, have a lot of Middle East connections, look after money for a bunch of wealthy Columbians, and trade very aggressively. They file all the right reports with the regulators.'

'Yeah, right.' They say that those who can do, and those who can't, teach. In the City, those who can do, and those who can't, regulate. 'And these other guys – the Dodgy Dozen?'

'Much the same. Middle Eastern money, whatever that means these days.'

'When did they put on these short positions?'

'Two days ago.'

'This sucks. Let's get the police in.'

Now Paul looks troubled. 'Are you sure? What if they did know this was coming? Do you really want to get on the wrong side of people like this? Weren't the Jamaicans and the AFF enough? We could just let them take their profits, carry on quietly trading with them, and if you really feel uncomfortable, write a big cheque to some charity or other.'

Even as he says this, he knows it won't work. I'm Dave Hart, womaniser, drug addict, alcoholic and super-hero. And I'm bored.

THE PLODS are as uninspiring as you might expect people to be who never make six figures, let alone getting a shot at real money. The Detective Chief Inspector is possibly the only person I've ever shown into my office who thinks the 'Me Wall' is real: 'My goodness, Mister Hart, you do get around.'

But when it comes to markets, this guy's an expert. While his sergeant sits taking notes, he explains to Paul and me that a lot of rumours went around the market after the DTI bombing, about possible terrorist activity behind the scenes, about how the big supporters of Middle Eastern terror might be cashing in and shorting the market ahead of the latest outrage, but it really is a conspiracy theory too far, and besides, they have 'intelligence' – really? – that shows we don't have to concern ourselves too much. He doesn't quite tell us not to worry our pretty little heads about all this, because the big boys are in charge, but he comes close.

Afterwards, when Maria has shown them out, Paul looks relieved. 'There, we've done our bit. No one can ever say we didn't try. We told the police. They're the professionals, it's down to them now.' Arse well and truly covered, let's carry on trading. He gets up to leave.

'I'm not honouring those trades.'

Paul's half way out the door, but stops in his tracks and turns.

'You what?'

'Those trades. The billion plus euros of profit the Dodgy Dozen booked. I'm tearing up the tickets. They're not getting the money.'

'You can't do that. They'd sue. We'd be closed down. Our word is our bond. You can't renege on a trade after you've dealt.'

'I just did.'

'Dave, this is insane. What about the billion? Are you keeping that, too?'

'I'm going to bring in a group of wise men – the Bank of England, the regulators, PC Plod if he wants to be part of it – because I'm not satisfied about the bona fides of the Dodgy Dozen. I don't want you to do any more trades for these guys without my say-so. We'll sit on the money until the wise men give us a green light. And if they don't, we won't keep a penny. The whole lot goes to charity. I don't care if we get the biggest lawsuit in the world. We're Grossbank, and we're taking these guys on.'

Some bosses would delegate the task of breaking the happy news to the Dodgy Dozen, but I'm Dave Hart, and I love this stuff. We do a whole series of conference calls, tape recorded, to explain that we are investigating discrepancies in trading patterns around the time of the

DTI bombing, that the British authorities are involved, and in the meantime they can whistle for their money.

Their reactions range from puzzlement and disbelief, to rage and fury. The President of one of them, sitting in Beirut, tells me I'm a Zionist motherfucker and I'd better watch my back. Another assures me that I have no idea what I'm getting into, and if I'm really going to do this, then I must be crazy. I lean close to the speaker-phone, and in a hushed voice, whisper to him, 'Say, Mister al-Fawaz, do you hear the voices, too?'

Herman is concerned. 'Are you sure about this, Dave? Are you sure about what you're getting us into?'

Of course not, Herman. I don't have a fucking clue, but I'm flying again. The Silver Fox organises another press conference. The room is packed, not just with the financial press, but with TV and radio and mainstream news as well.

Paul and Two Livers sit on either side of me, but they both look as if they'd rather be somewhere else.

'Ladies and gentlemen, thank you for coming today. I'm Dave Hart, global head of investment banking at Grossbank, and the man ultimately responsible for our activities in the world's markets. As you know, a number of financial institutions have voiced concerns about certain unusual trading activities in the stock market ahead of the DTI bombing. Grossbank is one of those institutions, and I am announcing today that as a result of our internal enquiries, we are freezing certain trades carried out by a number of client banks and other financial institutions based in the Middle East and Latin America. We are not naming those institutions in the interim, but are inviting the Bank of England, the City of London police and the regulatory authorities to convene a working party to examine their trading activities. Until such time as we are convinced that there is no link here to global terror, we are freezing over a billion euros in trading profits.

'Given the legal uncertainties surrounding our decision, you'll understand that there is very little I can add to what I've just told you, but I'm willing to take a few questions.'

Pandemonium. I love this job.

'Dick Harper, *Wall Street News*. Is your action legal? Isn't Grossbank effectively reneging on trades?'

'Thank you, Dick. You're right. Our legal position is... delicate. That's why we can't name the clients involved, and why we're bringing in outside help. But if it's a choice between doing the right thing, and sitting quietly on our hands, I think you know where Grossbank stands.'

'Eddie Strange, *Daily Post*. You said the clients concerned are from the Middle East and Latin America. Is there a connection? Could it be that the drug cartels are working with the terrorists? Is there an Afghan connection here?'

'It's too soon to speculate. When we can say something concrete, we will.' I look around. 'One more question?'

'Angela Hargraves, *Her* Magazine. Aren't you worried for your personal safety in taking these people on? What if the drug cartels are involved, as well as the terrorists? Aren't you being incredibly brave?'

Well, yes, actually, I am – and doesn't it set your pulse racing? 'Thank you, Angela. The man behind this decision at Grossbank is...' I flick a switch on the podium in front of me and turn to the giant screen behind. Damn.

Instead of a huge picture of Herman, there's one of me, with my name in very large letters. I cast a vicious glance at the girl who runs the presentation team, but she simply shrugs helplessly and mouths 'Herman's orders.' I look at the Silver Fox, and he shrugs too. Damn, these Germans learn fast. '...it's me.' I nod modestly. 'Obviously, not just me alone, the board are right behind me on this.' A long way behind, actually. 'And so are my colleagues on the management committee in London.' I hold my hands out towards Paul and Two Livers, but they've both moved their chairs to the far ends of the stage, so they're out of camera shot.

AFTER THE PRESS conference, the chaos. The Bank of England had no idea I was going to involve them as 'wise men'. The regulators are equally baffled – no one's ever accused them of being wise before. And PC Plod has had his head chewed off by the Commissioner for not telling him Grossbank was calling on their expertise as well. Who's going to organise this working group? How will they work? What will be their powers? Don't ask me, I just made the announcement. There are phone calls, more interviews, photo shoots. Everywhere I go, colleagues are looking nervously at me for encouragement. I grin and call out across the trading floor to our traders, 'Grossbank rocks.' They yell back and give me the thumbs up. On the giant screen TV's on the walls, there is footage of me at the press conference in our offices. We are the news. We are Grossbank.

Naturally, with a thousand and one things to do – and fortunately with lots of highly trained, competent people to do them – I tell Maria I'm taking an hour out of my day to see my acupuncturist.

Three hours later, when I get back, I'm drained. I haven't been sleeping lately, and all the excitement has caught up with me. It's turned into a 3G afternoon.

I arrive back to find that I have visitors. Not from the 'wise men', as I thought, but the President of the Orinoco Banking and Finance Corporation, with a couple of his sidekicks. Paul Ryan has had them shown into a meeting room, and everyone's been waiting for me to get back.

I stifle a yawn, which some of the young guys seem to think is incredibly cool and brave. 'All right, let's see what they have to say.'

Paul has had a couple of security guards stationed outside the meeting room door.

When I go in, with Paul and Two Livers beside me, I find myself facing three villains straight from Central Casting. The President, early sixties with silver hair and a suntan, has a scar running down one side of his face that is even more impressive than mine. His two hoodlums – I mean colleagues – look like Mike Moss's cousins. One has a pock-marked face. All are wearing suits and ties and dark glasses, as if they've come straight from the set of *Reservoir Dogs*.

'Gentlemen – what an unexpected pleasure.'

The President, who is holding a pencil, snaps it in two. Silence.

We sit facing each other, three on three, and no one says a word. If these turkeys think they can come into my office and intimidate me, in front of my own employees, they're damned right. They're scary as hell and I'm shitting myself. Where's Mike Moss when you need him? Finally the President clears his throat.

'You have something of ours, Mister Hart.'

Really? Oh, you must mean the billion. I'll just go and get it right now. Do you have a wheelbarrow, or would you like to borrow one of ours? Instead of answering, I raise a quizzical eyebrow. It's not that I don't want to say anything, just that all the excitement has so drained me physically, mentally and emotionally that I'm buckling under a wave of fatigue.

'We've come for our money, Mister Hart.'

Silence. Paul Ryan glances to his left, to see if I intend to say anything at all.

'Mister Hart! You would do well to take us seriously. Do you recall your friend Oscar Rodriguez, who first chose Grossbank to float his company? Our mutual friend, Mister Rodriguez, who was responsible for bringing us together?'

I stare at him through half-closed eyes.

'He died, Mister Hart. Someone put a bomb under his car.' He crosses himself theatrically. 'Oscar Rodriguez, his wife and driver all died.' He glances at his watch. 'In Bogota. About ten minutes ago.'

How could he possibly know that? Unless... Beside me, Two Livers gasps. She turns to me, but my eyes are closed completely now, and my head slowly sinks forward onto the table. I take a couple of breaths, followed by a loud, rasping snore.

THE LEGEND has reached almost mythical proportions.

They're calling me the Ice Man now – Dave 'ice in his

veins' Hart. Scotland Yard are fretting that I've made myself into too much of a target – really, just by falling asleep in a meeting? I'm always doing that these days. I was shagged out, for fuck's sake. Wendy's fretting about whether I've made a will – for Samantha, of course, not for herself. Herman the German insists that I keep a low profile for my own safety, and Mike Moss agrees with him. Even Tripod Turner says he'd think twice about having dinner with me, in case we were machine-gunned to death by drug dealers, or given a kick-start into the next world by a waiter with explosives strapped to his body. I see his point.

Everywhere I go, I travel with Tom in the armoured limo, and two carloads of heavies who stay in contact by radio. Two bodyguards stay with me in the house, and I have a panic button beside the bed. All of this is so seriously curtailing my usual activities, that I wonder whether it's time to cave – so that I can get back to drugs and hookers.

But as ever, it's the least expected line of attack that proves to be the one the enemy choose. They opt for blackmail. They want to ruin my reputation. Yes, honestly.

It's the beginning of September, the run-up to the bonus season, and it's Two Livers' birthday. She's sitting at her desk, her chair pushed back, and she's reclining, eyes half closed, breathing heavily, while I'm crouching underneath the desk. Her dress is pushed up and she's not wearing any panties. You can guess the rest. I'd like to say I do this for all my employees on their birthdays, but I'd be lying.

Suddenly the door flies open, and Paul Ryan comes in. Two Livers jerks upright and smooths her dress down as he throws something on the desk.

'Have you seen these?'

'Seen what?'

'Photos of Dave – hard core photos of him with three hookers.'

There's a crunch as I bang my head on the desk, and Two Livers pushes her chair back to allow me to crawl forward on my knees and get out.

'What did you say?'

'Christ, Dave, I'm sorry – I didn't know you were there.'

'Dropped my pen. Got it now. Let me see these photos.'

Spread out on the desk are some high quality shots of me with three girls, all of us naked. There's a brunette – I think she was Katerina, from Estonia – a blonde – no idea who she was – and a black girl. I don't recall her either. We're not at my place, and I can't see enough from the shots to recognise where it was all happening, or even recall when, but boy, was it happening. There are fifteen pictures altogether, and I'm seriously impressed. Did I really do that? I could be a porn star.

'Look at this.' Paul passes me a note.

'Tell your boss to behave, or the press get these.'

Paul and Two Livers look pretty sick about the whole thing – they have these hangdog 'So what do we do now, boss' looks on their faces.

But I'm excited. So excited that I've dragged myself to the surface of my exhaustion, gasping for air, but ready to take on the world.

'Get me the Silver Fox.'

Two Livers also had a set of photos sent to her, and I had a set too. It looks as if that's it, though I can't yet be sure.

When the Silver Fox arrives, I have the gratifying and unusual task of giving him a PR assignment that even he hasn't taken on before. Meanwhile the team are worried that I'm not worried.

It takes a couple of days, but then Herman calls.

'Dave – I'm very embarrassed to have to talk to you like this, about a rather awkward and difficult, personal matter.'

I assume he has a problem. 'Herman, you can trust me. I'm a man of the world, I've seen it all – hell, I've done most of it.'

'I know you have, Dave. I have the photographs in front of me.'

Damn. So the bad guys are upping the ante. Fine with me. 'Oh, you got them? Great. What do you think?'

'What do I think? I don't know what to think.'

'But they have an impact, don't they? You can't tell me they don't challenge your perspective on investment bankers? The ugliness of global finance and the sensuality of the world that surrounds us. It's all there, Herman, and it's all for a good cause.'

'Dave, what are you talking about?'

'The calendar. The charity calendar that Ball Taittinger are preparing for us. Didn't you see my note? The children's cancer charities?'

'Dave – I'm worried about you.' Great, Herman, thanks a million. That makes two of us.

'I guess it hasn't happened yet in Germany, Herman, but in this country there's a fine tradition of the least likely people baring all for charity. The Women's Institute did it, rugby players have done it, trendy 'it' girls have done it, and now I'm doing it. It's just that I'm taking it to a new, more explicit extreme – though Ball Taittinger say they'll airbrush out the bits that go too far.' I know Herman hasn't hung up, because I can hear him breathing at the other end.

'Dave, I want to help you.'

'Then order ten thousand copies. Hang them in all the branch offices, all over Germany, and have an exhibition of the originals in the Grossbank Tower – that's what I plan to do over here. I've already called the President of the Orinoco Banking and Finance Corporation – told him he and his associates will all get personally signed copies when it's published. The City columns of the papers are going to start running the story tomorrow. Herman, this is going to be huge. And it's great for our image – it keeps us right out there, on the edge. That's where we have to be, Herman – edgy... and unpredictable... and dangerous.'

'We're dangerous enough, my friend. I can't allow you to do this.'

He hangs up. What kind of remark was that? We're Grossbank. We can do what we want, because Grossbank rocks. Doesn't it?

When I get home that night, I can't sleep. I realise I'm going through a kind of cold turkey – with all the security everywhere, I can't misbehave the way I'm used to, and my body is tormented by the absence of the poisons and the pleasures it's come to depend on. Half a bottle of whisky later I doze off on the bed, still fully clothed, but keep seeing faces hovering over me: black men with dreadlocks; ugly hate-filled faces of men and women in jeans and combat jackets carrying placards; smooth, evil men in sharp suits carrying nasty little machine-guns; and angry men with beards in Arab dress, their mad eyes filled with hatred. The rational part of my brain is wondering whether there's any other serious hate-group out there that I've somehow failed to antagonise, but I can't come up with one.

In the middle of all this, the phone rings. Thank God for that. I hope it's Dan Harriman, suggesting I sneak out and play hookey, or hooker, or something. I'm damned if I'll hide away in here forever. These schmucks think they can threaten Dave Hart? Think again, pal. You think I care? Bullshit.

'Hello, Dave, is that you?'

It's a familiar voice. Female, sweet, innocent. 'Sally! It's been so long. Where are you?'

She's crying. 'I'm here. In London. I've come back, Dave. I thought I could run far away and forget about you, but I was wrong. Wherever I went, there was news of you. You were in the papers, on the radio, on the television news at night. I couldn't escape. I've told Trevor. He's heartbroken. I don't think he'll ever understand. I feel so guilty, Dave, but I can't help myself. I love you.'

Am I dreaming or what? It can't be the drugs, and I've only had half a bottle of Scotch. This is it. I am definitely going to get inside those perfectly white cotton panties. At last. Tonight.

'Sally – where are you?'

'I'm at Euston station. I've just arrived.'

'Stay there. I'll be right over.'

I know – I should have told her to take a cab. She's only a woman, for God's sake. If it had been Ilyana, or sweaty Sveta, or Breathless Beth, or glorious Gabbie, or any of them really, I would have done. But this is Sally, and I've been waiting a long time.

I hang up, rush downstairs and grab my jacket and car keys. Tom's long since left for the evening, so I'll drive myself.

'Mister Hart, sir – where are you going?' It's one of the goons who's here for the night shift.

'Out. By myself.' I run to the front door, and step out into the street, where H1 PAY is parked.

'Mister Hart, sir – please wait a moment. Let me check the car first.' He's got a hand-held radio out and as he hurries after me, he's calling for a car to follow me.

'No time – sorry.' I definitely don't want a bunch of goons overseeing my great romantic moment.

I jump in, slam the door, put the keys in the ignition, and for a moment wonder if I should just wait a minute or two. Will it really make that great a difference? I promised Mike Moss I'd do as I was told. Fuck it. When have I ever done as I was told? Sally's waiting, and it really has been a long, hard chase.

I turn the key and there's a loud bang and a blinding white light. I feel rather than see the windscreen shatter in front of me and a great blast of hot air engulfs me.

Shit.